The
Black
Stiletto
Stars &
Stripes

The Black Stiletto

Stars & Stripes

The Third Diary—1960

A Novel

Raymond Benson

Oceanview Publishing
LONGBOAT KEY, FLORIDA

ISBN: 978-1-60809-072-3

Published in the United States of America by Oceanview Publishing, Longboat Key, Florida
www.oceanviewpub.com

10 9 8 7 6 5 4 3 2 1

PRINTED IN THE UNITED STATES OF AMERICA

For Randi

ACKNOWLEDGMENTS

The author wishes to thank the following individuals for their help: Judith May Holstun, James McMahon, Stephen Plotkin and the John F. Kennedy Presidential Library and Museum, Michael Romei and the Waldorf-Astoria Hotel, Joyce Savocchio, Pat and Bob, and everyone at Oceanview Publishing, Peter Miller, and my family, Randi and Max.

AUTHOR'S NOTE

While every attempt has been made to ensure the accuracy of 1960s New York City, the Second Avenue Gym, Shapes, and the East Side Diner are fictitious. John F. Kennedy's campaign appearances cited within are exact. The Kennedy Girls volunteers were a grassroots movement encouraged and supported by the Kennedy Campaign for President in 1960. Details in dress and duties differed state by state. While most of what appears here regarding the Kennedy Girls is correct, some liberties have been taken.

The Black Stiletto
Stars & Stripes

I
Martin
The Present

I was so scared I could've peed my pants.

It was the middle of the night. The brownstones and tall apartment buildings appeared ominously abandoned. The sidewalk was dark and unnaturally deserted. None of the streetlamps worked. More peculiar was the absence of traffic. There were always automobiles on New York streets and avenues, even at such a late hour. I don't know how I knew it was Manhattan. I didn't know the city well. I'd been there a couple of times and found the place unpleasant. I just knew that's where I was, but everything was very, very different.

I walked at a fast pace. Headed uptown, I thought. North. Along Third Avenue. Or was it Second? I didn't know. None of the street signs made any sense. They were supposed to be numbered as I moved across intersections, but I couldn't read them. It was as if they were written in a foreign language.

It was also quiet and cold. The silence was unnerving. Usually the city was a machine of constant noise, even during that time of night when most souls were safely tucked in bed and dreaming of more pleasant activities. The chill made me shiver, and I could swear I felt icy breath on the back of my neck. When I turned, there was nothing there, of course.

Still. I felt her. She was near.

A maddening urge grew stronger. I wanted to shout out her real name to the nothingness around me. I couldn't keep it in. That jewel of knowledge was a burden that materialized itself as a heavy, bulbous mass inside my chest. It was a cancer that would surely kill me if I didn't let it out soon. And yet, I couldn't. When I tried to say her name aloud, nothing happened. My throat closed and choked and sounded like nails on a blackboard.

I kept the pace up the ghostly avenue. The buildings blocked what illumination the starry sky might provide. Every now and then I thought I saw gray shapes moving in the blackness, but I knew my eyes were just playing tricks on me. Or were they? I didn't know for certain and this alarmed me even more.

She was coming after me. She was going to catch me.

I couldn't let that happen. That blade of hers was sharp and deadly. A quick slash across the neck and I'd be done for. Or perhaps she'd just perform one of her fancy *karate* kicks and snap my sternum in two. It would puncture my lungs and I'd die of asphyxiation. Or she could hang me from a lamppost with that rope she carried, coiled on her belt.

Most of all, I was afraid of her eyes.

I imagined what would happen when I came face-to-face with her. It was always the same. The holes in the black mask would reveal glowing hot embers. She'd stare right through me and I'd feel it. The panic would set in, and once that happened, it was all over. I'd lose control. I'd scream. I'd run. I'd turn blindly into shadowy streets that turned out to be dead ends.

Then, when I was trapped, she would pounce.

And that's exactly what happened as I hung a left and tried to cross the avenue to the other side. The eyes abruptly materialized in the shadows as I moved forward. They stayed with me, hovering along at my side as I trotted. I felt the anxiety bubbling and my heart pounding in my chest.

No!

I impulsively made a sharp right turn into a darkened street and bolted. Did I scream? I may have. I wasn't sure. Of course, my legs were lead weights. I couldn't run fast. It was painful to put one foot in front of the other. It was torture. Everything slowed to a standstill. The blackness constricted around me, creating a tunnel of sightlessness through which I groped. And then, as I feared, I came to the brick wall.

Dead end. Last stop. The finish.

Knowing full well what would have to come next, I trembled and whimpered like a coward. The despair was excruciating. Nevertheless, I had no choice but to turn around and face her. It was the only way I could exit the nightmare.

And what happened if it didn't work? What if it was real this time? What if she was really going to *get* me? What if she took off the mask and revealed the terrifying face beneath? Would I survive the shock? Would my poor heart cease to pump life through my veins?

"Martin."

The voice was indeed hers. Always the same.

She wanted me to turn around, and I had to obey. I had no choice.

"I'll tell them all who you are!" I cried. "Everyone will know!"

But once again, I couldn't speak the name. The effort produced such an agony. The mass in my chest was unbearable. I had to surrender. I had to succumb.

Slowly, I pivoted on my heels. My bladder felt as if it would burst as I struggled to control my fear.

There. I faced the piercing red eyes.

And the Black Stiletto leaped forward out of the void.

I awoke with a start. As I did a couple of mornings ago. And a couple of days before that.

It was such an unpleasant sensation. The jerk of my body, the vocalization of a stifled scream against my pillow, and the sudden rush of adrenaline—it never failed to ruin my day.

The panic attacks and nightmares began shortly after my forty-ninth birthday in October. I'd just come back from New York. I

should have felt great because it turned out to be a successful trip. I
saw with my own eyes that Gina was going to be okay. The physical
assault and near rape she suffered in Riverside Park were the main
reasons for the journey. Luckily the crime was interrupted by a couple of passersby. It wasn't a great way to start out her freshman year
at Juilliard, but I was happy it wasn't worse. Still, it tore my heart
out to see her broken jaw. She had to have it wired shut for six weeks
or so. My poor little girl.

Second, I successfully stopped Johnny Munroe's blackmail attempt. That was a *tremendous* weight off my shoulders. I hope I've
heard the last of him, but you never know. After that experience, I
fear other people out there might know the big secret. Will I always
have to look out for guys like Munroe?

After completing the business in New York, I felt marginally
better as I returned to the miserable life of a lonely unemployed accountant who takes care of a mother with Alzheimer's. The once vi-
brant, now shell of a woman I'd known all my life. My mom is a
stranger living in a nursing home, and she has ceased to know who
I am.

I believe in midlife crises. I experienced a minor one around the
time of the divorce from Carol, which was—gosh—eight years ago?
I was in my early forties then. I've heard that guys who have midlife
crises are usually around forty, give or take. I went through a tough
time at first, but it wasn't terrible. What I'm experiencing *now* is
much worse. In a year I'll be fifty. It's not a milestone I'm looking
forward to, and *that* exacerbates the anxiety. So, I'm convinced that
what happened over Carol was just a trailer for coming attractions;
I'm currently having my *real* midlife crisis.

The strain of dealing with my mom and everything that entails
has taken its toll. The panic attacks and nightmares erupt out of
nowhere. My bodily reaction is always the same: my heart pumps
hard and beats against my chest as if I'd just run a fifty-yard dash; I
sweat and feel clammy; an intense feeling of dread washes over me;
and I want to cry. The first time it happened I thought I was having

a heart attack. I almost called for an ambulance, but maybe ten minutes after it began, the torture ceased. I was all right, but the short ordeal left me weak. I learned later that a panic attack produced a sudden release of adrenaline. Once you've gone through that fight-or-flight sensation, your energy is depleted and you feel rotten.

That was happening a *lot*, and the really stupid part about it all is that I know what's bothering me.

I need to tell someone my mother's secret. The truth is burning a hole in my soul.

There's no question I could cash in on it. What the media wouldn't pay for that news! The True Identity of the Black Stiletto! The legendary crimefighter's life story as told by none other than her very own son!

But that would be a betrayal. Wouldn't it? Even though my mother granted me the rights to her life story, a tale that she painstakingly put down in a series of diaries and ephemera left to me, I knew I couldn't reveal it just yet. Not while she's still alive. And, according to Maggie, the end could be as much as two, five, or ten years away—or as little as months or weeks. Alzheimer's is a cruel, unpredictable disease.

So far my mother is stable. She had a little fainting scare a couple of months ago but she came out all right. She maintained a pleasant, contented demeanor. That was good, but it was also sad. Her memories were like select, individual sand pebbles on a vast beach. Most of what's there she can't access. As I said before, she rarely knows who I am, only that I'm family. She loves me.

I love her, too.

Judy Cooper Talbot.

The legendary Black Stiletto.

And I'm the only person who knows, except for an elderly retired FBI agent living in New York. John Richardson isn't going to tell anyone. I trust him. Of course, there could be other people in the world that perhaps know the secret. Like my father, for instance. If he's still alive. I still didn't know if Richard Talbot really existed or if that was all a lie. He allegedly died in Vietnam, but his photograph never graced a mantel in our home when I was growing up. I'm beginning to doubt that Vietnam story.

So many masks. So many secrets.

Right after my mom's birthday in November, I got lucky and found a job. It was a step backward, but I snatched it right up. I couldn't afford to miss paychecks any longer. I'd been out of work since last May and my savings were nearly drained. My daughter attended an expensive arts school in Manhattan—even though she received a substantial scholarship, it was still a burden on the wallet. With Christmas just around the corner, I desperately needed the income. The opportunity came at just the right time.

Wegel, Stern and Associates, Inc. was a mom-and-pop accounting shop in Deerfield. Actually it was just a pop shop. Sam Wegel was in his seventies and had run the business out of the same small office for forty years. His partner, Morton Stern, passed away a few months earlier, so Wegel was forced to hire some young blood to fill in.

I applied, interviewed, and was offered the job.

Sam explained that he wanted to spend less time at work and eventually retire. The only other person in the place was a fifty-year-old woman named Shirley who acted as receptionist, secretary, and legal aide. I figured I could be a big fish in a small firm and end up running the place. So I accepted.

Sam was a good guy, a nice Jewish fellow with a wife and three grown children, none of whom wanted to go into the family business. It wasn't long before I became something of a fourth kid to him. He even invited me over for dinner with his family, which I appreciated. He's already invited me for Thanksgiving, but I told him I'd probably spend the holiday with my mom, even though the food at Woodlands is terrible. I certainly wasn't going to show up at my ex-wife's place and have turkey and stuffing with Carol and Ross, the guy she's probably going to marry. Maybe Maggie and I will have Thanksgiving together. I hope so.

Now, a month later, the job is what it is. I do income tax returns for regular, ordinary people. I used to be a corporate auditor and accountant. I worked in the Chicago Loop and made pretty good money. Now I tell Mr. Whatzenblatt and Mrs. Whozenstein what they can and cannot deduct. It's boring, tedious work, but it's a paycheck. And the hours are fairly flexible. Sam understands about my mom. It's a good thing the Deerfield office is near Riverwoods, where the nursing home is located. I can stop by and visit on the way home to Buffalo Grove.

So at least the employment component of the crisis has been taken care of.

The other things—my daughter's assault, the blackmail attempt, my mom—her care and the frikkin' elephant in the room that's the Black Stiletto—*those* things still weigh heavily on my mind. If only I could tell Gina. She would understand. She'd probably think it was cool as hell that her grandmother was a mythical vigilante. I'm just afraid she wouldn't keep that knowledge to herself.

Should I come clean to Maggie? Lord knows she wonders what skeletons reside in my closet. She definitely suspects something is wrong. After all, she's a doctor. Dr. Margaret McDaniel. Boy, things sure have changed between us since I first met her.

She's the physician who makes calls at Woodlands, where my mother has lived for the past couple of years. At first I couldn't stand the woman. I thought she had a bug up her ass or something. She was very stern and businesslike. Her bedside manner was off-putting. Okay, I thought she was the B-word. In particular I didn't like her questions about all the scars and ancient wounds my mother has on her seventy-three-year-old body. I refused to answer how my mom got them. I pretended not to know. There was no way I could tell Maggie that my mom was the Black Stiletto.

So if you'd told me two months ago that I'd be dating my mom's nursing home doctor, I would've said you were nuttier than an Almond Joy. But it's true and maybe not going too badly.

Even though we got off on the wrong foot at first, hey, I'd always considered her good-looking. Striking, in fact. Bright blue eyes. Terrific body, from what I could discern beneath that white lab coat. Just a few years younger than me.

I finally got the nerve to ask her out after I returned from New York. Our first date—for coffee—was awkward. I was nervous. I hadn't dated since I got divorced. It was very strange to be back in that game. I think Maggie felt the same way. She told me she'd never married, which I found surprising. I thought she was divorced, too. We mostly talked about my mother. No surprise there.

The second date was better. We both found our attempt at conversation to be much easier. The wine at dinner helped immensely. By the end of the evening we were actually laughing and enjoying ourselves.

On the third date, we kissed. I'd almost forgotten how to do it.

There's no telling where it's going, but whatever the thing is, I'm willing to give it a shot.

Currently, we weren't too busy at Wegel, Stern and Associates. Folks didn't start to bring in their stuff until after the holidays. Then it was supposed to be a madcap four months to April 15. Sam warned me it would be hell and that I couldn't take off during that time period. I said it was no problem.

When I got to work, Sam wasn't there. I didn't think he'd show up because it was snowing. He often took the day off or "worked from home" when the weather was bad. So I drank a lot of coffee and went through the motions of filing some guy's extension. Mostly I sat at my desk and gazed out the window at the white wonderland forming outside. Typical Chicago weather in early December.

I hated it.

Gina smiled at me from her high school senior photo. The frame stood right next to my in-box, where I saw it every time I reached for something new to do. She's such a pretty girl. When I think of what happened to her, my blood boils and my soul breaks. Her face was so bruised and battered. I felt so sorry for her. But she bounced back pretty well. She only recently had the wires removed and could resume eating normal food. I'm still amazed she insisted on continuing her studies. Her mother and I suggested that she take the semester off to recover, but Gina's always been a willful girl. She was determined to make an impression as an actress and dancer at school, so she wasn't about to drop out.

The psychological damage was something that couldn't be established yet. Sometimes a trauma's aftereffects can suddenly erupt weeks or months later. She's seeing a counselor at school, but that's all she told her mother and me. It's heartening, though, that every time we speak on the phone, Gina sounds happy and energetic. I believe she's going to come out of it all right. We just have to take it a day at a time.

She's planning to come home for the Christmas holidays. That's great.

I clocked out early and went to see Mom on the way home. When I got there, she was asleep. Afternoon nap time. Apparently she slept a lot now. Was her body doing that involuntarily so she could escape the frustrating blanket of fog that was her waking life? If I was in that situation, I'd want to sleep as much as possible. Or be dead. I couldn't imagine what was going on inside Judy Talbot's head. Anything at all? Ever since the disease struck her hard, my mom had become more quiet and subdued. She used to have tremendous energy and was extremely sociable. That's all gone now.

Maggie wasn't at the nursing home, so I didn't bother staying long. I sat with my mom for a while and watched her breathe. She was still a pretty woman, although she looked frail. I knew, though, that she had strength in those skinny arms and legs. The way she'd kicked Roberto Ranelli in the balls last summer was a sight not to be believed. Every now and then I caught glimpses of the person she once was.

I even saw the Black Stiletto in her, although I couldn't mention that name in her presence. It triggered something painful for her. She became distressed if I so much as whispered anything about her alter ego.

There's so much I still don't know about her. I've read only two of the diaries she left behind. One might think I would have devoured them all in one sitting, but I couldn't do that. I find the process of going through the books very upsetting. I don't know why. I went through the whole summer without reading the second one. When I finally caved in and finished it, I wasn't compelled to learn any more. When I returned from New York, I wanted to forget all about the Black Stiletto. Simply go about my business as if my mother was just Judy Talbot, the woman she had always been to me.

But then the recurring nightmares started, the panic attacks multiplied in frequency, and I was in a state of upheaval.

Against my better judgment, I thought perhaps it was time to find out more about Mom's past. Maybe that would ease my anxiety.

When I got to my house, I phoned for a pizza to be delivered, and then went into my makeshift home office. I had hidden the diaries and the strongbox in the back of a file cabinet drawer and covered them with manila folders. Everything else—the costume, the knife, the guns, the ephemera—sat in a safety deposit box at the bank. It's where this stuff should've been, too. I kept it nearby in case my curiosity drew me back to my mother's tale, even though I found it very disturbing.

I removed the strongbox and unlocked it with the key I kept in the desk drawer. I'd already solved the mystery of one of the trinkets—the roll of 8mm film. There's still the presidential campaign button, the heart-shaped locket, and the gold key. I removed the button and examined it. It was obviously from 1960, as it had the Democratic presidential candidate's and his running mate's faces on it. "Kennedy/Johnson" it proclaimed.

Reaching under the folders, I grasped the third diary, the one that would have been from that year, and pulled it out. I then closed and locked the strongbox, stored it away, and shut the drawer. I carried the diary into the living room and sat in my comfy chair.

I breathed deeply. I fought the unease that crept up my spine. It was going to be painful, but I couldn't put it off any longer.

I opened the diary and started to read, and I was back in the world of the Black Stiletto.

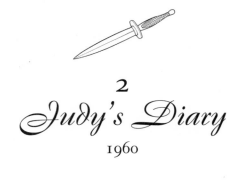

2
Judy's Diary
1960

JANUARY 1, 1960

Good morning, dear diary. Or should I say good afternoon? I slept past noon, and boy, am I hungover. Yuck. I feel crummy. It was a great party, though. I think. What I remember of it, ha ha.

After I went back downstairs last night, the champagne really flowed. I made the mistake of also drinking a couple of Jack Daniel's with Coke. By the time midnight rolled around, the gym was spinning. I never got sick, though. I don't recall how I made it up to my room, but somehow I did.

The only thing I *do* remember was what Lucy told me, just before the clock struck twelve. She and Peter made a date for their wedding. It'll be in May, but now I've forgotten the exact day. She asked me to be her maid of honor, and I'm pretty sure I slurred, "I'll be happy to, Looshy!"

Gosh, it's 1960. I can hardly believe it. A whole new decade. What will it bring? What kind of changes will we see? A bunch of them, or none at all? There's a presidential election this year. It'll be the first time I can vote in one. Actually, I was old enough in '56, but I didn't do it. I don't know why. I was too young to care then, I suppose. A new president always brings some changes, right? Now that I think about it, there's a lot going on that could use some change.

There's a bunch of trouble in the world. The Communists over in Russia are a big concern. They have bombs. We have bombs. Now that Cuba is also Communist, people are worried that it's so close. Will it lead to war? Gosh, I hope not. And then they're training astronauts to fly into outer space. Will we go to the moon or to Mars? Wouldn't that be something? And there's a firecracker about to go off right here in America. The Negroes are demanding equal civil rights. Will Dr. King lead his people to victory? I hope there won't be any violence.

Well, my stomach tells me I shouldn't be concerned about any of that right now. I need to go to the kitchen and put something in my belly before I *do* get sick. Maybe some toast and orange juice. I'm not sure I can handle eggs right now.

Okay, Judy, put on your robe and make an appearance. I don't think more beauty sleep is going to make much difference, ha ha!

LATER

It's nearly midnight again and I just came back from Bellevue Hospital.

Oh my Lord, Freddie had a heart attack today! Dear diary, I'm so worried. The doctor says he's going to be okay, but still, I've never seen Freddie look so bad. I swear I thought he was going to die in my arms.

When I left off earlier, I went to the kitchen to get some breakfast. Freddie was there at the table with his newspaper and a plate full of uneaten scrambled eggs. They were cold. I didn't know how long they were sitting there, but it must have been a couple of hours. Freddie was pale and had one arm around his chest. His brow was furrowed and he looked extremely uncomfortable.

"Freddie? What's wrong?"

He just shook his head. "I must have had too much to drink last night. I have awful gas pains."

Freddie never had hangovers. He had the ability to swallow

booze as if it was water and smoke a couple of packs of cigarettes at the same time. It never fazed him.

"Have you taken any Alka-Seltzer?" I asked as I went to the fridge to get the orange juice.

"We don't have any."

"Well, shoot, Freddie, why didn't you get me up? I'll run out and get some for you." I poured a glass of juice and looked back at him. It was then I could see this was more serious than gas pains. Freddie was wincing and couldn't respond.

"Freddie?"

Then his expression changed for the worse. His eyes popped open and he gasped for air. One hand clutched the edge of the table as he tried to stand. He didn't get very far. I put down my juice and rushed to him—just in time to catch him as he toppled into my arms.

"Freddie!"

I gently laid him on the kitchen floor. He writhed in agony and was short of breath. When he attempted to speak, he merely made choking noises.

"I'm calling an ambulance!" I didn't want to leave him, but I had to. The phone was on the other side of the kitchen. I darted to it and dialed the operator. It seemed like it took forever to get connected to the right place, but I finally blurted out where they should come. After I hung up, I moved back to Freddie. He was breathing a little better, but his eyes were wet and there was absolutely no color to his skin. The immediate distress seemed to be passing, though.

"Try to relax, Freddie, an ambulance is on the way," I told him.

All the time we waited, I prayed I wouldn't lose him. Not Freddie—my substitute father, my trainer, my friend. I even cried a little, but I was careful not to let him see. I kept thinking about everything they were saying on the news about smoking cigarettes and how bad they can be. Freddie smoked a ton a day. Could that be the cause?

Well, dear diary, the ambulance arrived about twenty minutes later, which seemed like an eternity. I went downstairs to the front of the gym to let them in. The fellows rushed upstairs with one of those stretchers on wheels. One of the guys asked me to wait in the other room, but I wouldn't leave. They checked Freddie's vitals and asked him a few questions, which he was surprisingly able to answer. Eventually they got him on the stretcher and carried him down and outside. I insisted on going with them in the ambulance. I threw on a pair of training pants and a sweatshirt, tennis shoes, and grabbed my purse. I looked like I'd just rolled out of bed—which was true—but it was no time for vanity.

When we got to the hospital, they wheeled him right into the emergency area. A nurse asked me if I was a relative. I explained that I was the only family Freddie had, even though we weren't related. She handed me a clipboard and ordered me to fill out some papers. I answered the questions I could and gave it back. And then I waited. And waited. And waited.

At one point I went to the pay phone and called Lucy. No one answered. She and Peter must have gone out to do something fun on New Year's Day. It was cold outside, but the weather was clear. I just wanted to speak to somebody. I didn't have anyone else's phone number with me or I would have called Jimmy or one of the other gym regulars.

I was there four hours before the doctor came out to talk to me. By then it was around ten o'clock. Dr. Montgomery was very young. I thought he looked like he was just out of medical school.

Sure enough, it was a heart attack. Dr. Montgomery said Freddie would have to stay in the hospital for a while, probably a few weeks! But he was stable and they'd given him drugs and stuff to make him comfortable. I asked if I could see him, but the doctor replied that Freddie was sleeping now. Dr. Montgomery suggested I go home and get some rest, too, and I'd most likely get to see the patient tomorrow.

So now I'm back at the apartment. I hadn't eaten all day. I feel pretty lousy. I'm going to make some eggs and then go to bed. I guess I'll have to close the gym in the morning.

Please, God, if you're really up there, please make Freddie better. Please, please, please!

JANUARY 2, 1960

It's been a long day.

I put a sign on the gym door saying we were closed "due to illness." Then I took the bus to Bellevue, and luckily, I was able to see Freddie. First the nurse on his floor told me the doctor wanted to talk to me. So I was stuck doing nothing *again*, this time in a small waiting room. Apparently, the floor was dedicated to heart patients, because a lot of pamphlets and literature about cardiac emergencies sat in trays on the table along with magazines that were several months old. I didn't have to wait too long, though. This time a different doctor showed up. His name was Abramson. He was older and looked more experienced than Dr. Montgomery. He introduced himself and asked what my relationship to the patient was. I told him that Freddie's my landlord and employer, repeating that I was the only family he had that I knew of. The doctor nodded grimly, which I didn't take to be a good sign.

"How is he?" I asked.

Dr. Abramson didn't immediately say, "Oh, he's fine," or "He'll be okay." Instead, he made a shrugging gesture and rocked a flat hand back and forth to indicate "not so bad, not so good."

"We're still waiting on all the tests, but Mr. Barnes definitely suffered a serious heart attack, what we call a myocardial infarction." He went on to explain that a major anterior coronary artery was blocked. I didn't understand a lot of the medical terms, but he put it as plainly as he could. The crux of the matter is that Freddie's condition is severe enough to warrant a long hospital stay.

When I asked if he could operate, Dr. Abramson looked at me like I was crazy. "There is no treatment like that for this sort of thing," he said. "Not yet, anyway. There's a lot about the heart we don't know." I felt kind of dumb.

He told me I could go on to Freddie's room, but I shouldn't stay long and I had to take care not to "excite" him. What was I going to do, make him do jumping jacks? I told the doctor Freddie and I were like father and daughter and that it would do him good to see me.

Freddie didn't have his own room. A curtain separated the two sides, and an old man covered with tubes and stuff was in the first bed. I quickly skipped over that space and went around the curtain. Dear diary, I stopped breathing for a second. I had never seen big, strong Freddie look so pathetic. He was in bed, of course, and he had an oxygen mask on his face. There was a plastic tube in his arm that coiled up to one of those bottles containing clear liquid. His eyes were closed. There was a little more color in his complexion, but somehow he seemed smaller and older. I wanted to cry.

"Freddie?" I whispered. I moved to the side of the bed and gently placed a hand on his. "Freddie?"

His eyes fluttered open. When they focused on me, he smiled beneath the oxygen mask. With his other hand, he reached up and removed it.

"Hello, Judy." His voice was soft and weak.

"Oh, Freddie." I indicated the mask. "Shouldn't you be wearing that? You don't have to talk."

He barely shook his head. "It's okay. I can take it off for a few minutes at a time. I have to eat, too, you know. They gave me breakfast this morning."

I didn't know what to say. "It ... it looks like you have good doctors."

Freddie rolled his eyes. "They're all quacks when it comes to heart attacks. They don't know what they're doing. I just have to rest for, God, I don't know how long."

"They said you'd be here for a few weeks."

He nodded. "Judy, you'll have to run the gym. I won't be training anyone for a while. Can you take over?"

"Of course I can! And if the guys don't like me training them, then tough cookies. Don't you worry about it. And I'll tell the regulars they should come visit you."

Freddie winced slightly and said, "Wait a week or so before you do that."

I laughed. "Okay, Freddie."

He sighed heavily. "I'd kill for a cigarette."

This time I shook *my* head. "I'm afraid that's not allowed."

"I know. I have to quit. For good. It's gonna be hell. I'm not sure I can do it."

"Sure you can, Freddie. I'll help you."

"I have to limit my drinking, too."

"That shouldn't be as difficult."

"I'm part Irish. Didn't you know that?"

I laughed. "I don't think I did. But it makes sense." After a little pause, I asked if he was in pain. He said, no, they'd got him on painkillers. There was a piece of paper on the tray by his bed where the doctor had written names of medicines he'll be taking. I copied them down so I could spell them correctly: quinidine and nitroglycerin. I always thought that second one was an explosive, like dynamite. What do I know?

After a while, I could see he was growing tired, so I left him alone. I didn't really want to go home yet. I thought I'd let him rest a while and then after I had lunch I'd see him again. Downstairs I called Lucy from a pay phone and told her what was going on. She offered to come up and sit with me, so I suggested we have lunch somewhere near Bellevue. And that's what we did. I can't remember where we ate, but it was a diner very similar to the East Side Diner. I wasn't much company, I'm afraid. Lucy told me not to worry. Freddie would be all right. Lots of people recovered from heart attacks and lived a long time. Yeah, maybe so, but I think *more* people *didn't* recover and an incident meant that their time on earth was now limited.

Lucy talked mostly about her and Peter and the wedding. It kind of went in one ear and out the other. I was actually thankful when we got up to pay our checks.

I visited with Freddie for a few minutes again in the afternoon, but he seemed even more tired than before. I thought it best to leave him be. Surely he'll regain more strength as the days pass.

He'll be okay.

I said that over and over to myself as I took the bus back to the East Village.

So a little while ago, I made myself some dinner and watched TV alone. It was strange being in our apartment without Freddie there. It made me very sad. The only thing that perked me up was something I saw on the news.

Today Senator John Kennedy announced his run for president. I like him. He's very handsome and he seems smart. I can't believe so many Americans don't want him to be president because he's Catholic. Why should that make a difference? Someone asked him if he was concerned about that, and Kennedy replied that the only thing we should care about is whether or not a candidate believes in the separation of Church and State. What a great answer!

After I cleaned up the dishes, I became restless. I needed to release some tension. I thought about going down to the gym and working out with the weights, but I also wanted some fresh air, even though it's cold outside.

Tonight the Black Stiletto is going to make her first appearance of 1960.

3
Judy's Diary
1960

JANUARY 3, 1960

It's late at night. Actually it's early morning, 2:00 a.m. I just got back to the apartment and I'm hurt. I don't know how badly yet. My face is a real mess and every bone in my body feels broken.

The Black Stiletto slipped out around 10:00. I did my usual running-along-the-roof of the gym, hopped to the top of the next building on 2nd Street, found my favorite telephone pole, shimmied down, and I was on the street. No one saw me. It was cold outside, so I wore my warmer Stiletto outfit. I was equipped with the knife strapped to my leg, the small blade hidden in my boot, my rope and hooks, a flashlight, and my backpack.

I was angry about Freddie. I hated seeing him in that condition, so it made me want to take it out on a street thug or two. Would I find any robberies in progress? Someone trying to hold up a liquor store? I actually hoped I would. So I headed west toward the Bowery, which was always a hot spot for crime. Much of that long, north-south thoroughfare was pretty seedy. Unfortunately, it must have been too darned cold for the crooks to be out. They were all inside getting drunk. If I hadn't tied one on so spectacularly on New Year's Eve, I might've stepped inside one of the dives and joined them.

A little farther west was Little Italy. I darted from shadow to shadow until I found myself at Mulberry and Grand. For a moment

I felt a pang in my heart. I thought of Fiorello and how much I missed him. So much time has passed since we were together, but it also seems like yesterday. If it wasn't for Fiorello's death, there would be no Black Stiletto. It's ironic that he was my boyfriend and lover, and yet he was a killer, a Mafia soldier who took orders from criminals. I was naïve then.

Some of the Italian restaurants were still open. I smelled the rich food in the air and my stomach growled. The dinner I'd made myself didn't exactly equal a steaming plate of pasta and meatballs. As I hid in a dark doorway, I watched patrons leave the establishments, walk to the corner, and hail taxis. I might have been crazy to just squat there and shiver, but the street brought back warm memories.

Eventually it was time to move on, so I did. I went south, past Broome and Grand Streets, but there wasn't a crime to be found anywhere. I figured I'd give myself another fifteen minutes—because I was freezing my tail off—and then I'd head back home.

There appeared to be more activity on the streets south of Canal Street. I never spent much time in Chinatown except to go eat the fabulous food with Lucy or Freddie. It was a very different world, almost as if it is its own little country within the much grander city. Of course, that's what it is. A community that existed by its own rules and customs. It was intimidating in a way. I'm pretty sure all white people felt as I did—we were outsiders. The Chinese were happy to feed us, do our laundry, and take our money, but beyond that their lives were a mystery.

There were more restaurants in Chinatown than in Little Italy, and many were still open for business. The odors of egg rolls and cooked pork permeated the air and once again my tummy made rumbling noises. What would happen if I walked into a place and ordered some chicken and broccoli and fried dumplings to go? I now had more of a hankering for that than I did the pasta.

But I kept going, flitting from doorway to doorway, staying out of the beams of the streetlights, and gazing at the strange buildings covered with Chinese writing. Many places also had the names in

English, but most did not. Some of the English translations were kind of funny, like the "No Louding" sign in front of a door or the one in a shop window that said, "Be careful do not break it, it will get a breakage." The neon signs were colorful and exotic, and suddenly I felt like I wasn't in America anymore. I've never been out of the U.S.A., but I thought this was what it must be like.

All the shops were closed, but I spent some time looking in the windows at the various dresses—they call them "cheongsams." I know that 'cause it was written in English in one place. There were also all kinds of flat sandals and scarves. I thought I might have to return during the day—not as the Stiletto!—and buy something. It was all very pretty. I could just imagine Freddie's face if I walked into the kitchen one night dressed up in all that silk.

As I continued my exploration, I heard voices of people on the street and inside the bars and restaurants. Their language was musical and their laughter contagious. I suppose it was similar to the Japanese that Soichiro spoke, but it was also vastly different. It *was* more sing-song, for the Chinese held vowels longer, producing a tone behind them. I guess they were vowels, but how should I know?

When I got to Bayard Street, I decided I'd had enough. If I was out much longer, I'd be the Black Icicle, ha ha. I crossed Mott Street and took a left on Elizabeth. A dark storefront window caught my eye. It was full of toys and dolls. It was strange to see dolls with Asian faces. I wasn't used to that. The girl dolls were dressed in little cheongsams, too. Boy dolls wore loose trousers and a long jacket with a high, stiff collar. A little sign said "doll in Mao clothe" in English and Chinese. I then realized it was an effigy of Mao Tse-Tung! Would that be considered Communist propaganda? Probably not. This was America, and after all, it was just a child's plaything.

As I stood at the window, a car pulled up to the curb directly across the street from me. I swiftly moved to the dark doorway and crouched where I couldn't be seen. The New York cops were still out to get me, and I couldn't take too many chances. But come to think of it, during my journey through Little Italy and Chinatown,

I didn't see a single policeman. Strange. I usually can't go out at night without spotting at least one patrol car.

The vehicle across the street was a black Buick. It looked shiny and new. I don't know much about cars, but I know enough. Somebody wealthy owned this one. There were two men inside, the driver and a passenger. The car idled in front of Lee Noodle Restaurant. The lights were on inside the place, but I couldn't see the interior because there was one of those Asian decorative folding screens standing in the window.

I didn't want to move while the men sat there, so I waited. After a moment, the passenger got out of the car. He was Chinese, probably in his twenties, maybe early thirties. It's so hard to tell how old Asian people are. The man wore a heavy coat but no hat. He strode purposefully to the restaurant's front door and tried to open it. It was locked; the place was closed for the night. He knocked loudly. And again. Finally, an older Chinese man appeared. The newcomer barked some words. He sounded angry. The older man unlocked the door and let him inside. Both disappeared from view. The car's engine continued to run. Exhaust poured out the back and created a thick, gray cloud that filled the street.

It was getting colder by the minute, and I remember thinking that whatever business that guy had inside the restaurant, it had better be quick so I could get home and make some hot chocolate!

And that's when I heard the four gunshots, followed by a woman's screams.

I didn't hesitate. I blindly ran across the road, skirted behind the idling car, and burst through the door, which the older man had left unlocked. I entered the small restaurant and beheld a shocking tableau. The old man lay on his back between two tables. His white shirt had two black-red holes in the front, and blood seeped across his chest. Another Chinese man, also gray-haired, was crumpled half-on, half-off a table. He, too, had been shot dead.

The passenger from the car looked younger up close. Probably early twenties. He pointed a handgun at a terrified woman and a teenage boy, both Chinese. They clung to each other in fright. She was crying and babbling in her language. It was clear that the bad guy was about to shoot them, too.

The gunman caught sight of me and turned the gun in my direction. I immediately performed a *Yoko-geri*—a side kick—and disarmed my opponent. This surprised him, and I didn't give him a chance to react. I moved in to deliver a resounding punch to his jaw. His head jerked appropriately, but he didn't fall back. I immediately alternated the delivery and threw a blow with my left fist—but he deftly blocked it with a *Harai-te*—a sweeping gesture that powerfully knocked my attack out of the way. Before *I* could comprehend what had just happened, I felt a tremendous strike in my stomach. He had kicked me! And then, as I was in the process of doubling over, he landed three swift wallops to my face with moves I'd never seen before. Needless to say, I went down.

The woman screamed louder.

The gunman started to run out, but he had to get past me to reach the door. I had the presence of mind to stick my leg up as he jumped over me. He tripped and crashed into a table, pulling off the tablecloth and condiments.

By then we had company. The driver entered the restaurant. He, too, was a young Chinese fellow. He went straight for me as his pal stood. I rolled and rose to my feet just as the newcomer attacked me with martial arts techniques that were beyond my comprehension. Dear diary, I had attained a black belt in *karate* and *judo*, but these two guys had something else going on. Looking back, I figure it was the difference between Chinese and Japanese martial arts. Whatever it was, they had me at a disadvantage.

I held my own, though. The next thirty seconds was a flurry of hand blocks, front and side kicks, and my "crescent moon" kicks—one of which successfully knocked the second guy to the floor. *Judo* throws were impossible. I simply couldn't get close enough to my opponents. They had the ability to hit and slap me repeatedly and rapidly, and it hurt like the dickens. I tried my best to anticipate the maneuvers with what Soichiro taught me, but the blocks didn't work. It was as if their technique had been developed specifically to combat my own. The two men moved incredibly fast, using their entire bodies acrobatically to deliver excruciating jolts with their fists, spear hands, and feet.

It didn't take long for them to have me against the wall. I was doing my best to defend myself, but I was losing. It was only then that I got a good look at their faces. The gunman, on the left, had pockmarked cheeks and a scar that ran from the left corner of his mouth along the edge of his chin. The other guy wasn't as distinctive, but I noticed he had blue eyes instead of brown, the way most Chinese do.

I couldn't take much more punishment, so I turned to the last resort—I drew my stiletto and pointed the blade at them. By then, the two men were working in tandem. Pock Face feigned a kick, so I prepared to block it, but it was Blue Eyes who actually delivered a kick I didn't see coming. He knocked the knife out of my hand and it went flying across the room. Then Pock Face performed a back kick, similar to the *Ushiro-geri* that I knew, but *different*, and it whacked me hard in the face. I went down with stars in my eyes and a ringing in my ears. I think I may have lost consciousness for a second or two, for the next thing I knew, the woman was screaming again. I looked up and couldn't believe what I was seeing.

The teenage boy was now fighting the two killers, and he was using the same techniques as his opponents. The woman—who was undoubtedly the boy's mother—was pleading for him to stop. There was no translation needed: "Stop it, they'll kill you!"

Dazed, a bit broken, and, yes, bleeding from the mouth and nose, I forced myself to get up. I didn't know how old the kid was, but if a fourteen- or fifteen-year-old boy was going to come to my aid, then, by God, I was going to his!

So I joined the melee. And that kid was good! He held his own. I remember at one point he was behind a table that was still covered with someone's dirty dishes. The boy grabbed the tablecloth, pulled it, and flung it so that all the plates soared at Blue Eyes like missiles. The tablecloth itself spread in the air and covered the man's head like a canopy. Now blinded, he was momentarily helpless. The kid looked at me and nodded. That was my cue. I let the cloth-covered intruder have it with simple American boxing triple punches.

But Pock Face got the better of me when I wasn't looking. I must have still been shell-shocked from before, because I should have sensed him coming. I've *always* been able to anticipate attacks, but this time it didn't work. Something hard and heavy hit me on the side of the head, and all the noise around me ceased. It was as if I had been dunked underwater.

Everything went fuzzy, and then someone was lightly slapping my face.

"Lady! Lady!"

I held up a hand so he'd stop. My vision was blurry, but I could tell it was the boy. He was kneeling beside me.

I heard his mother whimpering. I turned my head. She had thrown herself over the body of the older man and was wailing with grief.

Then I became aware of another familiar sound. Police sirens headed our way.

"You go now!" the boy said. He held out my stiletto.

"Where?" I looked around the restaurant.

"Men leave. Now you go! Hurry!"

I took my knife and sheathed it. He helped me up. I hurt all over.

Dear diary, we trashed that restaurant. As I recall, there were maybe ten tables all together in the place, plus a bar, cash register counter, and a swinging door to the kitchen. By the time it was all over, there were three tables still standing untouched.

I indicated the woman and the dead man. "Your mother?"

The boy nodded.

"Your father?"

He nodded again, tears welling in his eyes. He then indicated the other dead man. "My uncle."

The sirens were louder and closer.

"Thank you," he said. "Now go!"

He didn't have to tell me again. The last thing I wanted was for the Black Stiletto to be implicated in a double homicide in China-town.

So I limped out of there. The cold air hit me like a train, but it helped revive my senses. I got myself together and took off north on Elizabeth, kept to the shadows, and made it safely back to the gym.

4
Maggie
THE PRESENT

The Woodlands facility encompasses just a small part of my practice, but it's probably the most fulfilling. I visit the nursing home twice a week and monitor a number of patients, whom the staff call residents. A nursing home is generally the last stop these people make during their journey through life. No one likes to say it, but it's where a person goes to die. The staff—and I—try to make that experience as pleasant and comfortable as possible. For the patients who still have some time left, I treat all kinds of ailments. Dementia is probably the most common one. Alzheimer's is one of my specialties, although I must admit there's a lot I—we—don't know about the disease. There are medications that can treat the behavioral manifestations, but as of today there is no cure.

My private practice is in Lincolnshire. I share it with three other physicians, all of whom specialize in internal medicine and geriatric care. I can't tell you how proud I was when my name was etched into the glass door—"Margaret H. McDaniel, M.D." It was a long, hard road to get there, and I've managed to keep it going for twelve years. I opened the office when I was thirty-one. Now I'm forty-three, and I can't imagine another life. I take my profession seriously.

I want to be as diligent as possible when it comes to my patients. With Alzheimer's, the more you know about a patient, the better. You're dealing with a person's entire *life*. By that, I mean memories.

We all take memories for granted until you start to lose them. That's why I like to know a patient's complete history, his or her biography, anything that can help me help the patient regain some foothold in what has become a very elusive past.

And that's why the case of Judy Talbot concerns me so much.

Judy—I like to be on a first-name basis with my Alzheimer's patients because it helps me communicate with them better—was already a resident of Woodlands when I started there. She's seventy-three years old, but the disease makes her appear older. In her case, the onset of Alzheimer's was sudden and rapid. Within a couple of years she was at an advanced stage, whereas the majority of patients take six to ten years to go through early to moderate to advanced stages. Her case is not unusual, just rare. At the moment, Judy still has use of language, but she finds it difficult to recall vocabulary. She speaks only if necessary, and usually it's a generic phrase that is appropriate to any situation. "Thank you," "yes," "no," "that's nice," "hello," and "goodbye." Her long-term memory seems to be completely gone, although Martin tells me she'll occasionally surprise him by coming out with a sentence or two that refers to something that happened in the past. Judy has not shown signs of aggression, outbursts, or wandering. She has not experienced sundowning. The patient is content with sitting and staring at a television or out the window. She is one of the calmest patients with Alzheimer's I've ever seen. The staff at Woodlands makes sure she takes daily walks through the hallways and goes outside to the garden on pleasant days. At one time, Mrs. Talbot must have been very athletic, for her muscle tone is extraordinary for a woman her age and in her condition. But while the shape of the muscles is still there, she is terribly underweight and therefore thin and frail. Despite that, she often surprises the staff with her strength. I understand there was an incident prior to my joining Woodlands in which she incapacitated a homicide suspect by kicking the man in the groin! I wish I'd seen that. And from hearing that story, all the scars and wounds on the woman's body trouble me even more.

There are surely memories associated with them.

I once asked Martin, her son, if his mother had been in the military. Some of my early work was with war veterans, and I know what combat wounds look like. To me, it appeared that Judy Talbot had been through a war. There are numerous scars on her skin, including a large one on her right shoulder that goes down to the top of her breast. I'm certain it was caused by a knife of some kind. Whoever did the stitching was an amateur. It's the kind of job that's done on the battlefield when no professional doctors are at hand. More disturbing are two old gunshot wounds. One is on her left shoulder, just below the collarbone, and the other is on the left side of her abdomen.

Now, if Judy Talbot didn't get those kinds of wounds in military combat, then how did a suburban single mother acquire them?

Martin claims he doesn't have a clue.

I don't believe him.

In the past couple of months, I've grown to like Martin a lot. We've started dating—I guess that's what you'd call it—and we enjoy each other's company. When I first met him I found him to be a bit *nebech*, to use a term my Jewish grandfather used to say. He's not an unattractive man; if he lost twenty pounds, he'd look great. At first he was unemployed and he seemed to be very nervous around me. Now I know it's because he found me attractive, which is flattering, because I don't consider myself as such. Martin has a job now, and he's less nervous, but he tends to become stressed and anxious. I understand his job as caretaker for his mother isn't easy. Alzheimer's can be harder on the family than on the patient. But, to be honest, I believe there's more to his mother's story than what he's told me. I think that's the cause of Martin's stress, not so much his mother's illness. Something happened to her—and maybe to him— that was traumatic. I once suspected Judy Talbot had been abused by a spouse or someone else. Martin assured me that wasn't the case, but he also never knew his father. Martin's father was an early casualty in Vietnam, or so he claims. I'm not sure I believe that, either. Is Martin lying or does he not know himself?

The other possibility is that Judy was somehow involved in criminal activity. Could she be a wanted fugitive who has hidden under an assumed identity for years? If so, I feel it's my duty to find out the truth.

Martin and I have a dinner date tonight. There's nothing wrong with that—I'm not officially his mother's primary care doctor, although she doesn't really see him anymore. I like Judy, and I like Martin. I want to get closer to him, but that's not going to happen until I can fully trust him.

I met Martin at a place called Kona Grill in Lincolnshire. They serve American Asian cuisine and sushi, and they have a great happy hour from five to seven. The appetizers are half price then, and you can make a meal of them. We'd been there together once before and enjoyed it. It's convenient, too, as I can pop over from Woodlands, and he can stop there on his way home to Buffalo Grove from his office in Deerfield.

He was already there, working on a margarita. I'm not a happy hour-drink person and only occasionally consume alcohol, usually wine with a nice dinner. Martin, from what I gather, tends to have a daily cocktail. I refuse to nag him about it, though. It's how I lost my last boyfriend. He accused me of treating him more like I was his doctor than his lover.

"You look nice," he said after he kissed my cheek.

"Thanks, but you say that every time you see me," I replied with a laugh.

"Well, it's true."

"Martin, I've been working all day. I imagine I look tired."

"That's why you could use one of these." He lifted his glass. "Picks you right up."

"Coffee picks me right up. Have you ordered food?"

"Not yet."

When the waitress came, I asked for water. Martin and I decided to split a pizza, which they call "flatbread," and a California roll. That was plenty for me.

"I just saw your mother," I told him.

"I was there yesterday, but you weren't."

"I know."

"How was she today?"

"About the same. I think she likes me. She perks up when she sees me."

"She does that with any visitor. Wait until you see how she acts when she sees Gina. Mom really brightens up. I wish Gina could see her more often. You don't think Mom won't recognize her, do you? When Gina comes home for Christmas, it'll be four months or so since she saw her."

"If the bond is as strong as you say, then she'll remember. Your daughter's picture is right there on her dresser, so your mother sees that every day."

"I hope you're right."

"How's your job going?"

Martin shrugged. "You know, like I told you before. It's not what I'm best at or what I enjoy doing the most, but it's work. It beats collecting unemployment. Sam was in today. He's such a character. All he did was complain about all the Christmas stuff—Christmas music, Christmas decorations, Christmas this and that. He thinks Hanukkah should get as much attention."

"It does around here, doesn't it? This whole area has a large Jewish population."

"I know. He's just being funny."

"My grandfather was Jewish."

"Really?"

"Yeah. But my grandmother wasn't, so it didn't stick. He was a character, too. He'd send me chocolate coins—'Hanukkah gelt'— for my Christmas stocking."

The food came and we dived in. It was then that I could tell something was bothering him. He usually ate fast and talked a lot. He was rather quiet this time and picked at his food.

"Something wrong, Martin? Are you okay?" I asked.

"I don't know. I told you about it before. I have these weird dreams sometimes. When I wake up, I feel anxious and crummy the rest of the day." He waved a hand at me. "I'm all right."

"Have you ever had any history with depression? Not just you, but your mother, too?"

"Hmm, I haven't. Well, not what I'd call clinical depression. Everybody gets depressed now and then, right? After my divorce I was depressed. I was depressed while I was unemployed. But I'm okay now. That was normal. Wasn't it?"

"Sure, unless it starts affecting your day-to-day functioning. What about your mother?"

"She drank quite a bit while I was growing up. I think me going off to college really set her off. That's when our house kind of went into decline. I noticed she was drinking more when I came back to visit. But, you know? She still kept fit. She had a punching bag in the basement and whaled on that thing every day of her life. She used to run, too. I don't know if she was a true alcoholic or not, because she never seemed drunk, you know what I mean? She held it very well."

"That doesn't mean she wasn't—isn't—an alcoholic."

"So, yeah, I think Mom might have been depressed for a few years."

I took a chance and asked him again. "Martin, her behavior could be tied to however she got all those scars."

"Maggie. Not that again."

"But it could be important! Martin, she has *gunshot wounds*! No ordinary suburban Mom has gunshot wounds."

"I told you I don't know how she got them. It was before I was born, and she never said. I didn't know she had them until you told me."

I knew he was lying. He averted his eyes and kept eating. So I said, "Then I don't understand why you're not more interested in finding out what the story is. If she was *my* mother—"

"*Okay*," he snapped. "Geez, Maggie. Don't you think it bothers me, too? I'm pretty freaked out about my mom, you know. Just the fact that she's in a nursing home is distressing."

"I know." I put a hand on his forearm. "I'm sorry."

He started getting jittery and distracted. He placed a hand on his chest and breathed heavily.

"Martin?"

He didn't answer me. The poor man had an expression of absolute *despair*.

"Martin, what's wrong? Are you all right?"

He nodded furiously and reached for his glass of water—and knocked it over, spilling it all over the table, and a little on my dress.

"Oh, crap, I'm so sorry," he said, but the inflection was one of someone about to start crying. I told him it was all right, and started wiping up the mess and dabbing my wet clothes with my napkin.

Then he said, "I'll be right back," and abruptly got up from the table and walked quickly toward the restrooms. I knew something was terribly wrong. From what he's told me, I've suspected he has some genuine problems with depression and anxiety, and now I'm convinced.

After ten minutes I became worried. I got up and was prepared to approach a manager and ask that he check the men's room, and then Martin appeared. He looked pale. His eyes were red, as if he'd been crying.

"Martin, come with me." I took his hand and led him back to the table. "Tell me what you're feeling."

He described heart palpitations, shortness of breath, and intense anxiety. A feeling of "impending doom," he said. I told him he was probably having a panic attack and that it would subside. For the next five minutes I talked to him soothingly.

"You're not dying, you're not having a heart attack, you're only experiencing a rush of adrenaline that isn't supposed to happen. It will pass, Martin. Just breathe deeply and try to relax. Would you like to leave the restaurant?"

He shook his head.

After a while he did indeed calm down.

"I'm sorry, Maggie."

"Don't be silly. I'm very familiar with the symptoms of an anxiety disorder. Many of my patients have it."

"What do you do for them?"

"I send them to a psychiatrist. Someone you can talk to, and who can prescribe the appropriate medication to help you."

He shook his head. "A shrink? I don't want to see a shrink. Can't you prescribe something?"

"Nope. I'm not a psychiatrist. I don't know that family of drugs well enough. The regimen needs to be custom tailored to the patient, and only a qualified psychiatrist can do that. And besides, I shouldn't be treating you if we're going to be seeing each other."

I swear he did a double take. "What?"

"You heard me."

"We're going to be seeing each other? Really?"

"This is our, what, fourth date? I'd say we're seeing each other."

He took my hand. There was such a cute look on his face. "Maggie, that...that makes me happy."

"Feel better?"

He laughed a little. "Yeah."

The rest of the meal went well. I didn't bring up his mother again. When we left the restaurant, we agreed that he'd call me soon. We parted with a kiss, and I told him not to worry. I said that if he had another attack, to just remember it would pass and there were things he could do about it.

As I drove home, I thought about what I'd said and hoped it wasn't premature. Yes, I did like him. He could be very sweet. He was smart, although he tended to denigrate himself at times. He could make me laugh. Most of the time he was good natured, and it was obvious he loved his mother and daughter. But there was a wall between us, and that was his mother's past. I was determined to solve the big mystery, or else I couldn't really commit to Martin. Not in any long-term, meaningful way.

When I got to my little house in Deerfield, I looked up a friend who worked as a private investigator.

5
Judy's Diary
1960

I'm a mess, dear diary. I'm sore all over and my face looks like I got hit by a waffle iron. I have a busted lip, a bruised right cheekbone, and my right eye is swollen. The vision in that eye is blurry. My abdomen screams when I move too sharply, my forearms ache from all the blocking I did, my collarbone feels like an elephant stepped on it, and my neck hurts. On top of all that, I got my period today, so I'm not the most agreeable girl in the world.

But nothing was broken. The damage isn't as bad as it could have been.

I kept the "closed" sign up yesterday so I could sleep in. I didn't get up until after noon, which is unusual for me. When I saw myself in the mirror, I wanted to cry. Actually, I did a little. But I examined every inch of my body, tested my limbs and movement, and determined I would be all right without having to see a doctor. It looked worse than it actually was.

Everyone at Bellevue Hospital stared at me when I went to see Freddie in the afternoon. I guess they figured I *belonged* there, ha ha. I was afraid Freddie would have another heart attack when he saw me. His jaw dropped and tears came to his eyes, but I quickly told him I was fine.

"What happened to you?"

"Oh, you know me, boss," I answered with a whisper. "The Stiletto ran into some trouble last night."

He winced like he was in pain. "Oh, Judy. When are you gonna stop all that? You're gonna get yourself killed."

I shook my head. "You know better than to ask me that. Last night I saved two people's lives, but it cost me. That's all. I'm glad about it. But what about you? How do you feel today?"

I sat with him for an hour or so. He was still weak and grew tired quickly. We did talk about what to do about the gym. I had to admit I would need some help running it, at least temporarily, until he was able to come home.

"I was thinking of asking Jimmy if he'd like to be an assistant manager for a while," I said. Jimmy's the really nice Negro who was a gym regular even before I started working there. You know, dear diary, I've known him for years. I guess he's in his late thirties. Freddie thought that was a good idea. He told me what I should pay Jimmy and left it up to me to work out his schedule. I didn't know what else Jimmy did for a job, but if he didn't accept I wasn't sure who my second choice would be.

Last night I was tired and still sore, but I scoured the newspaper for a story about the Chinatown shootings. I didn't find anything, so I went to bed.

This morning I opened the gym on time. All the regulars who came in looked at me and asked what happened. My story was that I got mugged. A couple of the guys were sweet, they wanted to "go find the bastards and kick their asses." Then they asked why the gym was closed the last two days and where was Freddie. They were all shocked and saddened to hear about the heart attack. They promised to go visit him in the hospital, but I told them to wait a few days.

As guys came in throughout the day, I got the same questions, over and over, so I ended up getting a marker and writing on the back of a boxing tournament poster all the details about Freddie, when visiting hours were, and what happened to me and that I was all right. Still, they all expressed sympathy and support. Louis and Wayne and Corky—they're all such great guys. Even Clark, the young Negro I train, had tears in his eyes when he heard about Freddie.

Jimmy came in this afternoon, so I pulled him aside to ask him about helping out. He said he works nights as a dishwasher at a restaurant, so the extra hours during the day would be welcome. We figured out a schedule that was mutually beneficial. I'd do most of the work, of course, but Jimmy would be available to spell me for some time off.

Now it's evening, after dinner, and I'm finally able to relax with the newspaper. Finally, there's some news about the Chinatown incident. And sure enough, the headline in the *Daily News* is BLACK STILETTO IMPLICATED. Great. Just what I didn't want. The article went on to say that two men, owners of the Lee Noodle Restaurant, were shot and killed by an unknown assailant. Witnesses reported a sighting of the Black Stiletto at the scene of the crime. What witnesses? There were no witnesses! Perhaps they were the mother and son. They certainly saw me. Anyway, the Stiletto was wanted for questioning, of course. Police believed it to be a robbery gone bad. Ha. I knew better. That was no robbery. Those bad guys had gone there to execute the two men, plain and simple, and Pock Face was about to kill the mother and the teenage boy, too, if I hadn't waltzed in.

It was all very disturbing. I keep thinking about the devastated expressions on that boy and woman's faces. She had lost her husband. The boy had lost his father and uncle. I don't know if the uncle was related to the mother or to the father, but apparently he was a close family member if he co-owned the restaurant.

I decided I wanted to find out more, and especially see if that brave Chinese teenager was okay. If only the Stiletto could talk to him. He spoke English, after all. Perhaps he would tell her what was really going on that night.

JANUARY 14, 1960

I haven't written lately because I've been terribly busy at the gym and going to see Freddie. But I have some time now before I go out with Lucy to see a movie. *Cat on a Hot Tin Roof* is playing at the Bleecker. I didn't see it when it was out a couple of years ago. Lucy and I *love* Paul Newman. He's a dreamboat and a half! I'd follow him anywhere. All he'd have to do is blink those blue eyes at me. But he's married to Joanne Woodward, so I guess that's not gonna happen any time soon. The movie is on a double bill with *Suddenly, Last Summer*, which I've already seen, so I doubt we'll stay for that. I didn't like it very much, anyway.

Ugh, the radio just started playing that awful "Running Bear" song. I can't believe it's number 1. When, oh, when is my Elvis going to put out another record? He's supposed to come home from the army this year, and I think it's soon!

My bruises are finally starting to fade. My lip is healed, but scabbed a little, and my eye is back to normal. I was afraid I'd lose some vision; that blurriness lasted three days. I had resolved to go see an eye doctor if it didn't show improvement by the fourth day, and thankfully it did. I'm still a little sore, but I'm much better. Needless to say, the Stiletto took some time off since that night in Chinatown.

However, today at noon while Jimmy filled in for me, I went back to Elizabeth Street with the intention of having lunch at a Chinese restaurant, but I also wanted to see where the shootings had taken place. The streets in Chinatown were full of people, despite the cold weather. Mostly Chinese, but I did see a few Caucasians, probably there for lunch like me. The Lee Noodle Restaurant wasn't open. A sign on the door was covered with Chinese writing, and the single English word, "Closed." I picked a place across the street and sat at a table by the window. From there I could see Lee Noodle. I watched the building while I ate—had some delicious hot and sour soup, mu shu chicken, and hot tea—but I saw no signs of life.

Then, just as I left my money on the table and got up to leave, I noticed lights on in the restaurant. I hadn't seen them come on, but I was certain they were off a few minutes earlier. I left the restaurant and crossed the street. There's a door next to the restaurant that leads to the apartments on the upper floors of the building. Apparently the family lived—hopefully they still did—in one of the apartments, because the name Lee was on a mailbox inside the door. As nonchalantly as I could, I put my face and hands to the restaurant's glass door and peered inside. From there I couldn't see the full restaurant, just the archway to the right that led to the dining room. I could make out half of the cash register counter, so I took a chance and knocked on the door. After a moment, the woman I'd seen that night appeared. She held up a finger and waved it back and forth. "Closed! Closed!" she said loudly behind the door. I didn't know what I expected, but I simply smiled, nodded, and moved on. I guess I was hoping to see the boy, but then I realized it was a weekday and that he was probably at school. I don't know what the Chinese traditions are concerning mourning, but I suppose it made sense that he'd be back to a normal schedule by now. Although nothing would ever be normal for him again. He had witnessed the murder of his father and uncle and participated in the defense of his mother and himself. I wondered if he talked to his friends about the Black Stiletto and how he had fought alongside her.

A little voice in my head said I should forget about what happened that night and go on with my life. But my instincts, that gut feeling that has driven everything I've done since *I* was a teenager, told me that Chinatown hadn't heard the last of the Black Stiletto.

6
Judy's Diary
1960

I haven't written because I haven't had anything to say until tonight. For the past couple of weeks it's been business as usual—running the gym, going to see Freddie, and getting my body back to normal. Freddie's doing better. He's very restless. He feels fine now and wants to leave the hospital, but the doctor wants him to stay two more weeks. He's afraid Freddie won't take it easy once he gets back to the gym. I agree. Freddie'll want to take over again. He's got to realize things aren't going to be the same.

The Stiletto went back to Chinatown twice. I really wanted to find that teenage boy again, so I watched that restaurant and building for a couple of hours on two different nights. I nearly froze to death, it was so cold. We've had snow in New York and it's pretty slushy out. After a few days, the streets and sidewalks get all yucky with black icy mush and it's a mess. Snow is always pretty when it first comes down, but then it turns into the kitchen sink.

Anyway, tonight I was finally successful. Third time's the charm! I met Billy Shen Lee. He told me the proper Chinese way of saying his name is Lee Shen. They put their last names first. His first name is Shen and his last name is Lee, but everyone but his mother calls him by an American name. He goes by Billy at school, and that's what he wants me to use. He's fifteen years old and he's a sophomore in high school.

So this is what happened. I put on my Stiletto outfit and slipped down to Chinatown. It's tricky there, because lots of people are on the streets. It was only about 9:00, so I was taking a big risk. But I figured the only time I'd catch him was earlier because he's a kid. When I went there before, I found a hiding place. It's sort of an alcove in a building that's under construction or repairs with scaffolding in front, and it's on the other side of the street from the restaurant. It wasn't directly across, but the angle was good enough that I could see the place. As I did the last two times I was there, I crouched on a big piece of plywood in the darkness. People constantly walked by, just a few feet from where I was sitting, but they didn't see me. They'd have to actually *look* into the shadows. With the scaffolding, stacks of plywood, snow and all, I couldn't imagine anyone wanting to do that. Was it cold? You bet! I was beginning to think I was plain crazy for doing it and was about to give up and leave for good, when suddenly there he was.

The boy emerged from the door that led to the apartments. He had on a heavy coat and walked with purpose to the south. He passed my position—across the street—and kept going. I didn't know what to do. I hadn't completely thought it through. There were still people out. I couldn't just step into view and shout, "Hi, kid, remember me?"

So I sat there and watched him. I figured if he turned a corner and left Elizabeth Street, then I'd just have to get up and follow him. But he didn't. He went into an open convenience store. A few minutes later he appeared, carrying a paper bag with some groceries in it. I surveyed the street and—lo and behold—it was actually pretty clear. As soon as he was even with me on the other side, I stood and went, "Psst! Hey, kid!" I had to say it twice before he turned to look. I stepped out of the shadows so he could see me. He stopped and stared. His mouth dropped open. I beckoned for him to cross the street. He hesitated, looking both ways. "Come on, I want to talk to you!" I shout-whispered.

He finally did what I asked. The boy approached me cautiously.

"Hi," I said. "Remember me?"

"Sure." His eyes were wide. He kept looking back and forth along the street.

"Don't worry. Big deal if someone sees us."

"I can't be seen talking to *you*," he said.

"Why not?"

"If they see me, they'd—I have to go."

"Wait. Who's they?"

"I'm sorry."

He started to walk away. "Please wait. Come here, we can stand in the shadows here. We'll whisper. I just want to talk to you for a second. I promise."

Warily he followed me into the darkness. I leaned against the building's wall. I nodded to the bag. "Whatcha got?"

"Milk. Rice." He shrugged.

"What's your name?"

"Billy."

"Billy Lee?"

He nodded, and then he explained about his real name. Billy Shen Lee. I told him I was the Black Stiletto. "I know," he said. Stupid me.

I asked him about that night. What had happened.

This was his story, in a nutshell. His father and uncle (his father's brother) owned the restaurant, but they had borrowed money from the "Tong" to open it, and they also had to pay protection money. For the last few months, though, the men were unable to pay the Tong because Billy's uncle had some medical problems. The Tong grew impatient and killed them. Now Billy's mother must sell the restaurant back to the Tong.

I didn't know what a Tong was. Billy explained that it was a group of Chinese criminals. I said, "Oh, like the Mafia?" and he nodded. I told him I'd had dealings with the Italian mob and that maybe I could help him and his mother. He nervously shook his head.

"You can't go after the Tong! Too dangerous!" he said.

"Don't you want to see them brought to justice for killing your father and uncle?"

"Yes, but it's no use. Even if they are arrested, my mother won't testify against them. She would forbid me to as well. The Tong would kill us."

It was the same old story. Apparently the Chinese gangsters worked just like the Italian ones. If you didn't do what they told you to do, they hurt you. If you ratted on them, they killed you.

"How are you and your mom doing?" I asked.

He shrugged and looked down. "Okay." It was obvious that wasn't true. "I have to go," he said again.

"Okay. But hey, I have one more question."

"What?"

"What was that fighting style you did? I've never seen that before."

"We call is *wushu*."

"It's like *karate*, right?"

He shook his head. "Not really. Actually it's called Praying Mantis *Wushu*. It comes from Southern China. I take lessons at the youth club."

"Well, you're very good. You held your own against those guys."

"Not really."

"Can you teach me some of those moves?"

Again he looked out to the street. He was terrified of being caught talking to me. "I could get in big trouble. *Wushu* is only for Chinese men."

"That's what they told me about *karate* and *judo*, too. Look, I'll pay you. I'll bet you and your mom could use some money, right?"

That got his attention.

"Maybe. But—where?"

"Do you know of a room somewhere? Some place where we wouldn't be bothered?"

"Well—there's the restaurant. It's empty now, until the Tong takes it over."

"That's perfect! Billy, that's great."

So for the next few seconds, we agreed on a price—I'd pay him $25 an hour, which sounded like a million bucks to him, and agreed we'd meet at 10:00 the next night.

He started to move away and cross the street, but then he stopped and turned to me. "Oh. Thank you for helping us. That night."

"My pleasure, Billy. I'm happy to meet you."

Then he smiled. He was a cute kid.

So, dear diary, it looks like I've made a new friend and I'm going to learn some new martial arts moves.

And I'm also determined to learn more about the Tong.

7
Judy's Diary
1960

Freddie's coming home on Friday, so I've been getting everything ready in the apartment. I've been a nice tenant and did his laundry and actually cleaned up the kitchen! I also tidied up the gym so it'll look shipshape when he sees it. Jimmy's been a big help, and Freddie and I have talked about keeping him on part time so Freddie won't have to work so much. Of course, knowing Freddie, he'll want to resume his old ways, but I'll have to police him. I really do feel like he's the dad I never had.

I've met with Billy three times. I sneak down to Chinatown in my Stiletto outfit and he lets me in the restaurant from the inside. It's a good thing his mother goes to bed early. Just like Soichiro was a *sensei*, in Chinese the word for teacher or master is *sifu*. Billy's no *sifu*. He's just a kid and doesn't know a lot, but he's been teaching me what he can. He admits he's not an expert and may be instructing me incorrectly. I'm just learning basic stuff right now. It's actually called "*Chow Gar*," which is a branch of the broader Praying Mantis style of *wushu*. I guess you could say that Japanese martial arts employ more straight-line fighting styles, whereas the Chinese use more circular techniques. So far, I'm just learning exercises that involve my arms, hands, and trunk. One of the concepts behind *Chow Gar* is the *Gen*, or "shock power." That's when the power of the blows comes not from just your fist or foot, for example, but from within your whole body. It's almost like a reflex, similar to the movement you make when you pull your hand away from a hot stove if you accidentally touch it. The exercises are very herky-jerky compared to *karate*. Billy and I also do drills together, like "grinding arm." That's when we push the backs of our wrists together and press outward against each other, at the same time doing a "grinding" motion with our arms. You have to keep your body in the correct stance. It's very hard on the torso and waist. I can already tell I'm building muscles I didn't know I had.

Billy's told me more about the Tong, and I also asked Freddie about it. Freddie told me that the Tongs—there are more than one— came over from China in the 1800s when Chinatown was settled. Apparently there's a Tong network in all the major cities where there are Chinatowns, like San Francisco. Freddie said the Tongs are the "children of the Triads." The Triads are large organized crime groups in China, and right now they're mostly situated in Hong Kong. The Tongs here are generally independent, but some have ties to specific Triads. The stories Freddie told me are incredible. In the early part of this century, there were Tong wars in Chinatown. Gang members had gunfights in restaurants, nightclubs, theaters, and even in the streets. Now it's kept hidden, more like the Italian Mafia today. Of course, Freddie warned me to stay away from them, that they were very dangerous. After what I saw that night in January, I believe it.

Billy filled me in on the more immediate situation. He told me the two killers we fought were members of a Tong called the Flying Dragons. They're fairly new in Chinatown, but they're loosely associated with the Hip Sing Tong, one that's been around since the beginning. The Hip Sing Tong actually does good things for the community, as it's known as one of several "benevolent" organizations that have been in existence in New York since the Chinese first immigrated. But they also have a long history of criminal activities, too. One of the biggest gang wars in the 1920s was between the Hip Sing Tong and their rivals, the On Leong Tong. The Hip Sing Tong has a building on Pell Street called the Hip Sing Association, but Billy said no one knows where the Flying Dragons' headquarters is. Since it's one of the small Tongs, its members are young men, usually aged 16 to 24, hoping to prove themselves so they can join a bigger Tong.

Those two hoodlums that night were in their early twenties, like me, maybe even younger.

FEBRUARY 12, 1960

Freddie's home! Yea!

Jimmy and I were planning a welcome home party for him, but Freddie specifically told me not to do it. Now that I think about it, he was right. We don't want Freddie to get too excited. He's got to stay calm and relaxed for a while, at least another month, before he can resume work. Freddie hates the way his diet has to change and he has to quit smoking. So far, he's doing pretty well, though. Unless he was sneaking cigarettes into the hospital, he went six weeks without one. The challenge comes when he's around other people smoking, and at the gym it's going to be tough. There's no way we could ban smoking in the gym. Everyone would just go somewhere else.

I have the details about what Freddie can or can't eat, so I sautéed some fresh fish I bought on Canal Street—from a Chinese fish market—and potatoes and carrots. I also gave him that record "Theme from a Summer Place" by Percy Faith that everyone loves. When he was in the hospital, he heard it on the radio and liked it. Lately, I've been listening to this wild "exotica" music from Polynesia and Hawaii. Once, when I was over at Lucy's, Peter was there and he played a record called *Les Baxter's Jungle Jazz*. It was strange but beautiful, so I bought it. Then the salesman at the Colony store on Broadway told me about Martin Denny, so I bought his *Quiet Village* record, and I *love* it. I like the way you can hear birds and crickets and stuff in the background. Makes me feel like I'm on some island wearing a grass skirt.

Anyway, it's good to have Freddie back.

FEBRUARY 18, 1960

Today Lucy and I went shopping to look for a wedding dress for her and a bridesmaid dress for me. We went to fancy Fifth Avenue shops, and she said she was buying. I offered to pay for my own dress, but she wouldn't have it.

She didn't like anything we saw, so we went over to Macy's. Lucy ended up getting a beautiful white Casablanca gown that's curve-hugging and tight to emphasize her hourglass figure.

Mine is similar, but not as flowy, and it's pink. I love it! I rarely dress up in formal gowns. I felt like a princess!

FEBRUARY 26, 1960

Billy and I had a scare tonight!

We were drilling with the "Iron Palm" and "Iron Arm" conditioning exercises where we hit each other's palm with a fist, back and forth, over and over and over until your palm is numb, and then slap our forearms against each other on both sides, simulating a blocking maneuver, over and over and over. Ouch. Well, we were in the middle of it when the restaurant door started to open with keys rattling in the door.

"My mother! Hide!" Billy whispered.

The only place to do so was behind the counter where the cash register was. I started for it, but Billy snapped, "Not there!" So I rushed over to where tables and chairs were pushed against the opposite wall. The door was opening just as I was climbing behind a table that was on its side, the top facing outward. She didn't see me.

I stayed still and quiet as I heard Billy talking to his mother in Chinese. Then she went to the cash register counter and got something out of a drawer. More dialogue in Chinese, and then she left.

Close call!

Billy said she wondered what he was doing. He replied that he comes down to practice *wushu* every night. She needed a ledger or something from the drawer. Apparently the Flying Dragons want more and more records of the restaurant's business. She will be forced to hand over the place soon, but they've given her a couple of months to come up with the money her husband owed. Billy is afraid they'll have to move because they won't be able to afford the apartment upstairs.

I told him I wanted to start hunting for the killers, but Billy said I'm not ready yet. I'm nowhere near a point where I could face them again.

He's probably right.

8
Martin
THE PRESENT

The panic attack I had last night at dinner really shook me up. It was awful. I thought I was dying, I really did. You know the feeling you get when your hand gets caught in the cookie jar? Or when the teacher suddenly announces that you're wanted down at the principal's office? Or the sudden realization that something terrible is about to happen and it scares the shit out of you?

That's what it felt like, only magnified about twenty times. It brings on a crushing urge to start crying for no reason at all.

So I'm concerned about it, but I also feel embarrassed and humiliated. I can't imagine what Maggie thinks of me now.

She was very good to me, though. The fact that she's a doctor helped. She was very kind at the restaurant and talked me down. The date ended with a small kiss, so I guess that's a good sign. I do like her and think she's gorgeous. I hope I'm not going to be sheepish around her from now on.

As I entered Woodlands today, I thought about what Maggie had said—that I should see a shrink. I sure don't want to. The idea of taking antidepressants is depressing, and I don't mean that to be funny. But it's true, I need to do something. I have trouble sleeping; my mind races and I imagine all kinds of horrible fictional scenarios as I toss and turn. If I manage to fall asleep, I have nightmares and wake up disturbed and anxious. It's so weird because whatever's wrong with me started only recently and has gotten worse very quickly.

Nevertheless, I put on my happy face when I walked into Mom's room. She sat in front of her portable television watching a soap opera. That rocking chair I got her has seen some good use. She displays complete contentment as she sits in that thing, just like Mrs. Whistler in the painting.

"Hi, Mom!"

She looked up and smiled. The elusive twinkle in her eyes made a brief appearance. Something, somewhere in the deep recesses of her mind, an electric pulse stimulated a nerve that told her that I was someone she cared about. Would she remember the exact relationship today?

I leaned over and gave her a hug and kissed her cheek. "Can you say hello to your son, Mom?"

"Hello," she said. She actually kissed me on the cheek in return. That was rare.

I sat on the edge of her bed, near the rocker. "What are you watching?"

"Oh, I don't know." She turned back to the TV, the smile remaining on her face.

"Are you following the story?"

"What?"

"Are you following the story on the TV?"

"Oh, I don't know."

We went through our ritualistic same-old, same-old conversation. What did she have for breakfast? Had she been for a walk yet? How was she feeling? I got the usual generic answers and we slipped into the predictable clueless silence that invariably takes over when I visit. It's almost as if I've run out of the small talk I can have with my mother. I can't discuss anything of importance because she wouldn't know what I'm going on about. If I try, she acts like she understands, nods her head, and says, "Oh?" or "Is that so?" or "I'm sorry to hear that" or any number of other conditioned responses.

So I watched the soap opera with her and my mind wandered. My thoughts went back to the restaurant and the panic attack. My eyes darted to the dresser, where several framed photographs sat. Gina's senior picture. One of me and Mom. My high school graduation pic. Me and Gina. Mom when she was young.

Mom when she was young...

The Black Stiletto.

My mom was the Black Stiletto.

The sudden rush of adrenaline jolted me and I almost grunted. A wave of anxiety rolled over me, and I knew I had to get out of that room. I couldn't let Mom see me have a panic attack.

But before I could get up or say anything, she turned her head and looked at me. She had tears in her eyes. She reached over with one hand and placed it on mine, which was resting on my knee.

"I'm sorry," she said. A drop rolled down her cheek.

"Mom, it's okay. What's wrong?" I asked. Then I felt like *I* was going to cry.

"I understand," she said as if she was right there on my wavelength.

"You do?"

"She was—"

Oh my God, was my mom about to say something about the Black Stiletto?

"What, Mom? What was she?" I found myself becoming more anxious and choked up.

Mom wrinkled her brow. Whatever was on the tip of her tongue was inaccessible. She struggled for a moment, trying to put it into words. She squeezed my hand.

"For the sake of the baby," she said.

"What? Mom, what? What was for the sake of the baby? What baby?"

"Had to stop."

"Stop? Stop what? Being the Black Stiletto? Is that what you're saying?"

At the mention of the name, she turned back to the television and the tears flowed freely.

"Mom?" Despite my growing alarm, I got up and put my arms around her. "It's okay, don't cry."

At that moment, a nurse knocked on the open door and came into the room. "Everything all right in here?" she asked cheerily, but then she saw us and became concerned. "Is everything okay?"

I let go of Mom and said, "Oh, my mother's upset about something. I don't know what it is."

The woman came over to Mom and said some encouraging words and asked her how she was doing. Mom replied appropriately and seemed to settle down as the nurse took a tissue and wiped her face. I explained that she just started crying for no reason, but I knew that was something that can happen with Alzheimer's patients.

As the nurse gave Mom her attention, I made an excuse to leave, for I couldn't handle being in the room any longer. I'd felt something painful pass between my mom and me. Perhaps that empathy thing she has was working. She felt *my* anxiety and didn't know how to respond to it. So I said goodbye, kissed Mom on the cheek again, and got out of there.

Maybe Maggie's right and I *should* call a shrink.

When I was home that night, I decided to phone Carol. The ex. She works as an administrator for a medical group, so I figured I'd ask her if she could recommend a psychiatrist. Her group is in my health insurance's network of providers, and as much as I was loath to tell Carol I had an anxiety disorder, she's the only other person besides Maggie that I know around here who I could talk to about it. Maggie didn't know anyone in my network.

Carol and I have a cordial relationship. After all, we share a terrific daughter. Our time together in New York when Gina was recovering from the assault was awkward, to be sure, but I think we were both glad the other parent was present. I can't be around Carol for an extended period of time, but we don't hate each other like some divorced couples.

She greeted me on the phone with a noncommittal, "Oh, hi, Martin, how are you?"

Lying, I said I was just fine and then asked if she'd heard from Gina.

"I talked to her yesterday," Carol said. "She's doing okay, I guess. Her schoolwork is going well and she feels better. Her jaw isn't as sore."

"That's good to hear."

"But, I don't know, when I talk to her she seems to dwell on the assault a lot, have you noticed that?"

I hadn't. "Don't you think that's only natural? It's only been a little over a month. She just got her jaw unwired."

"I know, but when I talk to her she always brings up the police investigation. How they haven't caught anyone yet, how they're dragging their feet, how there's a serial rapist out there that they can't find. The way she talks sounds very angry."

"Well, wouldn't you be angry, too? I know I would. I *am* angry."

"Me too, of course I am, but you should talk to her, Martin. She just, I don't know, it sounds like she's putting a lot of hope into the guy getting caught. I don't want it to consume her, you know what I mean? She should continue talking to that therapist she's been seeing and try to forget what happened."

"Carol, it's going to take time. Something like that can't happen overnight."

"Oh, I know. I just worry about her."

"Well, I do, too, but she convinced me she needs to work it out in her own way, and she's smart and mature enough to do so."

"I know, you're right. Talk to her, will you? See if she brings it up."

"Okay. Last time I spoke to her was about a week ago, so I'm due to check in with her."

The conversation went a different direction as Carol talked about work for a minute. I couldn't find an opening to smoothly veer the topic back to psychiatry, and then she hit me with, "Oh, say, I hear you're dating someone!" She said it like it was great news, as if it was the best thing that could happen to *her*.

"Uh, where did you hear that?"

"Gina told me you're seeing your mother's doctor? Is that right?"

Drat that Gina! I had merely mentioned to her that I'd gone out for coffee a couple of times with Maggie. Gina got all excited about it, like it was a big deal.

"Oh, we've just had coffee together. And a couple of dinners. That's all."

"What's her name? Dr. McDaniel, right?"

"Yeah. Margaret. Maggie. And she's not Mom's doctor, really, she's just the one who makes calls at Woodlands. Mom still sees Dr. Schneider, although, come to think of it, I can't remember the last time she did. Maggie's been the one who's been doing everything these days."

"So it sounds like she's your mom's doctor."

"Yeah, I guess it does."

"Is she nice?"

"My mom? Sure, she's a sweetheart."

Carol laughed. I could still manage to amuse her. "Martin!"

"Yeah, she's nice. Look, it's nothing. We're just friends."

"If you say so."

"Really."

"Okay. Well, maybe you might want to bring your friend to a party."

"Yeah? What, are you throwing a Christmas party?" I asked.

"Sort of. It'll be a reception, too."

I was so dumb. I didn't know what she was talking about. "For what?"

"Martin, Ross and I have decided to get married. We're going to have a small get-together at his house over the holidays while Gina is home. We'll have the ceremony there, and then a reception."

Ross Maxwell. The rich lawyer she's been dating for a while. I suppose I should have anticipated that happening at some point, but I was in denial. Carol had been dating him for months. She gave me the date and time, but they went in one ear and out the other. I think I was in shock. My chest cavity suddenly felt like every organ had just been dug out of it with a hoe, leaving an emptiness I hadn't felt since those weeks following the divorce.

"Martin?"

I didn't know what to say. "Uh, wow. That's, uh, well, congratulations!"

"Thanks. Martin, if you're comfortable with it, feel free to bring your doctor friend. We're sending out invitations this week. And hey, listen, if you don't feel like you can make it, I understand. I won't feel bad."

"Do you *want* me to come?"

I could tell she was on the fence. "Only if you're okay with it. I'd like us all to be friends, you know. Ross likes you—"

"No, he doesn't. He hates my guts."

"Oh, that's not true. Stop that."

"He looks down his nose at me. I'm a lowly unemployed loser and he's a big shot lawyer."

"Martin, stop. Besides, you've got a job, now."

"I guess you can call it that."

"I'm not going to get into this with you, Martin. Either you come or you don't, I'll leave it up to you. You'll get an invitation, and I'd love for you to come if you're all right with it. Now what did you call about?"

Somehow asking her for the name of a shrink at that point would sound like I was mocking her plans to get married.

"Never mind. I gotta go. Tell Ross congratulations for me."

"Okay, I will. Talk to Gina, all right?"

"I'll do it. Talk to you later."

After I hung up, I felt another panic attack coming on. I couldn't believe Carol's news would upset me as much as it did, but there you go. I had no qualms about pouring myself a couple of shots of tequila and becoming a couch potato for the next several hours until it was way past my bedtime.

9
Judy's Diary
1960

MARCH 6, 1960

Elvis is home! Hurrah! First Freddie, and now Elvis! There was
footage of him coming home from the army on TV the other night.
They said he's going right into the studio to make a record that will
come out at the end of this month. I'm so excited! I can't wait!

Speaking of Freddie, he's doing better. He wasn't very happy during his first couple of weeks at home. I guess he was depressed. He
kept complaining how he was only 45 years old and that he was an
"invalid." I told him he's *not* an invalid and that as soon as he gets his
strength back, he'll be as good as new. But he shot back with how he
won't be able to do what he used to do. He can't smoke, he can't drink
as much, he can't train (for now); all he can do is sit behind the counter
at the front of the gym like a cripple and watch everyone. Well, when
he said that I got angry. I told him to stop feeling sorry for himself
and be thankful he's alive. For goodness sake's, he could have died!
As he grows stronger, he'll be able to do more. I told him to stop acting
like a baby and *be patient*! That shut him up. I'm sorry I made him
feel bad, but someone had to do it. I think he has a better attitude now.

The Stiletto hasn't made any appearances on the streets except
to go to Chinatown to meet with Billy. We're still doing mostly drills
and exercises, except he showed me a couple of moves that I'm having trouble understanding. In fact, we're sort of making them up as

we go along. I want to move along faster, too. I'm afraid I'm probably doing everything all wrong because I don't have a proper *sifu*, but Billy's doing the best he can. I suppose I'm integrating the *wushu* techniques with what I already know of *karate*; in a way, I'm developing my own personal technique of martial arts. I don't know if that's a good or a bad idea in the long run, but it's working for me right now.

Billy told me about a *wushu* tournament that will take place next Saturday at the youth club he attends. It's free for spectators. I plan on going—not as the Stiletto, of course. I'll be in disguise—as Judy Cooper!

MARCH 12, 1960

Interesting developments in the Chinatown case today, dear diary!

Today I went to the *wushu* tournament at a Chinese youth club on Mulberry Street just west of Columbus Park. You'd have to be Chinese to know it was a youth club, because there was no English on the outside. I was a little nervous. I didn't want to be where I wasn't wanted, but Billy assured me there would be white folks there. All I saw were Chinese people of all ages going in and out. I finally got up the gumption to enter the building. A couple of Chinese men sat at a table inside the door. They didn't say a word, but one gestured to several flyers and handouts. They were all in Chinese, but I picked them up anyway and thanked the men in English.

It was a small gymnasium with a basketball court—hoops at both ends—and surprisingly full bleachers on two sides. A taped outline on the bare floor designated the "ring," only it was square. Judges sat at a table along one side.

The voices and shouts echoed loudly as they tend to do inside a gym. The adults appeared to all be sitting on one side, so I headed there. It was so crowded I had to take a seat pretty high up, so naturally they all stared at me as I climbed to an empty spot next to some gray-haired Chinese men. It was a look that said, "What are *you* doing here?" but then they turned their attention back to the action on the floor. Every once in a while I'd get another scrutiny, but for the most part I felt comfortable. I noticed Billy's mother sitting six rows below me with a group of women. Thankfully, she'd only given me the one curious and slightly disapproving glance. For the most part, I'd say everyone ignored me, even though I think I was the only white girl at the tournament. There were a handful of Caucasian males in the audience, and they gave me the look-see, too.

The gym floor and the other bleachers were full of Chinese teenagers and young adults, almost all boys. There were no girl participants, but there were many sitting in the bleachers. A few teams were in competition. Billy told me that a *sifu* named Lam Sang was the grandmaster in Chinatown. I was pretty sure I spotted him at the table. Maybe he was the head judge, I couldn't really tell. Another guy did all the talking between bouts. Lam Sang was an elderly, but very fit, gentleman dressed in a traditional *wushu* uniform, which is different from the Japanese *karate* and *judo* clothing. Instead of a *karategi*, the Chinese wear a jacket with loose sleeves and cuffs, a mandarin-style collar, and buttons called "frog" closures. The pants also fit loosely and have cuffs. There's no question that it looks "Oriental." The uniforms look like they'd be comfy.

I spotted Billy sitting on the other side with a group of boys, all dressed in the same brown-and-white uniform. I hoped I hadn't missed his bout.

The tournament consisted only of barehanded fights. They got points for striking the head, trunk, and thighs, but were penalized for the back of the head, neck, or groin. Each bout had three rounds of two minutes each, with a minute rest in between. The competitors had to stay within the square. I recognized some of the moves Billy had taught me, but most of it was *way* over my head. I sat there simply fascinated. It was like when I witnessed my first Japanese martial arts tournament at the Second Avenue Gym. I was dumbfounded. I couldn't believe human beings could actually *do* what I was witnessing.

And it looked so *rough*, too, and yet it was beautiful to watch.

There was more of a dance between opponents in *wushu* than in *karate*. As I observed the matches, I realized what I was doing wrong when I drilled. Seeing *wushu* in action was a lot different than attempting the simple exercises with Billy, so I did my best to study the moves.

Finally, I saw members of Billy's team start matches with a team wearing purple-and-white uniforms. In between each match, one of the judges delivered a brief speech in Chinese.

Eventually, Billy got on the floor. His opponent was a boy that appeared to be the same age, size, and weight. I heard Billy's mother clap and shout something. My stomach had butterflies in it. I wanted to shout, "Go, Billy!" but I didn't want to draw attention to myself.

The opponents faced one side of the audience and made a gesture with their arms and hands—they held them in front of their chests as if they were praying, but the left palm lay flat against the right fist. The boys "saluted" the other side in this manner, and then they did the same to each other.

The match began. Billy and the other boy circled each other once, and then went at it. Their arms and hands flew at one another, slapping and hitting, almost as if they were playing patty-cake as fast as they could, but with intense aggression. Then, suddenly, there'd be a leg and another leg and a kick and punch and kick and punch and a punch and—you get the idea. The other boy broke through Billy's defenses once and landed a blow on my friend's chest. I could tell it hurt, but Billy barely flinched. He deftly blocked a second attack and "grinded" his opponent's arms away—and then he swiftly shot his right hand forward and hit the other boy's face. Apparently Billy got points for that. His mother applauded. Round one ended. It appeared that Billy won it.

The fight continued after a brief break. The other boy managed to hit Billy a couple of times on the shoulder. They continued to block each other, and then Billy's opponent moved in closer and his attacks became fiercer and lightning fast. I was amazed that Billy could keep up with him, blocking the whiplike thrusts and slaps as if he knew what was coming. Before you knew it, the round was over. The other boy won that one.

The third round began like the first with a lot of sparring that landed no targets. No points for quite some time. But after deflecting his opponent's assault for over a minute, Billy suddenly smacked the boy on the jaw. He didn't stop there; he kept assailing his target so fast I could barely follow the movements of his arms. I felt the audience lurch forward in their seats—this was an exciting match!

And then—just when the bout reached a fever pitch—it was over! The two boys saluted each other with fists to palms and then stood at attention as Lam Sang and his assistants tallied the score.

I thought it was a slam dunk, and sure enough, Billy won!

I watched him return triumphantly to the bleachers and sit with his team. I felt proud and happy for him. His mother stood and said something to the other women. They smiled and nodded congratulations. His mom stepped down to the floor and made her way toward the front door.

Billy's opponent looked angry. I followed him with my eyes as he resumed his seat on the other side of the bleachers.

And that's when I saw Pock Face.

He stood next to the bleachers. Although he was a young man, he wasn't a member of any team. He was dressed in street clothes. I quickly scanned the faces of the other boys, but didn't see Blue Eyes.

Pock Face wore a scowl. He must have spotted Billy's mother, for he strode across the gym toward the entrance and crossed over to our side. He caught up with her near the door. She looked frightened when he approached. He gestured for her to come closer. When she did, he leaned in and spoke into her ear. She nodded furiously, as if apologizing for something, and then she hurried out the door. The poor woman was terrified.

Pock Face stood where he was for another minute or two until the next match began, and then he left.

That was my cue. I politely excused myself as I made my way down the bleachers to the floor and went outside. I looked up and down Mulberry, but I didn't see him. At first I was angry that I let him get away, but then I looked straight across the street and saw the guy. He was walking west through Columbus Park to join a group of boys who were smoking and laughing around some benches. Tong members, I was sure of it. So I went to the corner and crossed at the light. I nonchalantly entered the park and stopped to buy a hot dog from a street vendor. With my food, I wandered near the cluster of hoodlums and sat on an empty bench. I felt safe. It was broad daylight. The weather was cold, but it wasn't snowing.

Pock Face smoked a cigarette with his buddies and then moved on. He continued west to the other side of the park. I got up and followed, but when I got to Baxter Street, the western edge of the park, I stopped. My prey had crossed the street and stood on the other side in front of a brownstone. There he huddled with two other young Chinese men. I had to keep going south on the park side so I wouldn't be conspicuous. I needed another excuse to stop, so when a Caucasian woman came toward me with a big German shepherd on a leash, I went, "Oh, what a beautiful doggie!" She stopped and let me squat and pet the animal, but all the while I kept Pock Face in view. I made time-killing conversation with the woman about how I wanted to get a dog. Just when I ran out of things to say and sensed that she wanted to move on, Pock Face headed south. I said goodbye to my new canine friend and kept going.

Then, the gangster abruptly stopped walking and bounded up the steps of a brownstone at the southern end of Baxter Street. With a key, he opened the door and entered the building.

I got you! I thought.

Now I know where one of the killers lives, and the Black Stiletto will pay him a visit tonight.

Wish me luck, dear diary.

10
Judy's Diary
1960

MARCH 13, 1960

It seems like every time I come home from one of the Stiletto's adventures, I write that I "escaped with my life." Tonight—earlier this morning—was no exception—but I came out the victor.

Around 10:00 I put on my outfit and slinked to Chinatown. I had no idea if Pock Face would be home or out with his gang. My effort could have been futile, but I had to give it a shot. I found a shadowy spot in Columbus Park, right across from Pock Face's brownstone on Baxter Street. It was still cold out, so I told myself I'd give it an hour and no more. If I didn't see him, I'd try again another night.

I remember sitting there on a park bench thinking I was nuts. There I was, decked out in my leather outfit—a *costume*, according to the papers—sitting in below freezing temperature, at night, in a deserted park, watching a house where a Chinese gangster may or may not live, and hoping I could exact some justice for a teenage boy I barely knew. How many twenty-two-year-old girls in New York City did that kind of thing? How many other smart and attractive young females in Manhattan spent their days boxing and learning *karate* and *wushu* and then spent nights prowling the metropolis wearing a mask and looking for trouble, when they could be dating men, getting married, and having babies? Okay, forget those last two things, but the dating men part would be nice. It's been a while since John and I—you know—dear diary. But I didn't have any prospects. Not a single possibility. I loved all the regulars at the gym, but I couldn't see going out with any of them. Plenty have tried. I didn't think it was right to mix business with pleasure. I learned my lesson with that chump Mack. Actually, the guy at the gym I think is the most attractive is *Jimmy*. He may not be the brightest man in the world, but he's fit and muscular and he's very sweet. He looks fabulous in boxing trunks. But he's a Negro. Can a white girl date a Negro? I don't see why not, but I'm sure most people think it's something taboo. Maybe one day in the future it will be acceptable for races to mix, but right now it would be asking for a whole lot of woe.

That was the kind of stuff going through my head, dear diary, as I sat in the cold darkness and felt sorry for myself. Then all of a sudden the brownstone door opened and Pock Face emerged. I knew it was him. He was wearing the same winter coat he'd had on earlier. No hat.

He headed across Baxter to the park, in my direction.

I hopped off the bench and hid behind a tree. Should I confront him right there? Or was it better to follow him to see where he went? Maybe he was going to the Flying Dragons' headquarters. I thought it might be useful to discover its location.

The young hoodlum crossed in front of me and moved east, stopping momentarily to light a cigarette. I stayed on his tail, darting from trees to shadows, until he reached the other side of the park and crossed Mulberry Street. From there he turned north. That's when I realized I hadn't thought the evening through. I've been guilty of that in the past and I've got to stop it. I need to get better with *planning*.

There were more people out than I liked, making it more difficult to follow him. I stayed on the park side of the street, watching him stride with purpose to Bayard, a one-way street going east. There, he turned right. I had no choice but to navigate around some shocked pedestrians and run across Mulberry. Fine, so the Chinatown newspapers would report a Black Stiletto sighting. Whatever, at that point I had committed myself to the task.

When he got to the intersection of Mott and Bayard he must have sensed something, possibly the surprised reactions of pedestrians behind him, for he stopped and slowly turned. He caught me standing ten feet away. Our eyes met. He stood his ground and beckoned with his hand for me to come closer. And, dear diary, we had an audience of about twenty people. Even drivers of cars or taxis passing by on Bayard could see us. It was going to be a very public encounter.

Fine.

I took the initiative and attacked first. I ran at him and performed a *Tobi-geri*—a jump kick—by leaping into the air and striking him with a side thrust from my left leg—but I sensed he was ready to block the blow, so in mid-jump I changed the maneuver to a *Nidan-geri*—a double kick. That's when you leap as you would with a jump kick and strike the opponent's torso with one foot, but then you sort of jerk your body upright in midair and slam the guy's face with the jumping foot. You have to leap quite high to accomplish it.

My strategy worked. He indeed blocked the first kick, but didn't expect the second one. My boot slammed into his cheekbone with such force that he cried out. I landed badly because of my split-second decision to alter the maneuver. I fell to the pavement on my side, but I rolled with it to deflect a full impact. Pock Face's legs buckled and he landed on his behind!

He recovered quickly, though, performed some kind of circular kick with his legs parallel to the ground, and got me right in the stomach. It hurt, but it could've been worse. My opponent didn't have the kind of balance and leverage he needed to back the attack with the power it needed.

We simultaneously got to our feet. He moved in and launched an onslaught similar to what he did that night in the restaurant. His arms and fists snapped out at lightning speed, hitting me in the face and shoulders. It took a few seconds of getting the stuffing knocked out of me before I remembered some of the blocking moves Billy had taught me. Lo and behold, they worked. My newfound prowess surprised Pock Face. I could see it in his eyes. *How did she learn to do that? Why isn't she on the ground, howling in pain? What am I doing wrong?*

His puzzlement worked to my advantage. He hesitated and then I let him have it. I remembered what I'd seen at the tournament and applied the graceful-yet-shockwave style arm and hand attacks with what I already knew in *karate*. The result was, well, something new, I think. Pock Face tried his best to block me, but everything I did wasn't on his radar. Several of my blows hit their targets and caused considerable damage. He retreated as I moved forward without stopping the barrage of punches and kicks. I felt invigorated. If it was a tournament bout, he would've already stepped out of the ring and I'd be the winner.

He whirled around and took several steps backward to put some distance between us. There was a brief respite. Only then was I aware of the growing audience that surrounded us. It had doubled in size. I didn't understand the murmurs and shouts, but I didn't need subtitles. Some people shouted for us to stop. Others cheered us on. It was grand entertainment, and only in Chinatown.

I'd been afraid he'd draw his handgun, but for some reason he didn't. Perhaps he wasn't carrying it. But the switchblade he suddenly flicked open was long and sharp and certainly not inconsequential. He swished it around and lunged at me. The spectators moved farther back for fear of being accidentally slashed.

I deftly spun and avoided the thrust, but Pock Face had made a big mistake. He had chosen to have a knife fight with the Black Stiletto. There was no way he was better than me with a blade.

I drew my stiletto—and everything Fiorello taught me came rushing back. The dance you do in a knife fight was very different from the steps you make in *karate* or *wushu*. I knew the moves; Pock Face didn't even know the music.

Like miniature swords, the two blades whooshed back and forth, occasionally striking the other with scrapes and clangs. At one point my stiletto struck his hand. Blood spurted, but he kept hold of the switchblade. Pock Face then saw an opening and he lurched at me with his entire body. Fiorello's training paid off in spades. I performed a split-second twist of the trunk while continuing to bolt forward—awkward and doable only by someone fit and lithe like me—and his blade missed me by less than an inch. By then he was at my side, his momentum carrying him past. All I had to do was fling the stiletto as if I was throwing it at the ground, and the knife punctured the back of his thigh. He screamed and went down hard.

I kicked the switchblade away from him and then dropped onto his back with my knee in his kidneys. That took most of the fight out of him, but he struggled to buck me off. No such luck. I grabbed an arm and pulled it behind his back and up across his shoulder blade. He grunted in agony.

"Stop squirming or I'll break it!" I spat.

With my other hand I took hold of the rope at my belt, looped it around his wrist, and successfully wrapped it around his other arm. It took nearly a minute to hogtie him, but when I was done, Pock Face was helpless, lying on his stomach with his hands and feet secured together behind him.

Only then did I look up at the throng around me. All Chinese. All dumbfounded. Completely silent and in shock.

I nearly gasped when I saw Billy among them. He stood in the front and watched me with eyes wide and jaw dropped. I nodded at him and said, "Call the police." He didn't move. "Hurry!" The boy jumped and rushed to the pay phone a few yards away on the corner. I watched him pick up the receiver and then I stood and addressed the audience.

"Go home, the show's over. The police are coming, and unless you want to be witnesses and give statements, you better get out of here!"

No one moved. Either they didn't understand me or they weren't about to miss any more excitement.

"Fine," I said. "Just make sure you get the details right. The Black Stiletto took down the murderer of Mr. Lee from Lee Noodle Restaurant." I pointed to Pock Face. "He was the killer. He killed Mr. Lee and his brother!"

Billy returned. I said to him, "Tell the cops everything. You'll have to identify him as your father's killer."

The boy stared at me like I was asking him to do the impossible.

"It's the only way," I insisted.

Finally, he nodded, just as we all heard the sirens.

"That's my cue to leave." I sheathed my knife, and then, on a whim, I saluted the audience with the fist-to-palm gesture. Most of them acknowledged it with smiles and small bows.

Then I ran home and here I am, safe and sound.

I feel good.

11
Maggie
The Present

I suppose I should have felt devious for having my boyfriend—can I call him that yet?—investigated. The thing is, I do like him. But there are some awfully suspicious mysteries about his mother that I think he knows about. I wouldn't want to get more involved if there was something, dare I say criminal, in their past? I have to be honest with myself. I'm too old to mess around with serial dating. I'm in my forties and I have a busy, productive practice. If I'm going to invest my time in something that might develop into a relationship, I want to be somewhat confident that I'm making a good decision.

I explained this to Bill Ryan when I went to see him last week. He told me women have prospective boyfriends checked out all the time. It was nothing new. That made me feel a little better about what I was asking him to do. Bill is a former cop, probably fifty- or sixty-something. A little heavy, not too bad. I'm not sure why he retired early, but now he's a private investigator. I know him through my networking group. We meet once a month for breakfast in Highland Park. I hired him because I thought he'd be considerate, reasonable, and, most importantly, discreet.

Today he called and asked that I stop by his office in Northbrook. He had me sit in front of his desk and he went over what he'd discovered so far.

"I started with Illinois, because it's easier to begin in the present and work backward," he said in a gravelly voice that might have been comedic in a different setting.

"I looked into Judy Talbot's records and also searched for information about Richard Talbot, the father. Public records are all straightforward. They moved into that house in Arlington Heights in 1970. Prior to that, she and little Martin lived in two different apartments, both in Arlington Heights. Her first records in the state begin in late 1963. Then they were in Ohio for a few months. Then they were back in Illinois until 1965. For some reason they went to St. Louis, Missouri, for a few months, and then they got another apartment in Arlington Heights, Illinois, from 1965 to 1969. So far, I haven't found anything on any Richard Talbot. Military records from that period, especially if they involve the Vietnam War before it escalated into the conflict we know, are pretty hazy, I'm afraid. But I'll keep looking."

"What kind of work did she do?" I asked.

"That's the funny thing," Bill said. "She has no employment records. Zilch. Not in this state, anyway. Tax returns showed she earned around thirty grand a year up until the New Millennium. Her profession on her return was listed as 'consultant,' whatever that means. After that she lived on savings until she was near poverty. The house was all paid for. Her current bank is Village Bank and Trust, and she has no money in any accounts now. That's why she's in a nursing home. I'm trying to get statements prior to the ones from Village Bank, but that's hard because banks in Arlington Heights turned over a lot since the sixties. In the sixties and seventies, thirty grand a year wasn't too shabby. Her credit rating is clean."

"So what was she consulting? Who was sending her money?"

"That's the next step."

"You mean Los Angeles," I said. "Martin told me he was born there and they came to Illinois when he was a baby."

"An investigation in L.A. can get expensive, Maggie. You sure you want to do this?"

I told him I did, heaven help me.

*   *   *

Martin and I had dinner together on Saturday night, this time at Fleming's Steak House in Lincolnshire. I told him that was way too expensive, but he insisted on taking me. He wanted to "make up" for embarrassing me at Kona Grill the other evening. I told him I wasn't embarrassed and to forget about it. But we went to Fleming's anyway. I'm afraid I allowed myself to indulge in the bottle of wine he ordered, and besides, that was the best way to enjoy the steak, baked potato, and vegetables. Everything was delicious. Well, the wine went to my head and my inhibitions went out the window, just like they're supposed to when you drink wine. I ended up going home with Martin.

His house probably needed a maid service to give it a once-over every couple of weeks, but it wasn't the bachelor nightmare I was afraid it might be. It was actually quite nice. There were framed duplicates of the photos Judy has in her room at Woodlands, along with several others of Martin and his small family. Gina is an attractive girl.

He lit a fire in the fireplace and then asked if I wanted another drink. I told him no, but he brought out some sherry that I sipped. Incongruously, there was a vintage Kennedy/Johnson campaign button on the coffee table. I asked him about it and he said it was his mother's. He said he found it among her things and just happened to be looking at it and left it there. Martin had suggested earlier that we could watch a movie on DVD, but that never happened. As we sat on the sofa, one thing led to another, and he got up the nerve to kiss me. I kissed him back and before long we were making out.

We ended up in his bedroom and I spent the night. I had been proceeding on the side of caution, but for some reason that night I simply wanted some intimacy and Martin was there. He was charming at dinner and he said all the right things when we were at his place. Perhaps I wanted to be seduced; it had been a long time since I'd been with a man. Despite my reservations about his past, I went ahead and made our relationship official. Whether or not it was a mistake, it's too soon to say. I do know that it went well, it was a pleasant experience, and he was an adequate lover. Being the first time for us, of course it was a little awkward and we fumbled a bit, but in the end everything was fine.

However, during the night, I woke up to hear him talking in his sleep. He was having a nightmare; that much was apparent from his distress. It was difficult to understand his words, but I clearly heard him say "Not you, Mom." I shook him and he started violently. It took a moment for him to calm down and realize he'd been dreaming. I asked if he remembered what was so disturbing, but he said he couldn't. I didn't tell him he mentioned his mother.

I suggested again that a therapist could be useful to him, and he admitted that he was planning to seek one out. I told him I could try to get a referral for someone in his medical network, but he preferred to find a doctor on his own.

We went back to sleep.

In the morning I didn't immediately regret what I'd done, so I took that to be a good sign.

12
Judy's Diary
1960

MARCH 15, 1960

Last night was a disaster, dear diary.

It's late afternoon and I just woke up a little while ago. This morning Jimmy took over at the gym for me. From behind my bedroom door I told Freddie I was sick. I slept all day.

I got beat up again. Bad. I have a broken rib, I know I do. It was a good thing Freddie was already asleep when I got home last night or he would have forced me to go to the emergency room. I probably should have. Instead, I've wrapped my ribcage with that same stretchy wrapping they gave me a while back when I broke a different rib. I remember sticking the support wrap in a drawer somewhere, so I pulled it out. I'm sure if I went to a doctor he'd just make me wear it for a month or so, and I've already got one, so okay, I'll wear it for a month or so. I've been down this road before.

Other minor injuries—a swollen right eyebrow, another busted lip, a bloody nose, a black eye that's on its way, and *really* sore forearms, hands, and thighs. Oh, and shoulders. And neck. Dear diary, my whole body hurts!

But I'm alive.

What hurts the most is the headline of the *Daily News*.

"BLACK STILETTO DEFEATED!" in big, bold letters. Four photos accompanied the article. They were pictures of me lying in the middle of Pell Street, surrounded by innocent bystanders. In the fourth shot, the police had joined them. Yes, the police. An enterprising pedestrian must have had a camera I didn't notice. I was a bit out of it at the time. There were no photographs of my assailants. They had all run off by the time the street brawl had become the biggest news story on the planet.

Alas, it's true. I *was* defeated. Of course, it was a couple dozen against one, but I didn't think that would stop the Black Stiletto. I guess I have to know my limitations.

Most of the article was inaccurate, as they usually are. The reporter especially got the last part wrong. It stated that I was helped up by two policeman, handcuffed, and thrown into a patrol car, under arrest. I was "humiliated and broken in defeat." That's not exactly what happened, or I wouldn't be sitting at the kitchen table writing this now. And I wasn't humiliated. I was *angry*. The bad guys ganged up on me. It wasn't a fair fight at all.

The evening started out with me going to my regular *wushu* lesson with Billy at the restaurant. I was feeling good about catching his father's killer. I thought he and his mother would be very happy about it. But he met me outside and told me there would be no lesson and to meet him in a few minutes in our shadowy alcove across the street in the building under construction. I thought, *uh-oh*. Something had happened.

Billy showed up nearly ten minutes later and apologized. He said we can't meet for lessons anymore. He and his mother have to move out of the building. The Flying Dragons took over the restaurant and still claim his father owed the Tong $20,000! Pock Face's arrest made the situation worse. Billy said his mother wouldn't testify and forbade him to do so. She was threatened. And Pock Face was *released*! None of the charges stuck. Like the Italian Mafia, the Tongs had good lawyers and corrupt police and judges in their pockets. At any rate, Billy and his Mom were in a lot of trouble. If they don't do what the Tong says, they'll be killed.

I was horrified. Somehow my fight with the killer put my friend in danger. I guess it made sense, now that I think about it. Why would the Black Stiletto be avenging the murder of Mr. Lee and his brother unless she had a connection to the family?

"Who *are* these people? How can they have so much power? Don't the police have any say in what goes on in Chinatown?" I asked.

Billy rolled his eyes. "Not really. The Tongs pay no attention to white cops. There are more and more Chinese policemen in Chinatown, but it doesn't really help."

"Do you know any more about the Flying Dragons?"

"All I know is their leader is a guy named Tommy Cheng. The two men at the restaurant that night are a couple of his enforcers. I imagine the headquarters is on Pell Street. That's where the Hip Sing Tong is, and the Flying Dragons are their little brothers."

"Where are you and your mother going to live?"

He shrugged. "I don't know. Some dump. We're thinking of going back to China to be with my grandparents. At least we'd escape the Tong, but we'd be poor."

"I'm sorry, Billy," I said.

He replied that he understood and that he wasn't upset at me. His mother was, and she was also angry at him for talking to the Stiletto. It put their lives in jeopardy.

I immediately said I would make it right, but Billy held up a hand. "No," he said. "You must go away and forget about all this. I mean it. It's now too dangerous for you—and for us—if you're seen here. Ma'am—" that was the first time he ever called me "ma'am"— "I thank you for everything. I have enjoyed our time together. But I must say goodbye. I am sorry."

That's when I realized poor Billy was scared to death. The Tong had put the fear of God into him and his mother. For that, I was determined to take them all on. I wanted to find their little nest and fumigate them.

But I told him, "All right, Billy. It's okay. I don't want to make you uncomfortable. I understand." In other words, I let him off the hook. I thanked him for his lessons and paid him his last fee. Without him knowing, I slipped an extra $50 in the wad of cash.

We shook hands and said goodbye. I could tell he wasn't happy about what he had to tell me. He was genuinely upset. I might have felt bad about it myself, but somehow I knew—I *know*—Billy and I will meet again and I told him so.

I waited until he was back inside his building before I emerged from our hiding place. Even though I'd just promised him I wouldn't come see him anymore, I didn't exactly say I wasn't going to visit Chinatown. So just to make the evening's effort worthwhile, I decided to take a stroll. Instead of heading north toward the Village, I went south to see what kind of mischief I could find. Maybe I wanted another scrap with a Tong member. I had felt so good the previous night. The Black Stiletto had trounced a really tough guy—a murderer—and handed him over to the police. My extracurricular activities hadn't gone so well in a long time.

But ego and arrogance were my downfall. I was cocky. Having an audience the other night went to my head. I know that now. I was stupid and I'm mad at myself for not paying heed to what I'd told Billy.

There were a lot of pedestrians on the streets, as usual. I dashed between dark pockets of storefronts, step by step, along Bayard Street going west. I was seen. Fingers pointed. But I moved swiftly and didn't give anyone time to engage me in any way. I found a few unlit spots where I could stand, catch my breath, and observe the landscape.

I reached Bayard and Mott, the scene of my little scuffle with Pock Face and kept going south. By then, the buzz on the street was pretty strong: *the Black Stiletto was in Chinatown*. It must have been what I wanted. I hoped the Tongs would come out and play.

And they did.

Pell Street T-intersected into Mott from the east. There, a dozen toughs stood in the middle of the road, blocking any travel farther south. I either had to turn around and go north on Mott, or take the left turn onto Pell Street, which, from the intersection, looked clear of anyone but pedestrians. I chose the latter.

It was a trap.

As soon as I slipped to the sidewalk on Pell, more young Chinese men materialized out of the shadows in front of me. They'd been waiting. I looked behind me and the first mob had moved forward and now blocked the way out to Mott. I was surrounded by at least two dozen Tong members. Some of them carried weapons—clubs, bats, knives—but I saw no handguns.

Dear diary, I'd been in precarious situations before and I've also experienced fear, but I don't think I've ever been as scared as I was then. My stomach was in my throat. My intuitive danger alarms were going haywire. My heart pounded and my adrenaline pumped. It was fight or flight, no question about it.

I was the Black Stiletto! I could face all those hoodlums, right?

They proved me wrong.

Mustering up some bravado, I said, "You fellas don't want any trouble, now do you?" I don't know if they understood English or if they just didn't want to reply. They just kept moving forward, squeezing me in, leaving me no way out.

I drew the stiletto. "Stand back," I threatened, but my words fell on deaf ears.

The best route out of the situation was through the cluster in front of me on Pell. If I could get past them, I'd be at the Bowery and home free. There was no way they could outrun me. I could whip up a fire escape and fly over some rooftops before they knew where I'd gone. I just had to find an opening.

So I attacked first.

I think the element of surprise was on my side at the beginning. They hadn't expected me to make the opening move. I ran at the thugs with the knife whishing back and forth. A few stepped back, allowing me some advancement. For a moment I thought I saw doubt on their faces. But then a couple of guys deftly blocked me, and I felt the excruciating blow from a club on my side. My blade struck some meat and I heard a cry, but I had no idea what happened next. It was as if a swarm of bees had descended on me. The stings came from everywhere at once. Fists, feet, clubs—the onslaught was overpowering. Before I knew it, I found myself curled in a fetal position and lying on my side in the street. The blows were a flood of agony, sharp and powerful, tearing me apart and rendering me helpless.

Dear diary, I might have been killed. I remember crying out in pain and thinking it was hopeless—when I realized I still held my stiletto. In my mind's eye I saw Soichiro standing in his old *karate* studio, berating me for not breathing or not concentrating or not doing *something*. It was the motivation I needed.

I thrust my knife hand out and struck a calf. I swung it around in a curve, slicing ankles and shins. My targets yelped and retreated, but that didn't stop the crush of anger directed at me. The torment unleashed on my body increased in intensity, and I was sure I blacked out. It must have been what had happened, because suddenly there were police sirens in the air. They had come out of nowhere and were *loud*. The assault died off and finally stopped altogether. I felt the oppressive huddle of the mob disperse. I was alone on the street, a battered rag doll that couldn't move.

Everything became a blur. I was aware of the nearby heat from a patrol car's engine, and headlights illuminated my disgrace for everyone to see. Raising my head, I attempted to crawl out of the spotlight, but I heard a male Caucasian voice in my ear.

"How bad is it?"

I didn't answer. I squinted at the man kneeling beside me. It was a young patrolman.

"Can you walk?" he asked. "Do you need an ambulance?"

"Help...help me up," I managed to say.

He did. My body screamed in misery as the broken rib made its presence known.

"We're getting you out of here," the cop said. And with that, he snapped a handcuff on my right wrist. The other half locked onto my left, and suddenly I was in the backseat of the patrol car. Two young policemen got in the front, put on the siren again, and drove out of Pell Street.

"Do you need to go to the hospital?" my new friend asked.

"No," I managed to whisper.

I forced myself to sit up. We were traveling north on Bowery.

"Are you sure?" the cop asked again.

"Yeah."

"You could have been killed back there."

"I know."

"Stay out of Chinatown. It's not for you."

I didn't know what was going on. Were they arresting me? Were they taking me to the nearest precinct? Was the Black Stiletto finished?

To my surprise, they pulled over to the side of the road. The cop in the passenger seat got out and came around to the back. He opened the door, leaned in, and unlocked the handcuffs.

"Can you make it?" he asked. "Are you all right?"

I told him, "Yeah," although to tell the truth, I wasn't sure. He helped me out of the car and I stood unsteadily on the sidewalk.

The young patrolman then explained himself. "I admire you a lot," he said. "But Chinatown is no place for the Black Stiletto. It's a different world. Even the police don't understand it. Those Tongs are animals. Stay away, if you know what's good for you. Don't go back, okay?"

"Thanks," was all I could think of to say.

"Take care of yourself," the cop said as he got back in the front seat and slammed the door shut. The driver took off and left me alone.

I breathed deeply, despite the pain in my side. Examining myself, I saw the blood all over my outfit. I wiped my nose and mouth and flung red goo onto the street. Thankfully, the cold air helped revive me. My senses returned and I had the strength to get out of the streetlight and scram. I limped east until I found a shadowy, isolated storefront on a side street, and I fell to my knees. There, I rested and pulled myself together. I stayed there for several minutes until I talked myself into standing and moving on.

It's a miracle I made it home.

13
Judy's Diary

1960

As you can see by the date, I haven't written lately. I've been concentrating on healing and running the gym. Freddie's a lot better and has resumed his managerial position, but with limited activity. I still do the grunt work and Jimmy helps out. He's very sweet. The other day I was about to clean the locker room, shower, and toilets, which is always a disgusting chore. Jimmy offered to do it for me. I thought about saying no. Newcomers should not be subjected to that horrible job, but in light of my injuries, it was nice to take that one break. I also didn't want Freddie examining me, so I asked Jimmy to take a look at my ribs. He would know if I'd cracked one. It was in the locker room. I pulled him inside during one of his workouts. You should have seen his face when I lifted my sweatshirt and exposed myself in my bra to him! I hated to startle him, ha ha. Anyway, he got over his shock, examined me, felt around where it was tender, and confirmed what I already knew—it was a cracked rib. Wearing the wrap was the best thing I could do.

I couldn't talk to Freddie. On the day after the Stiletto's "defeat" in Chinatown, he got really mad at me. He almost started crying, he was so afraid that I'd get hurt. He said I should let it go, and that there is more to life than revenge. I told him I was sorry, but he blurted, "Do you know what a burden it is, knowing you're the

Black Stiletto?" That made *me* cry, and I shut myself in my room for a while. We haven't spoken much since then.

And then there's the so-called defeat. That was the big news for a while. Several of the New York papers ran stories about my demise. The cops who took me away from the scene claimed that I "jumped them, grabbed a gun, and forced them to release me from the handcuffs, even though I was badly hurt." I suppose they were covering their rear ends. So reporters speculated that I might be lying seriously injured in my Black Stiletto Cave or possibly even dead. "Have We Heard the Last of the Black Stiletto?" one editorial suggested.

The hard part was explaining how I looked to my friends—especially Lucy, who *also* got mad at me, but for a more selfish reason on her part. She didn't want me to look ugly at her wedding. It was unsaid, but I knew that's what she thought because she repeatedly asked me how long the marks on my face would take to heal. The guys at the gym are more curious and concerned about me now. I hope they don't put two and two together. After getting beat up in January and now again in March, they're starting to wonder how come a pretty girl like me is the victim of so many "muggings." They know I can defend myself, too, so it doesn't make sense to them. Jimmy thinks I enjoy getting in bar fights for some strange reason.

The only bright spot in my life right now is the new Elvis record. "Stuck on You" is a breath of fresh air.

I miss being stuck on someone.

April 15, 1960

Yesterday I had my second annual physical exam with Dr. Goldstein—remember him, dear diary? He poked and prodded me *down there*, and it was just as embarrassing this time as it was last year. He also checked my ribcage and asked how I broke a rib. I told him it happened at the gym where I work. He believed me. He wanted to take what he called an X-ray picture, but I wouldn't let him. I've heard those things give you radiation. Dr. Goldstein said I was doing the right thing by wrapping my torso, and if the pain was decreasing then it must be healing. He suggested I come back in a couple of weeks, but I don't think I will.

Things are better between Freddie and me. This morning at breakfast he told me he'd been too hard on me and that he was sorry. I apologized again for being a burden on him. He explained that I'm not a burden, that I'm like his daughter, and that he loves me. The burden is that he worries about me. At the same time he said he was proud of me and that my life as the Black Stiletto is the most courageous thing he's ever seen anyone do.

That made me cry again. We hugged and made up.

My rib is much better but it's still sore. The shiner is gone and my face looks better. I'm nearly back to my beautiful self, ha ha.

I haven't thought about Chinatown.

APRIL 18, 1960

You won't believe what I'm going to tell you, dear diary! Oh my God, *I* can't believe what I've done! And I don't know what I think about it!

Okay, here goes. We had a birthday party today for Jimmy. He turned 32 and this evening at closing time I brought out a cake. Louis and Corky had both brought some bottles of champagne. We knew Jimmy would be there, and boy, was he surprised. He was so funny, he got so self-conscious! If Negroes could blush, I'm sure he would have been bright red.

Freddie had a tiny sip of champagne and then went upstairs. He didn't want to be around drinking and smoking. I, on the other hand, had a lot of champagne. I was feeling a little loopy by the time a lot of the guys left to go home. Jimmy hadn't showered yet, so he went off to the locker room to do so.

I was all alone in the gym. They left me to clean up, so I did. Then I guess it was the champagne that did it, but I suddenly felt hot and bothered. You know what I mean. It had been so long since I'd felt a man's touch. I think it's the first time I ever really felt like I *needed* it.

So what did I do?

God, I can't believe it.

I locked the front door and then went to the locker room. I heard the shower running. Jimmy was the only person in there. It was one of those community showers, where several guys can get their own spigots in the same space. I slowly approached the archway.

Jimmy's back was to me. He was naked, of course, rubbing soap in his black curly hair. His muscles were well defined and he had the cutest behind. He looked really good to me. I didn't care if his skin was a different color than mine.

He happened to turn around. He yelped like a girl when he saw me and quickly covered up his privates. "Miss Judy! What are you doing here?"

"Don't be embarrassed, Jimmy," I said.

A few seconds passed with no one saying a word. It might have been comical, but I was too much in the moment to think it was funny. He just remained under the water, his hands over himself.

Finally he asked, "What do you want, Miss Judy?"

"Forget the Miss, Jimmy. Just call me Judy."

With that, I pulled off my sweatshirt. Then I took off the sweatpants and leotards. Jimmy's eyes were about to pop out of his head. He didn't know *what* to think!

Finally, I took off my bra and panties.

"Can I join you?" I asked. Without waiting for an answer, I stepped into the shower and stood under his water spigot. He was inches away from me. He smelled musky and manly. I reached out and rubbed the palms of my hands on his iron-steel chest.

"What are you doing, Miss Judy?" he whispered. "I could get in a lot of trouble."

"So could I."

He shook his head fiercely in protest, but I could already see that parts of his body were responding to my presence. "They hang me from a lamppost, Miss Judy. I can't do this."

"No one will know."

"Miss Judy!"

"Just this one time, Jimmy. I promise." I'm tall, and he's maybe an inch or two taller. I rose on tiptoe, wrapped my arms around his neck, and kissed him. Was it different kissing a Negro? I'd have to say it was. I don't know how to describe it. The taste was a little different, and his lips were very soft.

By then he was past the point of objection. Jimmy picked me up and carried me out of the shower. He laid me on a bench in front of his open locker. And we did it right then and there. I think I was noisy, for he had to put his hand over my mouth. Oh Lord, forgive me, but I must say I enjoyed it. Maybe it was because it was such a taboo, or maybe Jimmy was just a darned good lover, but it was indeed exciting.

Afterward, Jimmy was quiet and flustered. I think he was scared, too. "Don't worry, Jimmy, I won't tell anyone if you won't."

"No, ma'am."

"It's our secret, okay? And that's the only time, all right? Just forget about it."

He stared at me and finally nodded.

I got dressed and left the locker room. My heart was still pounding and I nearly collapsed on the gym floor because my legs were so weak. I was in a daze, but I made it to the cash register counter and sat down. Before I knew it, Jimmy came out dressed. He timidly walked across the gym to the front door. He stopped and looked at me. I smiled at him and said, "Good night, Jimmy. Happy birthday."

He swallowed hard and replied, "Thank you, Miss Judy. Good night." I got up off the stool and unlocked the door for him. Then he was gone.

I don't know if I made a huge mistake, dear diary. How many white girls have relations with Negroes? I'll bet not many! Was I

awful? Had I sinned? Did I do something really, really bad? I'm
sure everyone I know would think so.

Of one thing I am certain, though. As I climbed the stairs to my
room, I was aware of feeling better than I'd felt in a long time. All
warm and satisfied and happy.

Why should that be considered wrong?

APRIL 24, 1960

Jimmy's been avoiding me like the plague. I say hello, smile at him,
and try to engage him in conversation. I want us to be like we were
before, but he averts his eyes, mumbles an excuse, and moves away
from me. Now I feel bad about it. I hope he'll get over whatever it is
that's bothering him. Maybe I shocked him so badly that he doesn't
think he can relate to me anymore. I guess I'm a progressive young
woman when compared to most girls in this city.

I've been tempted to go down to Chinatown to see if I can find
Billy. Or I could go looking for Tommy Cheng and his little band of
Flying Dragons. What I wouldn't give to see all of them trussed up
and dressed in striped prison clothes! But a little voice inside me—
that old intuition again—tells me I shouldn't bother. That voice has
served me well, so I suppose I should listen to it. Still, it haunts me.
Billy was so distraught when we said goodbye. As a tribute to him,
though, I still practice what little *wushu* he taught me. I'm still developing my own style, combining it with what I know of boxing, *karate*,
and *judo*. Maybe someday they'll name a martial art after *me*, ha ha.

Lucy's been real nervous lately. The wedding is in a couple of
weeks. With all the arrangements and catering and details and
money involved with such an event, it makes me never want to go
through it. But then again, if I found the right man—who knows?

I told Lucy she needs to take a break and get her mind off of it,
so tonight we're going to see *Ben-Hur* again. It won the Oscar for
Best Picture, as I knew it would. We both want to see that chariot
race again!

14
Martin
THE PRESENT

The good news is I went to see a shrink. I never did say anything to Carol about it. I found Dr. Kessler on my own by looking at my health insurance's website and finding a provider. I knew nothing about him, but he was conveniently located and that sold me. He was in his forties, and he seemed to understand what I was going through. I told him about the stress I was under from dealing with a mother with Alzheimer's, a new job, and all the trivial crap that comes with being a middle-class suburbanite. When I described the panic attacks, he wrote stuff down in my chart and nodded like he'd heard it all before. He asked me questions about my mother's illness and its timing. I asked him flat out if Alzheimer's was hereditary. He said, "It can be," but he also told me not to worry about it. What I was experiencing now had no relation to Alzheimer's. I had an anxiety disorder.

I'm sure it was all the Black Stiletto's fault. It's like what Freddie told my mom in her diary—knowing my mother's secret was a burden. But I didn't tell Dr. Kessler that.

He prescribed an antidepressant that had a strong antianxiety component. The bad news is that it takes about a month to kick in. Only then will we know if it's the right medication for me. Dr. Kessler said every case is different and requires a custom-made treatment plan. Sometimes doctors and their patients have to experiment with different drugs to see which one works the best. That said,

Kessler thought the one he gave me would do the trick because I had a surprisingly common malady.

That evening, I decided to call Gina. We hadn't spoken in a while and, miracle of miracles, she picked up. Nine times out of ten I got her voice mail.

"Hi, Dad!" She sounded perky, like the Gina I've known her whole life. While she had a *terrifically* good attitude during her recovery after the assault, she did go through some periods of "blue," as she called it. It didn't help having a jaw wired for six weeks.

"Hey, why don't you come home for Thanksgiving?" I asked her. The holiday was the upcoming Thursday.

"I can't, Dad, I've got rehearsal." She had a small part in a play. Apparently, being cast rarely happened to freshmen at Juilliard. "But I'm coming for Christmas, you know."

"Yeah, I can't wait to see you."

"Are you all right, Dad? You sound funny."

I didn't want to worry her. "I'm fine, honey. Just tired. Working hard, you know how it is."

"How's Grandma?"

"She's fine. I'm sure she misses you."

"Does she even remember who I am?"

"Of course. I read her your letters when you write, and she has your pictures on her dresser. She knows who you are." At least I thought she did. You never really knew with my mom.

"Hey, did you get the news there?"

"What news?"

"Guess what," Gina said, grimly, "that rapist struck again. Another student at Juilliard got attacked and *killed* a couple of days ago."

Great, just what I needed to hear. "No, I didn't hear about it. I haven't been paying much attention to the news. Geez, Gina, you need to get out of that city," I said. "Your mother and I worry about you."

"It's okay, Dad, I'm a lot more street smart now," she said. "The girl that was attacked was coming home late from a party and was really drunk. She was all alone."

"Did you know her?"

"No. But the police called me and asked me to come to the station today to look at mug shots, like I did before. I was going to call you and Mom and tell you about it; you beat me to it."

"What happened?"

"I saw Detective Jordan again." I remembered him. He was the African-American NYPD guy in charge of Gina's investigation. "He said they think the same man who attacked me was the killer of this other girl. They showed me some of the same pictures I saw before, but also some new ones. Dad, I think I picked out the guy! I'm pretty sure I recognized him. He's white, in his twenties or maybe early thirties. But when I pointed him out to Detective Jordan, he simply nodded and said the man was just a person of interest and had an alibi for the nights in question, but they had to be verified. I asked what the man's name was, but Detective Jordan wouldn't tell me."

"How did he leave it?"

Gina lowered her voice. "*Well*, I asked for some coffee. He left the interview room and the mug shots were sitting there in a manila folder on the table. I snuck a peek at the back of the picture and got the guy's name and address! Ha!"

"Gina! Whoa!" That totally freaked me out. My anxiety level shot up exponentially. "What were you thinking? You could get in big trouble doing that."

"Nah, I didn't get caught."

"What good could that information do you, Gina?" Surely she wasn't thinking of—she wouldn't—

"Oh, nothing, I just wanted to have a name for the face."

"Well, you let the police handle it. There's no reason for you to get involved unless they want you to testify or something. All right?"

"Sure."

"Promise me?"

"Dad! What do you think I'm gonna do? Go all Black Stiletto

on him?" She laughed and I nearly shit in my pants. *What the hell made her say that?*

"What did you say?" I demanded a little too strongly.

"Dad, geez, I said, 'you want me to go all Black Stiletto on him?' You know the Black Stiletto? She's that lady from the sixties who put on a costume and fought crime like a superhero."

"I know who you mean, Gina. And don't you *dare* think about doing something like that!"

"Oh, right, Dad, don't worry. My X-ray vision isn't working too well these days, so I gave my costume to Goodwill."

"Gina, it's not funny."

"Dad, are you crazy? No one would do that *now*. That was a long time ago. I can't believe you would even say that. You weren't *serious* were you?"

I didn't know what I thought. Yeah, I guess I was serious. *Considering her bloodline—*

"Never mind, Gina," I answered. "Just be careful."

I didn't feel any better after saying good night to my daughter.

Right then and there I decided that Gina must never know the truth about her grandmother.

The next day after work I went to see Mom. Maggie was working, so it would give me a chance to see her too if she wasn't very busy. Things are going splendidly between us, I think. It's helped that I did what she suggested and saw a doctor. We've started sleeping together. I usually go over to her house in Deerfield. She's stayed at my place only once, the first time we had sex. I couldn't believe it at the time. I felt so lucky. Too bad my anxiety had to put a damper on things, but it was still a very nice evening. I wasn't sure if our relationship would continue in that vein until Maggie invited me to her house a couple of nights later. It's actually convenient for me, because my job isn't far. So I keep a toothbrush and some other toiletries over there now.

It's so weird to be dating again.

I arrived at Woodlands and went to the dementia unit—you have to punch in a code to get inside—and found Maggie in the common area. She stood at the nurse's station as she wrote on a clipboard.

"Hey, you," I said.

"Hey, you, too," she said. She rarely smiled when she was in work mode, but she gave me a warm one.

"How's Mom today?"

"Hmm, I had to prescribe some medication, Martin. Her blood pressure has been elevated the past couple of days. She's been complaining of pain, although she couldn't really put it into words. We figured out from her behavior that she's having headaches. Have you noticed her rubbing her head lately?"

"Geez, no, I haven't seen her in a few days. Is it serious?"

"I don't think so, but we need to watch her. I don't like the way that blood pressure looks. Want to see her?"

"Sure."

Maggie accompanied me to Mom's room. As usual, my mother sat in the rocking chair facing the TV. A reality game show was on. She was already dressed for bed. The staff usually helped her put on a nightgown and robe right after her dinner.

"Hi, Judy, look who's here!" Maggie said brightly as we walked in.

I also spoke in my "everything-is-wonderful voice." "Hi, Mom, how are you doing?"

The strangest thing happened. Mom turned to me and looked at me with those dark eyes that once displayed such a spark. She furrowed her brow and actually *flinched*. "Oh!" she said, as if I scared her or something.

"Mom, what is it? It's me, Martin."

"Judy?" Maggie asked as she sat on the bed beside the rocking chair. "Does your head still hurt?"

Mom answered, "No," but she continued to stare at me as if I was an alien.

"This is your son, Martin," Maggie said. "He's come to see you."

Tears came to Mom's eyes and she turned back to the television, although she focused her eyes past it. "I'm sorry," she said in a whisper.

"What are you sorry about, Mom?" I asked. I moved closer and squatted in front of her. Once again, Mom reacted by shying away from me, drawing back in her chair.

"No—" Her voice was almost a whimper. It was heartbreaking.

"I'll be right back, Judy," Maggie said to her. "Come on, Martin." She stood and gestured for me to follow her. At the door she said, "Your presence is upsetting her."

"No kidding. That's never happened before."

"It could be she's aware that she knows you but can't grasp who you are, so it frightens her. Don't worry, it's typical."

"It looked to me like she thought I was going to hurt her. Maggie—"

She put a hand on my shoulder. "Maybe you should go. She hasn't felt good today, so that probably has something to do with it too. Tomorrow she'll be just like she was before."

"I hope so. Should I say goodbye?"

Mom had resumed her Whistler's Mother pose in the chair. I'm not sure she knew we were still in the room.

"Looks like she's calmed down. Why don't you try again tomorrow?"

"You won't be here, will you?"

"No, but get Jane or someone to come in with you."

I nodded and we left the room. Maggie said, "I'm sorry about that."

"It's not your fault. It's kind of upsetting when your own mother is afraid of you, though." Actually, my mom's response was similar to what she did when I once asked her about the Black Stiletto. Maybe for some strange reason, *I* remind her of the Black Stiletto now.

Maggie told me what I already knew—that Alzheimer's patients in Mom's advanced stage are unpredictable. They can be lucid one day and totally out of it on another. I sensed it was something else, though. My mom's intuition is highly developed. She knows what people are feeling. I believe that in her own special way she empathizes with my anxiety disorder. She perceives something's wrong with *me* and she doesn't know how to handle it.

She probably doesn't remember writing me the letter that Uncle Thomas gave me last spring, but I think she's aware that I know she's the Black Stiletto and it disturbs her.

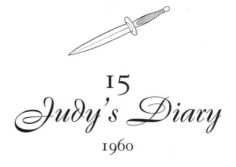

15
Judy's Diary

1960

MAY 9, 1960

It's four o'clock in the morning and I just got home. I've had, well, a pretty horrible night. It was a nightmare, and it really started yesterday (Sunday) afternoon at Lucy and Peter's wedding.

The ceremony was at St. Mark's Church on E. 10th Street. That was actually quite lovely. Lucy's parents had spent a lot of money to decorate the sanctuary with tons of flowers and the place was absolutely gorgeous. Lucy looked beautiful. Everyone said I did, too, all gussied up in my dress. Sherrilee, one of the waitresses from the East Side Diner, did my hair, put some curls in it, and gave it more shape than I've ever been able to do. Freddie and the guys from the gym said I was a "knockout," so that made me feel pretty good. Peter was handsome in his tuxedo. His best man was Doug Something, a guy he'd known since college. I thought Doug was a dreamboat, but it turned out he was married.

The reception was at the East Side Diner! Lucy and Peter had looked for a fancier place, but couldn't afford it. Manny offered to close the diner for a few hours on late Sunday afternoon, so Lucy took him up on it. It turned out great. We played the jukebox and danced. Manny made steaks for around fifty people, paid for by both Lucy's parents and Peter—I don't know where Peter's parents were, and I didn't ask. Hard booze had to be brought in because the diner served only beer and wine.

Jimmy was there. He looked sharp in a suit that was probably ten years old. I've never seen him dressed up before. When champagne was poured, I was standing next to him, so we clinked glasses. He still acts funny around me. I'm convinced the truth of the matter is that he carries a torch for me, but is afraid to act on it. I'd told him our encounter in the shower was a one-time-only thing. But who said I had to keep that rule? I felt attractive, I was drinking, and I had that itch again. I have to admit I was on the prowl. But I looked elsewhere first. I figured Doug wasn't available, Jimmy wasn't available, and none of the other gym guys interested me, so I started talking to some of Peter's friends, none of whom I knew. That turned out to be a dead end.

Doug introduced me to his wife Patty. She wore a button on her dress that said, "Vote Democrat." I asked her about it and she said she volunteers at the New York Democratic headquarters. "There's an election this year, you know," she said. Another guy named George also wore a button. He works in Peter's office.

"Do you think Kennedy will get the nomination?" I asked them. I'd been following the senator's campaign since he announced his candidacy in January.

"I don't know. It might be Humphrey or Stevenson. I like Jack Kennedy, though," Patty said.

"I do, too," George echoed.

I told them I thought I was a Democrat, but this would be my first year to vote for a president. I confessed my admiration for Kennedy.

"Why don't you come volunteer, Judy?" George asked. "We could use more people. It's going to get real busy this summer."

At first I couldn't see me doing something like that. I'm not really a politically minded person, but I was interested in current events and the civil rights movement. It might give me something new to do. I told Patty and George I'd think about it. She gave me the details of where I should go on Park Avenue South if I decide to go for it.

I suddenly had a vision of the Black Stiletto standing on a street corner and handing out political literature, ha ha. Wouldn't that be a riot?

So I continued to drink and I danced with Peter and with Lucy and with Freddie and with George and with Doug and with Louis and with Corky and with—gosh, I think I was the belle of the ball there for a little while. I kept requesting that someone play Elvis songs on the jukebox. "Stuck on You" is still number 1!

The party started to wind down around 7:00. Lucy and Peter left and reappeared dressed in street clothes for the ritual rice throwing and goodbyes. They're off to the Bahamas for a honeymoon! I can't imagine what that would be like. It sounds so exotic and exciting. I know they're islands in the Caribbean, but I'm not sure exactly where they are. Close to Cuba, I think. I told Lucy not to get too sunburned. She laughed and whispered that she may not be spending a whole lot of time outdoors, if I knew what she meant. Then she winked and we both laughed. I gave her a hug and a kiss and told her to be happy and be careful. I embraced Peter, too, and he gave me a wet smacker right on the lips. Lucy said, "Hey! What was that?" Peter blushed and said that he was entitled to kiss the maid of honor and she was entitled to kiss the groom. I think that was just an excuse—I have a feeling Peter's wanted to kiss me ever since he met me!

After the newlyweds left, there were only a handful of folks still at the diner. We were all a little drunk. I saw Jimmy sitting at a booth and he was staring at me. I thought, *what the heck*, and went over and sat across from him.

"Hey, handsome," I said, "you're not drunk, are you?"

He smiled a little and said no.

"Well, I am. Want to take me back to the gym?"

The smile vanished and he narrowed his eyes at me. "Miss Judy, it was wrong what we did. I ain't ever doin' that again. We be friends all right, but tha's all." He said it in a stern voice, almost like he was angry.

"Jimmy, I—"

He held up a hand. "No. I can't have no white girl gettin' me in trouble. Good night, Miss Judy. I'll see you tomorrow." With that, he got up and left the diner. I was stunned. I felt—*rebuked!* Dear diary, maybe it was the champagne, but I was angry. I wanted to pick up the sugar jar and throw it at his back as he walked out the door, but I didn't. I sat there and fumed for a bit. Corky sauntered over, sat across from me, and slurred, "How ya doin', Judy?"

I can't explain my actions. I snapped, "Fine!" and abruptly stood. I headed for the front door and heard Corky call, "Was it something I said?"

I wanted to catch up with Jimmy and slap his face. I wanted to tell him that he couldn't reject me like that, and that I refuse to be humiliated. I didn't care if people found out about us. I just wanted to release a lot of pent-up frustration and tension.

But I didn't see him on the street. He had vanished. I ran to the corner of 5th and Second and peered up and down the avenue. I dashed back to 4th and did the same thing. Nothing.

So then I was really mad and felt like spending an hour punching the speed bag in the gym. But I had a better idea, or thought I did.

I went home, put on the Stiletto outfit, and slipped out into the night. At least I waited until after sundown, but I made a mistake by not stuffing my trench coat in my backpack to wear over my outfit if I had to. And there came a point when that was a necessity.

For the first hour or so of my adventure, I ran and climbed and jumped, making my way uptown. It was cathartic to release all that anger. The effects of the champagne disappeared with the sweat.

Before I knew it, I was at 59th Street, the bottom of Central Park. I rarely ventured that far from home base. It was nearly 11:00 by then, and I was tired. I could have used that stupid overcoat to put on so I could ride the subway or a bus back to the gym. So that made me angry again, this time at myself. How could I be so dumb? I was stuck as the Stiletto and had to make my way on foot.

First a rest was required, so I squatted in between the Plaza Hotel and the building immediately west of it. The weather was springlike and unseasonably warm for early May. I was sweating like a dog. I figured I'd sit there for fifteen minutes to get my wind back and then take off downtown. The second mistake I made was allowing myself to daydream. I started thinking about the wedding and the party, about Jimmy, about Billy in Chinatown, and whether or not I should volunteer for the Democrats. *I wasn't paying attention.*

Misfortune reared its ugly head. Two beat cops walked right in front of me. They were patrolling 59th Street. In hindsight, I can't believe my senses didn't pick up on them. Usually, I know when someone is around a corner. The only explanation is that I wasn't concentrating. I was lost in my thoughts.

So the two cops were less than six feet away from me. I froze, hoping they wouldn't turn their heads, for I'd surely be seen if they did. It was no good. One guy glanced my way and stopped walking. The other one kept going until he realized his partner had halted, so *he* turned and saw me. It was one of those moments when time stood still. I must have resembled an animal looking into headlights.

The first cop drew his weapon. "Freeze!" he shouted.

"Holy crap," the other one said. He also drew his gun. Then they both stepped back, out of my reach. "Is it really her?"

Cop #1 asked me. "Are you her?"

"I'm not Mayor Wagner," was the lame pithy answer I gave.

"Stand up. Slow. Raise your hands where we can see them!"

I did. I thought my goose was cooked. The NYPD had finally caught the Black Stiletto. Where was my friend, the cop from Chinatown who let me go? These two were big and beefy and they meant business.

"She's got that knife, Sean," Cop #2 said.

"I'll get it. Run and call for backup. I'll hold her here."

"You sure?"

"Go!"

Cop #2 ran toward the Plaza, leaving me with "Sean."

"If I ask you to pull out that knife and drop it, you'd just throw it at me, wouldn't you?" he asked.

"No."

"I don't believe you. I'm going to take it myself. And no funny stuff. Keep those hands above your head." He indicated the handgun. "This is pointed right at you."

"It's all yours, Sean." I jutted out my leg, knee bent, providing him better access to the sheath. Actually, it was a *wushu* position that Billy taught me. I didn't know how to do the move that normally accompanied it, but I had developed my own "power strike" with my elbow. My target was just the right height, too. I breathed evenly and deeply, preparing myself for the bout to come, and waited for Sean the Cop to move closer.

When he did, I quickly swung my left arm down on his gun arm. A split second later, my right elbow slammed into the curve between his neck and shoulder. It never would have worked had I not been a tall girl.

The handgun flew out of his grip like butter. The blow to his neck surely sent an electric shock down his spinal cord; he went down like a rag doll. I quickly leaped over him and ran out into 59th Street toward the park. Traffic was heavy, as it always is in that part of town and, Lord, I was nearly hit by a taxi. The driver blasted the horn and screeched to a stop, causing the car behind it to ram the back bumper. A chain reaction occurred down the line for several cars. I kept going as more horns honked and drivers yelled and cursed at me. I managed to dodge between vehicles in the traffic going the other way and reached the sidewalk before Sean the Cop had retrieved his gun and given chase. He wasn't as brave as me, though; he refused to dart blindly into traffic. Instead, he blew a whistle, held up his hands at the oncoming cars, and crossed the street with impunity. By then, though, I was in the darkness of the park.

I've been in Central Park only a handful of times during daylight. At night it was a pretty creepy place. The pole lamps lining walkways were inadequate for illumination, so everything took on a dim, glowing essence, as if I'd entered a land of ghosts. I've always heard Central Park was once one of the most beautiful landmarks of New York City. I wish I'd seen it then. Now all you hear is how dangerous it is to go there at night, and sometimes broad daylight isn't so safe either.

Needless to say, I didn't know my way around. Once you get inside the park, there are paved pathways that web out from major corners and then twist and turn like a maze for *fifty blocks* all the way to 110th Street. There is little signage. Sections have a lot of trees and are slightly hilly. There are bodies of water all over the park, like the one I skirted around as soon as I was inside. I remembered a skating rink being in the southeast sector because Lucy and I went there once. We also rode a carousel, but I wasn't sure where that was.

Sure enough, I found the Wollman ice skating rink. It was deserted and gray in the dim lighting, although I thought I made out some dark human shapes sitting in spots around it.

By then I heard sirens, so I kept running and following the path that appeared to curve west. I either had to find a place to hide, which was risky, or find my way out on the north-south western border, Central Park West. The Upper West Side was becoming a trendy area of town, so it would be alive with people at that hour. Both options were chancy.

The path suddenly curved more southwest than I wanted to go, so I took a fork heading north, or at least I thought it did. It went through some very foreboding territory, as it was thick with trees and boulders that were part of the landscaping. I saw embers on the ends of cigarettes here and there. The Black Stiletto wasn't the only one stalking the park. I didn't have the time or inclination to stop and find out if the other folks were friendly.

In the distance, men shouted. I distinctly heard, "She went this way!" My senses were wide awake now! If a cop or anyone else came near me, I'd know it. I could hear a twig snap twenty feet away. My internal danger radar was on full alert. But if I didn't slow down, I'd wear myself out too quickly. My heart was beating a million miles a minute and I was panting for breath.

The path rounded a rock outcropping and the landscape leveled out. The carousel stood in front of me. It was wonderful, too, colorful and old-fashioned. The horses were beautifully painted and there were other characters you could "ride" as well. But that was in the daylight. At night it looked just plain scary. And since I had unwittingly run out of possible hiding places, I moved on, intending to pass the carousel and keep moving north until I found a trail that led west. But as soon as I was within twenty feet of the attraction, two black shapes materialized from the shadows between the wooden horses and stepped in front of me. One had a knife.

"Looky here, wha's dis we got here?" the armed one said.

"She wearin' a mask!"

"Get out of my way," I said.

"Or what, missy?"

"Hey she got a knife, too!"

That was my cue. At that moment, both men were looking down at my leg—which swiftly rose for a *Mae-geri*. The front kick caught the creep's knife hand. The weapon went sailing off into the night. Without a second's hesitation, I stepped in and performed the attacks Billy had taught me. They weren't real Praying Mantis moves, but they worked for me. I mimicked that fast and repetitive slapping style of fighting, hitting with my fists and open hands. The creeps didn't know what kind of storm had unleashed at them. One went down quickly. The other seemed to have more stamina, so I whirled around a got him with a *Mawashi-geri*, a roundhouse kick. Hard, under the chin. I'm pretty sure I heard his teeth crack when his lower jaw drove into the upper.

I paused long enough only to check the sounds in the air. Voices. Police. I saw flashlight beams cutting through the darkness of the trees.

No time to dawdle! I shot out of there on the path leading north.

Before I knew it, I'd reached 65th Street. Some streets go through the park so cars and taxis can get to other side without having to go all the way around. I started to follow it west, but vehicle headlights brightened the area so much that I'd be seen. The road was also curvy and narrow, with no sidewalks.

Unsure what to do, I looked behind me and heard the cops reach the carousel. They probably found my handiwork lying on the ground.

I kept going north.

After a few moments of running in black nothingness, I stopped to listen again. I had no idea where I was. The path twisted a few times, and I lost my sense of direction. I didn't know which way was west anymore. I considered going back to the 65th Street transverse and taking my chances, but I chose to move forward.

Suddenly, I reached a wide-open field. No trees, just a flat, grassy plain. Kids obviously played soccer or football there during the daytime. I didn't want to cross the field and expose myself, so I trotted along the perimeter, staying close to the trees. Eventually, I heard cars just beyond the woods. It was another through road, but smaller and not as busy, so I slipped around the rocks and trees and followed it west.

Eventually, dear diary, I made it out of the park at 66th Street and Central Park West. I was about to move off the sidewalk and run across the avenue, when a police patrol car came rumbling up the road. There was no way I could jump for cover in time. The red-and-blue lights went on and the siren beeped. The car quickly pulled over to the curb, so I hightailed it back into the park. I had to hide after all.

The spooky trees were my friends then. I dashed toward the blackest, bleakest hole and followed it to the core of the small forest. My intuition served me well, for it was difficult to see directly in front of my face. I figured that was about as good as I was going to get, so I stopped and crouched behind a tree.

I waited. Heard voices in the distance. Saw no flashlights. I sat on the ground. It was a damp and cold.

The wilderness around me was full of ungodly dark shapes. If you'd have told me there were bears in Central Park, I would've believed you.

I stayed still and silent. Off in the distance, I pinpointed tiny moving beams of light after all. The cops were searching for me due east of my position. They moved along a path, which was a good sign. So far they hadn't ventured into the thickness of the woodsy area. Maybe they were as scared of it as I was!

My strategy had to change. It wasn't a chase anymore. It was all about stealth, and moving slowly and deliberately. I figured if the cops came my way, I'd covertly sneak to another tree, and so on, until they gave up. My senses told me there were two clusters of policemen, but they didn't consist of as many men as I'd feared. I listened carefully, following the passage of the closest group. Their voices were low, unintelligible murmurs.

Dear diary, it seemed like I sat in that cold, dark spot forever. It was at least an hour before the policemen abandoned the search. I detected no more activity anywhere near me. I stood, brushed off my behind, and *walked* out of the trees. A deserted, gray path led west. I took it, moving slowly in case I heard anyone. At that point I probably would have rather run into a gang of criminals instead of the NYPD!

I reached Central Park West, crossed the avenue, and went west on 64th Street until I hit Broadway. Although it was a busy thoroughfare, it was way after midnight. Not as many pedestrians, but it was still prudent to move quickly. I went back to the speedy, blink-and-you'll-miss-her Black Stiletto, darting from building to building and dashing across street intersections. It was a long way home, but I made it.

Remind me never to forget my street clothes again.

16
Judy's Diary
1960

MAY 21, 1960

I've been feeling down since Lucy's wedding. I probably made a big fool of myself by drinking too much, coming on to every male in sight, being ridiculous with Jimmy, and then experiencing that fiasco in Central Park as the Black Stiletto. That's why I haven't written much, dear diary.

I've been sneaking glasses of Freddie's bourbon. He's not drinking it, so I figure why let it go to waste? Freddie commented that I seemed to be getting "looped" every night and should maybe cut down. He's probably right, but I didn't answer him. Right now, having a drink or two after dinner hits the spot.

I saw Lucy when she and Peter returned from the Bahamas. She was tan and looked great. She's very happy. She told me all about going snorkeling and seeing gorgeous colored coral and weird exotic fish. The food was spectacular and the hotel was splendid. I'm sure I'll see all the pictures they took when she gets them developed. Lucy hated coming back to the real world. She's moved in with Peter, so visiting her is more of a schlep. He lives in the West Village. They want to buy a larger apartment somewhere. I told her it had better be on the East Side!

Peter got tickets for us to see that new musical playing Off-

Broadway, *The Fantasticks*. It's at the Sullivan Street Playhouse. Now
I can't get that song "Try to Remember" out of my head. I'd like to
see more theatre. I can count on two hands the number of times I've
been to a Broadway show. Sometimes famous stars appear. I'm silly
not to take advantage of it.

Mostly I've been working and training. I looked in the phone
book for instructors who taught *wushu*. Although I've been practicing and developing my own techniques, it would be nice to learn the
real thing. One studio I called said they don't teach girls. The person
who answered at the second place didn't speak English, so I gave up.
I once had an idea to open my own martial arts class for girls only.
Maybe I should do that. Would anyone register? Are there other
girls besides me who want to defend themselves? You'd think there
would be.

One day I went up to Park Avenue South to see the Democratic
headquarters. A young man and woman sat behind a table on the
pavement asking passersby if they were registered to vote. I realized
I wasn't, so I filled out the papers. I looked at some of the party literature and told them I hoped John Kennedy got the nomination.
The woman said, "As long as we get a Democrat in the White
House, that's the important thing." I'd read that President Eisenhower signed a new civil rights act this month that was supposed to
help Negro voters in the south. I had asked Clark about it and he
said the new law was a start but it didn't do enough.

Maybe I *will* volunteer. It would bring something positive to my
life again.

Meanwhile, the Black Stiletto hasn't made an appearance since
the Central Park incident. I haven't felt like it lately, but tonight I
do. It's Sunday evening, the weather is nice, and the night is calling
me. It's been a while since I've been to Chinatown. I want to see if
Billy and his mother are still in the apartment above the restaurant.
I'm probably crazy for showing my mask there again, but I have
nothing better to do.

MAY 22, 1960

Ugh, I have a hangover today. I guess I drank too much last night, but I was real blue. What's wrong with me? I should have been happy after what I did, but I wasn't.

Around 10:00 I dressed as the Stiletto and slipped out. The sidewalks were crowded with people. New York City in late May, you can't get much better than that. That meant I had to be extra careful dashing along the streets, dodging traffic, and not staying in one place too long. Sure, people saw me. Some of the reactions were pretty funny. Women screamed like they'd seen a mouse. A few men did, too! Others yelled at me, both positively and negatively. "Menace!" "Hurray for the Black Stiletto!" "Go get 'em, Stiletto!" "Someone call the cops!" You get the picture.

It's pretty difficult traipsing through Chinatown without being noticed. My plan was to check on Billy and then get out of there. I didn't want another gang of Flying Dragons to corner me. I've had my fill of getting beat up by mobs.

Elizabeth Street was quiet. The restaurant was closed, of course, and the lettering "Lee Noodle Restaurant" was gone. Plywood covered the windows on the inside. A construction permit was taped to the door. Another note said "Open Soon New Manjment" in English and Chinese. I bet I knew who the new managers were, too.

I also checked the mailboxes inside the building. The Lees were no longer listed. Gone. I hope Billy is all right. I suppose I'll never see him again.

Not wanting to tempt providence, I quickly got out of there. I moved up Elizabeth to Canal and was just starting to dash east when I heard shouts of distress in Chinese coming from a convenience store on the corner. A few people stopped to look, so I did, too.

Two young men wearing plastic Halloween masks were in the process of holding up the place! The elderly Chinese man behind the counter had his hands up. One guy—his mask was Mickey Mouse—pointed a gun at the man. Another crook stood next to the manager with his hands in the cash register drawer. His mask was Popeye.

Without hesitating, I opened the door, lunged at the gunman's waist, and tackled him. The gun fell on the floor and rattled like a tin can. It was a toy made of plastic! The boy behind the counter dropped what money he had, leaped over, and ran out of the store before I could stop him. I let him go since I had one of them. It wasn't difficult holding the kid down. I pulled off the Mickey Mouse mask, revealing a young Chinese teenager not much older than Billy. Meanwhile, the manager jabbered in his language and picked up a phone. I assumed he was calling the police.

"What's your name?" I growled at the boy.

"Chow!"

"Chow? That's your name?"

He nodded furiously. He was so frightened he started to cry.

"Are you in a Tong?"

He wouldn't answer. The boy just sobbed and said, "I'm sorry! I'm sorry!"

"Answer me! Are you in a Tong?"

Then he shook his head. "I want... I try to join... this initiation!"

"You had to rob this store to get in the Tong?"

He nodded and cried some more.

"What Tong? The Flying Dragons?"

When I said that, his eyes grew wide. "No! No!" I thought he said, "On lung, on lung." Was that Chinese?

"What's on lung mean?"

"No, *On Leong*!" Then I remembered what Billy had told me. On Leong was the name of another Tong in Chinatown. In fact, they're the main rivals of the Hip Sing Tong. That meant this kid wouldn't like the Flying Dragons, since they're associated with Hip Sing.

I got off of him and let the boy stand, but I held on to the back of his neck. I addressed the manager. "He's just a kid. He didn't get anything. Should I let him go?"

The old man didn't understand me. He let loose a string of angry Chinese. I asked the boy what the manager said.

"He says to let me go," the boy whimpered.

"Oh, really? That didn't sound like what he said. I think he wants you locked away."

"Please! I won't do it again! I promise! My parents, they kill me!"

I suddenly felt sorry for the kid. He was trembling. I turned to the old man again. "I'm letting him go, okay?" The fellow continued his monologue, but it didn't sound as angry. I squeezed the boy's neck hard and said, "All right, this is a warning. You don't need to join a Tong. Stay in school. Be a good kid." I looked down at the plastic weapon and kicked it across the floor. "And don't play with guns," I added. "Now run along before the cops get here."

The boy was out of there faster than a Texas roadrunner. The store manager didn't stop talking. He proceeded to berate me for letting the would-be robber go. I just shook my head at him and said, "He's just a kid! Tell the cops he got away." I was pretty sure the man had no idea what I said, so I left. A few pedestrians had gathered on the sidewalk outside, so I addressed them. "If any of you speak English, tell the police the two robbers were young boys and they got away." My statement was met with blank stares. I guess they'd never seen a Black Stiletto before.

That was it. I gave up and ran east on Canal. I never heard any police sirens. After making sure no one followed me, I made my way to the telephone pole, shimmied up, skirted across the roofs on 2nd Street, and climbed in my window above the gym.

What's weird is that I should have felt good. I hoped I'd scared that boy into not joining a Tong and that I'd done a worthwhile act. Instead, an overwhelming sense of frustration and failure took over. It was that Chinatown *thing* again, how foreign and alien it is. I had to admit I didn't understand it. I was definitely a fish out of water there, more than any other place in New York.

So after I removed my outfit and put on my pajamas and a robe,

I got Freddie's bottle of bourbon and poured a few glasses. I'm not sure what time I finally got in bed. Hence, the hangover today.

Bah, humbug. Grumble, grumble, toil and trouble!

17
Maggie
The Present

I'm looking forward to the Thanksgiving break. Tomorrow's the holiday and I'll be spending it with Martin. It's the first time in quite a while that I've spent Thanksgiving with a man. We'll have dinner at my house. I've already bought a turkey and the ingredients to make stuffing. I just need to run out after work and buy some vegetables and cranberries.

Woodlands is quiet today. The kitchen staff plans to prepare Thanksgiving dinner for the residents. Martin wants to come by and sit with his mother when they serve the food. I told him that shouldn't be a problem with our schedule, and I'd be happy to join him.

I went to check on Judy and found her standing by her dresser, studying herself in the mirror. Her right hand was lightly caressing her cheek.

"Good afternoon, Judy, how are we doing today?"

She slowly turned her head and smiled at me. "Fine," she said, and then she focused on the mirror again. I went and stood beside her.

"Who's that pretty young lady in the mirror?" I asked.

Judy smiled wider and shook her head. "I don't know!"

"That's you, Judy." I pointed to a photo on the dresser. "And that's you a few years ago." It must have been taken in the seventies.

The photo had the kind of color saturation common in those days. It revealed a much younger Judy Talbot standing by a tree in front of the house in Arlington Heights. She was very beautiful then. She is still a striking woman. Unfortunately, Alzheimer's steals so much of what makes a woman pretty. Judy now looks much older than her seventy-three years, and she has the mind of a four-year-old. It's so tragic.

She scanned the other framed pictures. "Where's my son?"

I pointed to a recent photo of Martin. "Right here. This is Martin."

Judy wrinkled her brow. "No, that's not…" Then she spied an early black-and-white shot from the sixties in which Martin was less than ten. Judy picked up the frame and said, "This is her." Alzheimer's patients often mixed up gender usage.

"Yes, that's him. That's Martin when he was little. He's all grown up now." I pointed to the recent pic. "This is Martin now. He comes to see you nearly every day."

"He does?"

"Of course he does. He'll come see you tomorrow around dinnertime. It's Thanksgiving tomorrow."

"Thanksgiving?"

"Yep, and we're having turkey and dressing. Won't that be nice?"

She actually licked her lips and nodded. I was pleased to see that the connection from her brain to her saliva glands wasn't broken.

"You want me to call one of the nurses so you can take your walk?"

She replaced the photo and moved toward the rocking chair. "Not now." She carefully lowered herself in the chair and started to rock.

I thought Judy was actually fairly lucid today. She had answered my questions with appropriate responses. I decided to try something. "Judy, Martin showed me a button that used to belong to you. It was a presidential campaign button for John F. Kennedy and Lyndon Johnson from 1960. Do you remember that?"

Judy continued to rock but turned her head to me. "What?"

"John F. Kennedy. Do you remember when he ran for president? You must have supported him."

She nodded and said, "I was a Kennedy Girl."

That threw me for a loop. A *what?* "What was that, Judy?"

No answer, just a smile.

"What's a Kennedy Girl? Did you meet Kennedy?"

She nodded. "He knew my name."

What? Was a "Kennedy Girl" one of JFK's many alleged girlfriends?

Oh. "So you did meet him?"

Judy's expression was dreamy. Apparently, she had latched on to a memory and relished it for a moment, but then her face abruptly changed. Her brow creased and the smile vanished. Her eyes narrowed and she whispered, "They tried to kill him."

I sat on the edge of the bed by the rocker. "You're right, Judy. They *did* kill him. In Dallas. Do you remember that?"

But she shook her head. "No, they didn't. I saved him."

She continued to stare at me intently. Whatever fantasy was going through her head was very real to her. I decided not to pursue it.

"I tell you what, Judy, I'm going to get Jane and see if she's free to walk with you now. It'd be good for you to get some exercise. You're looking pretty good. I noticed your blood pressure is getting better, too. That medication you're taking is helping."

I'm sure she didn't understand any of that, but I got up and told her I'd be right back. Jane was busy with another patient, so I tried Eric, one of the staff assistants. He couldn't get away from his current task either, so I went back to Judy's room—and found her slumped in the chair, unconscious. She was definitely not merely asleep.

"Judy?"

I rushed to her and immediately checked her vitals. They weren't good, so I picked up the phone and called a code blue.

There was no question about it. Judy had suffered a stroke.

18
Judy's Diary
1960

June 10, 1960

Today, on my day off, I went to the Democratic Party's New York headquarters on Park Avenue South and volunteered. I decided to go for it. I figured there wasn't much else in my life at the moment. All I had was my work at the gym. No boyfriend, no hobbies (well, not the kind of hobbies you normally think of as "hobbies," ha ha), and no circle of friends with whom I could gossip and shop like other normal young women in the city. I'm a misfit, no question about it. My only real female friend is Lucy, and now she's married and I don't see her as often as I did. I still work out and practice my martial arts, but that's it. As for the Black Stiletto, well, I haven't put on the outfit since that last night in Chinatown. I'm not sure why. The weather is nice—hot, in fact—and very conducive for night prowling. I just haven't had the urge lately.

So I thought that immersing myself in a new activity would be a good thing. I've been following John Kennedy's progress to win the candidacy—he just won the California primary—and I want to support him.

The place was busy and noisy! People were outside on the sidewalk handing out literature and registering citizens to vote. Inside, young men and women in their twenties ran here and there carrying stacks of paper or boxes or whatever. I could feel a definite energy in the air that was invigorating and exciting.

They put me to work right away. I agreed to hand out flyers and pamphlets in my neighborhood and spend some evenings registering folks to vote. Today, though, I stuffed envelopes in a room with ten other people. I sat next to a very nice couple and talked with them the whole time. Mitch Perry and Alice Graves. I suppose they're in their late twenties. Mitch might be in his thirties. He told me he's in "investments," and that his family came from Spain. I didn't think Perry sounded like a Spanish name, but he said his family had been "homogenized" over generations. Alice, on the other hand, looks like she has Latin blood. She said she's from Florida and thinks her ancestors were from South America. They're not married, but I got the impression they live together. When they mentioned going to clubs in Greenwich Village, I said I liked going to Café Wha? and listening to beatniks read poetry. Mitch and Alice also often go there, too, and they have friends in the Village. Mitch and Alice support Kennedy and hope he'll get the nomination, so we immediately bonded and became friends. A lot of people are for Humphrey, and there are even more for Adlai Stevenson. Lyndon Johnson (a fellow Texan!) is a wild card, but he hasn't declared if he's running or not. The Democratic National Convention is next month in California, so that's when we'll know for whom we'll ultimately be campaigning.

At any rate, I felt welcomed and wanted. It also gave me a sense of patriotic pride that I'm doing something for my country.

Who would have thought?

JUNE 19, 1960

I'm writing this at 12:30 a.m., but it's really still Saturday night to me.

I just got home from meeting a *man* at a party!

More on that in a minute. I haven't written, dear diary, because

I've been so *busy*. And that's a good thing, because I'm also having *fun*! I *love* working for the committee, and I've been doing more than what is asked. I like the people there and I think they like me. I've found myself suddenly in the middle of a group of...*friends*?

Besides Mitch and Alice, who I see a lot of these days, there's Chip Rangel, who makes all of us laugh. He probably weighs 280–300 pounds. He cracks jokes all the time and is always in a good mood. It's infectious. I believe he has a crush on me, poor thing. Because of that I don't get too chummy with him. Karen Williams, who's in her 40s, I guess, is a schoolteacher and she plays that same role at headquarters. It's become a running joke that whenever Karen tells us to do something, Chip says in a low voice, "Who made *her* boss?" Now he mumbles it every time she comes into the room, before she even speaks, and it's *hilarious*. I struggle to keep from busting out laughing and making a fool of myself. There's Mr. Patton, who's in charge, and Mr. Dudley and Mr. O'Donnell, Mrs. Bernstein, and Mrs. Terrano, and a whole bunch of other people. They're all nice and enthusiastic and fun to be around, even Karen when she's not worried about stuff getting done in time.

As we get closer to the national convention, things have become crazy. Everything's well organized, I'll give them that. It's just that there's so *much* to do and there aren't enough volunteers. I tried to get Lucy and Peter to volunteer, but they passed.

What do I do? We sell pins for a dollar or any donation, stuff envelopes and mail them, we deliver signs and literature around the city, we register people to vote, and try to talk intelligently to pedestrians who ask us about the Democrats. Most everyone I've talked to on the street is nice and stops to listen for a moment and maybe asks a question or two; others are downright rude and say nasty things as they walk on. I really didn't realize how divisive everyone is over politics before I started doing this. Most of my life I didn't pay much attention to Republicans or Democrats or politicians in general. Only recently have I discovered what a *hot button* it can be for some people. Geez! One guy started yelling at me that the Democrats were Commies and that I should "go back to Russia." All I'd said to him was, "Excuse me sir, are you registered to vote?"

Since none of us know who the candidate is yet, it makes our jobs a little tougher. On the other hand, there'll be a broad choice in Los Angeles. Actually there's a big disparity among the volunteers on who should get the nomination. There are quite a few for Kennedy, but also a bunch for Stevenson and Symington. The younger people seem to be more attracted to Kennedy. I think his campaign is the best. His younger brother Robert is running it from Massachusetts. He's some kind of hot-shot lawyer with the Justice Department.

After we argue about the best candidate, we usually get into the debate of who the running mates will be. Kennedy hasn't picked one yet.

So now that's my life outside of the Second Avenue Gym.

Back to *tonight*. I've gone out with Mitch and Alice a couple of times to Café Wha? and listened to music and poetry readings. We watched Kennedy on *The Jack Paar Show* the other night at their apartment on E. 52nd Street between Lexington and Third. Whatever Mitch does in "investments" must be pretty nice, 'cause I can't believe what a nice place they have. It's a very nice space on the sixth and highest floor of a big building. I didn't ask them, but it looked like they'd just moved in. The furniture was sparse and there were no decorations. But they have a great television!

Tonight Mitch and Alice invited me to a party in the Village and at first I balked because I didn't want to be a third wheel. Alice said she and Mitch love having me around and that I'm "fun." She also said I needed to meet more men and find someone I like so we can double date. So I went.

The party was in an apartment on Christopher Street. It was the same block where Studio Tokyo used to be. The building is still there, but since the fire it's been boarded up and under repair. It was the first time I'd been over there since it happened. It made me miss

Soichiro. I must remember to give his daughter, Isuzu, a call sometime.

I have never been to a party like this one! The hosts looked like
beatniks. Ron and Pam, a couple. He had a mustache and hair on
his chin and she wore sunglasses indoors. They were both dressed
in black. There were other people who looked like beatniks, too, the
kind of crowd I'd see at Café Wha? and the Village Vanguard. And
there were two Negro couples, too! The place was small, like many
New York apartments. It was just a one bedroom. I'd say there were
25 people or so in that living room, kitchen, and bedroom. There
was no way all of us could've fit just in the living room, so we spread
out into the three spaces. There was wine and vodka and bourbon
and beer and Coke, and a lot of smoking—the apartment was *full*
of smoke. Some of it was that marijuana stuff. A tiny group was
using the bedroom for that, and I didn't go in there. It made me a
little nervous being in an apartment with it because it's illegal. I've
seen people smoke it at jazz shows, though.

I thought the food was interesting. I'd never had stuffed mush-
rooms before. The stems had been removed and the caps were
stuffed with bread crumbs and parsley and cheese and I don't know
what else. Someone made a big pot of spaghetti and we ate it off of
paper plates. Jazz music played from the hi-fi and there was a lot of
chatter. People talked about politics, movies, art, poetry, books, theatre, and music. I'm afraid I might have come off too dumb. I like
all that stuff, but when I mentioned Elvis Presley I got a bunch of
dirty looks. Alice stood up for me, though, and admitted liking Elvis,
too. Most of the people there were for Kennedy, so that gave me
points.

Around 9:00 or so, I was on the floor next to the sofa. I was listening to an NYU professor talk about Jack Kerouac when a dark
and handsome man settled on the floor beside me. He wasn't quite
as beatnik looking as the rest. He did have facial hair though, what
he later told me was a "goatee." His name is Michael Sokowitz. He's
from Austria but is now living in America. He speaks with a Euro-

pean accent. I guess he's in his thirties. He told me he's a writer and that he's working on a lot of things, mainly a novel. I asked if I could find any of his books at the store, but he said he hasn't been published yet. We talked for about twenty minutes and then he said his eyes were watering from all the smoke and asked if I'd like to go somewhere and get coffee. I said sure. The smoke was getting to me, too, so we went to a coffee shop he knew over on Bleecker. There he told me he got his American citizenship two years ago. He came to the United States in 1957. Michael asked me where I was from and all that. He was surprised to hear I work in a gym. He said, "Women shouldn't fight," but I told him, "Sometimes they have to."

Michael has very intense brown eyes, did I mention that?

Sitting there with him was bizarre. He had such an exotic accent and looked like a Russian Cossack or something like that. I must say Michael created a lot of mystique about himself during that short little date. He made me want to know more about him and see him again. It sounds corny, but I find him mysteriously attractive.

After one quick cup of coffee and minimal chitchat, he asked me for my phone number. I gave him the one at the gym and said don't be surprised if a man answers. Freddie is used to taking messages for me, especially since I started volunteering. He said he would call me. After that he walked me to the crosstown, shook my hand, and said goodbye.

What an evening!

19
Judy's Diary
1960

JUNE 26, 1960

I went out as the Stiletto last night for the first time in, gosh, over a month. I've kept in shape though. I never stopped my exercises. My personal workout plan is a combination of everything I learned from Freddie and Soichiro, basic information I got from Billy, and my own inventions. It's a good thing I kept up the regime, because last night I needed the Stiletto's abilities in a very unique way.

What made me put on the outfit again? I don't know. I just got the urge to go out. It *had* been a while. Maybe I just needed that little vacation away from her after being beaten *twice* in Chinatown. The truth is that I missed—gosh, I almost wrote "her" again. I've noticed I sometimes refer to the Black Stiletto as someone other than me. Isn't that weird? Pretty soon I'll be like Anthony Perkins in *Psycho*, talking to himself in two different voices! Oh, my gosh, dear diary, that was the *scariest* movie I've *ever* seen! It just came out and *every-one* is talking about it. I love Alfred Hitchcock and I wanted to see it, so Lucy and Peter went with me. Lucy screamed several times and hid her eyes during the shower part. I screamed when the detective was killed and fell down the stairs. I couldn't believe Janet Leigh died so soon in the movie. Ewww! It was *shocking*! We walked out of the theater *stunned*.

I can't wait to see it again!

Part of the reason why I went out as the Stiletto was because I
was a little angry. Adam Clayton Powell claimed that Dr. King is
being controlled by Communists. What a terrible thing to say! As if
the Negroes didn't have enough problems trying to get equal civil
rights. Kennedy was in New York a couple of days ago, but I didn't
see him. Supposedly, he met with Dr. King while he was here. I
would like to someday meet Kennedy. If he gets the nomination and
I continue working for his campaign, then maybe I will.

I thought becoming the Stiletto again would be a good way to
blow off some steam, so I went out around 10:00 p.m. It was a hot
night. I figured I'd stay close to home and do my running, climbing,
and jumping just on the Lower East Side. People were out in droves.
I received lots of catcalls and hollers from pedestrians as I rushed
past them. I waved at a few of the nicer folks. But I didn't find any
crimes in progress, and luckily I didn't bump into any cops.

It was nearly midnight when I heard sirens near Washington
Square. A fire truck passed me with its lights blazing. Curiosity got
the better of me, so what did I do? Followed it, of course. I stealthily
flitted from building to building until I was at the southwest corner
of the park. Police cars, an ambulance, and a fire truck were posi-
tioned in front of a red brownstone to my west on 4th Street. It appeared to be a five- or-six-story brick building with cement trim.
The police had brought a spotlight and one of the men shined it up
toward the top. I had to cross McDougal and join a crowd of gawk-
ing onlookers to get a better view.

"What's going on?" I asked.

Everyone turned and dropped their jaws. Then came the onslaught of reactions. "It's the Black Stiletto!" "Holy cow, look!" "Are
you really her?" and all the usual exclamations. I held my hands up
and calmed them down.

"Hush, I don't want the cops to see me. What are they doing?"
And then I saw for myself. The spotlight encircled a figure standing
on a narrow concrete ledge in between the top floor windows. The
ledge was so small that the toes of his shoes extended beyond it. He

hugged his back to the wall, scared out of his wits.

"He's going to jump. Look," the fellow next to me said as he pointed.

"Oh, my," I responded. From the street, the guy on the building looked pretty young. High school or college age. "Who is it? Anyone know?"

A girl spoke up. "He's a student at NYU. It's going around that something happened with his grades, he failed or something, and he wants to kill himself before his father does it for him."

The firemen extended the truck's ladder, and one man began to climb toward the frightened kid. The boy yelled, "Don't come closer! I'll jump! I'm gonna jump!" I couldn't hear what the fireman said to him. My instincts were to run across the street and get up there to help the poor student. With one inadvertent movement of his shoulder, leg, or arm, he could lose his balance and fall.

Before long, the news trucks arrived. Reporters piled out and took pictures of the sight. I think one journalist had a movie camera. If the jumper wanted publicity, he certainly had it now.

A policeman with a megaphone spoke from the street. "Come on, son, make your way back to the window. You don't want to do this."

"I'm gonna jump!"

The cop tried a sterner approach. "Get down, *now,* before you cause some serious trouble not only for you but for the city!"

"I'm gonna jump!" The kid was a broken record.

By now, more people had gathered to witness the spectacle. They stood with hands over their mouths and holding their breaths in suspense. I was lost in the crowd. No one except those around me knew I was there. It probably wasn't the smartest place for me to be, but I was just as spellbound as everyone else.

At that point, a fireman appeared in the window to the right of the jumper. It must have been the same window from which the young man climbed out to the ledge. It was six or seven feet away from the boy. The fireman spoke to him, but we couldn't hear anything. I saw the kid shake his head violently.

The jumper and the rescue team were at a stalemate. The police and firemen were getting nowhere. I finally couldn't take the tension any longer and was compelled to do something about it. It may be the boldest thing I've ever done, but I pushed through the crowd and made my way to where the police had cordoned off the street. I addressed a patrolman, "Can I do anything to help?" His eyes bulged when he saw me, but at least he didn't draw his weapon.

"Uh, Lieutenant?" he called out. The man with the megaphone looked up and saw me. That started everyone pointing and murmuring. Now the crowd was looking at *me* instead of the jumper! The reporters' cameras flashed. Finally the lieutenant came over to me.

"You have three seconds to get out of here or I'll have you arrested," he said.

"Wait, maybe I can help," I said. "I'll go up there and talk to him. He might listen to me."

"Why would he listen to you?"

I shrugged. "Isn't it worth a try? Come on."

"You're wanted by the law. We can handcuff you right here."

"Not tonight!" I said as I abruptly darted through the barricade and ran toward the building. The lieutenant shouted for me to stop. Some patrolmen tried to grab me, but I wiggled out of their clumsy holds and jumped up to the building's stoop, which was a simple six steps up to the front door. There were two basement-level restaurants on either side of it, above which, at about shoulder level, were the lower platforms of exterior fire escape staircases. I chose the one on the right, leaped on, and started climbing.

The crowd applauded and shouted its approval. "Yea, Black Stiletto!" "Go get him!" "Hurray!"

I'm pretty sure some of the police drew their guns and aimed at me, for I heard the lieutenant shout, "Put away your weapons!" I didn't look down. So as not to scare the jumper, I moved slowly and eventually made it to the top level. The fireman inside the open window said, "The kid won't listen to me." I replied, "Let me talk to him."

The spotlight still outlined the boy. Now that I was closer, he appeared to be nineteen or twenty. The ledge he stood on was at eye level. He stared and shouted, "Don't you come near me!" Tears streamed down the kid's face.

I moved to the platform rail, indicated the ledge, and spoke. "Hey, was that hard to do?"

"Don't come near me!"

"Was it hard climbing out the window and inching along that ledge? Can I try it?"

"No! Go away!"

"Come on, I've never done that before. I'm going to try, okay? You look like you could use some company." I didn't wait for him to respond. I pulled off my backpack and set it on the platform, raised a leg, put my boot on top of the rail, and hoisted myself up. The entire fire escape creaked. I was afraid the rail wouldn't hold my weight, but it did. Once I was there, I realized how the kid was able to reach the ledge. There were decorative, horizontal cement grooves in the wall. I grabbed one, climbed the wall like a ladder, and then placed my right boot on the ledge. With my back flat against the wall, I slowly scooted toward the young man.

"Take it easy. I'm a friend," I said. "You know who I am, right?" The expression of terror on his face said it all. "Don't be afraid. I just want to talk to you."

"Don't come any closer!"

I still didn't look down. My boots barely fit on the ledge. It was an extremely precarious position, and I began to think what a stupid idea I'd had. A strong wind would be fatal, but one false move or shift of balance could be my downfall, no pun intended.

That's when I remembered something Billy taught me. It was part of the relaxation exercises he had me do before moving on t more aggressive practice. He called it *Tai Chi*, and said it helps you maintain the center of your body where it's supposed to be. It involves breathing and moving gracefully on very light feet. It was all about equilibrium and staying steady.

So I concentrated on that, emptied my mind, and blocked out the external stimuli. I forgot that I was six stories high and stepping on a tightrope of concrete eight inches wide. I smoothly moved along the ledge, and before I knew it, I was right next to the jumper.

"Hi. What's your name?"

The poor kid was trembling. "B-b-barry."

"Well, Barry, why do you want to do this? I heard it was something about school?"

"I f-f-failed. I have to d-d-drop out. My p-p-parents are gonna die."

I shook my head. "They won't die, but you will if you fall off this ledge. And I'm sure your parents don't want you to do that, no matter what happened in school. You're their son."

"My Dad hates me!"

"Barry?"

"What?"

"I didn't even finish high school. Dropping out of college isn't the end of the world."

He started crying. "I can't face him! He's ashamed of me!"

"I think he might be more ashamed if you kill yourself. Are you sure you really want to do that?"

He nodded furiously.

"Then what's taking you so long?"

That threw him. "Huh?"

I indicated the crowd below. "I mean, you've been up here for some time. I think if you were going to jump, you would have done it by now."

"I'm gonna do it! I'm gonna do it!"

"And you know what, Barry? If I was going to jump off a building, I'd pick a really big one. This brownstone is *Mickey Mouse stuff* compared to a lot of buildings you could have chosen in this city.

What is it? Five stories? Six? Why didn't you pick the Empire State Building? That would have been more dramatic. Now *that* would have made a statement! That would *really* make the news. At the very least you could've jumped off one of those new high rises they've been building in the Village, not this puny place. Or maybe a bridge! What about the Brooklyn Bridge? Lots of people jump off of that."

"Shut up!"

"Look, why don't we scoot on back to that window and climb inside. What do you say? I'll buy you a drink or something. Maybe you can go to another school. Maybe if you change the subject you study, you'll do better."

"My d-d-Dad wants me to be a lawyer."

"Is he a lawyer?"

"Yeah. A big one."

"And you don't want to do that?"

"Not really."

"What is it you want to do?"

His lips quivered. "I write plays. I want to be a playwright."

"Well, you should do that then. I believe everyone needs to do what they want, not what other people tell them to do."

"Y-you do?"

"Of course! Tell your father that you're not him. You're *you*."

Barry looked at me as if he'd never thought of that logic before.

I decided to change the subject. "Hey, are you registered to vote? Who do you think might be president this year? I follow Senator Kennedy. I think he'd make a great president. What do you think?"

Poor Barry thought I was nuts. We were a hundred feet off the ground and I wanted to talk about politics.

"I don't know," he finally said.

"Can you believe it's 1960? A whole new decade is waiting for us. What's going to happen? You think we'll send a man to the moon?"

"I don't know."

"I bet scientists come up with all kinds of new things. Maybe

they'll find a cure for cancer or heart attacks or strokes. You think
that will happen, Barry?"

He didn't answer.

"Don't you want to be here when it does? Won't it be great to be
able to tell your grandchildren that a man walked on the moon and
you watched it on television? I bet it'll be on TV when it happens.
Everything's on TV these days. Do you have a favorite show? I think
mine's *The Twilight Zone*. Hey, it's kinda like the Twilight Zone up
here!" I laughed, and then *Barry did too.*

I continued to talk to him about dumb stuff, and eventually
he relaxed. His terror subsided and he stopped shaking. I don't know
how long I stood on that tiny ledge, dear diary, but I did it and
couldn't have done it without the *Tai Chi* exercises. I don't know
how Barry was able to stand there. His adrenaline must have been
pumping the entire time. I was prepared to grab him if he started to
fall; the only problem would then be who was going to grab *me?*

Finally, out of the blue, Barry said, "I don't think I can get back
to the window. I'm too scared. I'm gonna fall."

I noticed he used a different word. Falling was different from
jumping. I took that as a positive sign and said, "Barry, if it'll make
you feel better, I'm going to toss my rope up there to the roof. Then
we can hold on to it as we make our way back. Okay?"

He got that frightened look in his face again and started to
panic. I believe earlier Barry had been so full of despair that his mind
couldn't comprehend the danger he was putting himself in by going
out on the ledge. Now it was as if he finally realized where he was.
"Whatever. Christ, help me. Help me!"

"Calm down, Barry. It's going to be okay. Take a deep breath.
Can you do that for me?" While I kept that up, I unfastened my
coiled rope and fitted the pulley hook on the end. "I'm going to
throw it now, Barry. Here goes."

I didn't want to break eye contact with Barry, but I had to. As I
faced the opposite direction, *sideways,* if you know what I mean, I

aimed for a section of the roof directly above the fire escape and made an easy underhanded pitch. The hook hit and clutched the edge. Perfect. I turned back to Barry and gave him my end of the rope. "Here. Hold on to it. Feed the rope through your hands as we go."

"I can't!"

"Look at me, Barry. See my eyes inside my mask?" He nodded. "Just keep watching them, okay? Look me in the eyes." He did. Then I started moving along the rope toward the fire escape, leading with my *back* so I wouldn't break eye contact. I fed the rope, hand over hand as I went. "Look, Barry, see how I move along the rope? Take it one step at a time. I'm right here."

It took us nearly ten minutes to move six feet, but I finally reached the point from where I climbed off the railing. "Barry, wow, I'm right above the fire escape! We've almost made it!"

At that moment, his right foot slipped. He started to toddle. His balance was not working in his favor. He was going to fall and we both knew it.

But he held on to the rope. Screaming, he wiggled and kicked as full panic set in.

"Barry! Stop! Don't move! Just hold on!"

And then he did fall. The crowd collectively gasped. But he gripped the rope and dangled below me. It was a good thing he was a kid and was relatively light. Still, it was a tremendous strain on my right arm as I held on to the line.

"Don't let go!" I shouted. "I'm going to pull you up."

Instead, the fireman from the window climbed out, rushed to the edge of the fire escape, and grabbed the rope, too. If he wanted, he could reach out and touch Barry's shoes.

"Look, Barry, that nice fireman is going to grab your ankles. All right?"

The officer didn't wait for an answer. He wrapped his arms around Barry's calves and pulled him in so the boy could stand on the railing. He was safe. The fireman helped him down and the kid promptly sat and put his face in his hands. Three other officers appeared on the platform and they all gave their attention to Barry. It was as if they'd forgotten I was still on the ledge.

Then the lieutenant with the megaphone broadcasted the order loud and clear, "Black Stiletto, come down immediately. You are under arrest. If you do not comply, we shall use force."

At that, the crowd booed! It was incredible. I heard shouts of "She saved the kid!" "What's wrong with you?" "Let her go!" "She's a hero!"

At that point, I figured it wouldn't be prudent to come down, at least not in front, where dozens of police and newspaper reporters were waiting to make my life miserable. So instead of climbing down to the fire escape, I went *up* until I reached my pulley hook, the end of the rope, and the roof.

The megaphone blasted again, but I paid the lieutenant no mind. I shimmied up, stood, coiled my rope, and put it away. I waved to the crowd—and they cheered. Before the cops could send men around to the back of the building, I darted across, leapt to the roof of the adjacent building, and so on, until I found a fire escape I could use. The police were looking for me everywhere. My advantage was that the scene had attracted quite an audience. 4th Street was packed. I descended at 6th Avenue. Bright lights, traffic, and people—those three things served as my cover. I ran, dodged pedestrians, zigzagged across streets heading south and then east. No one pursued me. I made it home safely.

This morning the Black Stiletto was on the front pages again. The *Daily News* had a great picture of Barry and me on the ledge, surrounded by the spotlight. The headline was "Black Stiletto Saves Jumper." The article said Barry was indeed despondent over his performance at NYU, but his father is quoted as saying that he loves his son and would never be ashamed of him. I hope that's true.

I think I did a good deed, don't you?

Time to go to the gym.

20
Judy's Diary
1960

JUNE 30, 1960

I had dinner with Michael tonight. He called the gym a couple of times and left messages for me, so I called him back and he asked me out.

Dear diary, I am smitten. I think.

He's the most *exotic* man I've ever known, even more than Fiorello. In fact, maybe he reminds me a little of Fiorello and that's why I'm attracted to him. Like Fiorello, Michael has an "Old-World" sensibility, speaks other languages, speaks English in a sexy foreign accent, and is handsome in a completely different way from American men. I don't know how to describe it. It's a "darker" handsomeness, the rare kind that reminds me of classical paintings and sculptures of Greek gods or even of Jesus.

While he's nice, there is definitely a wall around him, though. My crazy intuition's jury is still out. I don't feel the kinds of alarms I do when I meet a truly dangerous or evil person, but I do sense that there's something in Michael's past or background that was—or is—very unpleasant. He doesn't smile much. I try to tell jokes, but he doesn't get them. He takes things very seriously, and frankly, I'm not sure I can handle that. I like a few laughs now and then. *But*—he is most certainly attractive and he *is* nice and seems intelligent.

It's probably not going to develop into anything, but I might as well see where it goes for now. What else do I have to show for romance lately?

He took me to a Russian restaurant I'd never been to, and it's only a few blocks up 2nd Ave from the gym. I'd never gone in there because, well, it looked so *foreign*. I had a dish called beef stroganoff that was good—it had flat, wide noodles in a brown gravy with chunks of meat. I couldn't tell you what Michael had, but it wasn't very appealing to me. I started off with a beet soup called borsht, and I have to say I didn't like that too much. Michael spoke to the waiter in Russian. German is his native language, that's mostly what they speak in Austria, where he's from. So he speaks three languages that I know of. I don't think I could do that! He told me that a lot of people in America think he's either a Nazi or a Commie. I said that wasn't fair. I got the feeling he wasn't too happy with his decision of immigrating.

Our conversation at dinner was stop and start. There were quite a few periods of silence. That's another thing about Michael. He's not a big talker. I had to draw him out by asking him questions. At one point he asked, "When do I get to ask *you* questions about your life story?" He said it with one of the few smiles I saw all night, but I sensed he was a little annoyed. So I let the silences run their course. Don't get me wrong, it wasn't *uncomfortable*, just a little awkward.

Those eyes of his sure are intense. Despite the reservations I might have about Michael, that's what gets to me. His eyes have the ability to melt me. But in order for that to happen, things just have to warm up a little more, ha ha. (I can't believe I just wrote that!)

When we were done it was nearly 11:00. I drank a martini with vodka in it that was pretty strong, plus wine with the dinner, so I was a little loopy. He knew it, too, and probably could have taken advantage of me if he'd wanted, but he was a gentleman and just walked me home. We did have a dynamite kiss in front of the gym door!

He said he'd call me again soon.

I must have had a stupid grin on my face when I walked in, because Freddie said it looked like I'd enjoyed my date. He wanted to meet Michael, but I said to Freddie, "You're not my father." I think that hurt his feelings. Freddie got up and went into his room. I knocked on his door and said I was sorry, I didn't mean it the way it came out, and that I'd been drinking. He said, "Never mind, I'm going to bed." So I did, too.

JULY 5, 1960

Holy cow, Lyndon Johnson announced his bid for the presidency today. That throws a monkey wrench into the convention, which starts next week. It also came out that Kennedy might have something called Addison's disease. I don't quite understand what it does to you, but some of the politicians are questioning whether or not Kennedy is healthy enough to be president. I'm nervous! Johnson's okay, I guess. I like him better than Symington. At any rate, things are extremely busy at the headquarters. It seems like we hear news about the convention every few minutes, and it's becoming really complicated. I gave Jimmy a few of my days at the gym so I can spend more time volunteering.

Mitch and Alice and I went to a bar nearby on Park Avenue South last night where they were celebrating 4th of July. I can't help but feel like a third wheel when I'm out with them, so I invited Michael to meet us there. We had plans to watch the fireworks from the roof of the gym later. Mitch and Alice seemed surprised when he joined us a little late. They vaguely remembered him from the beatnik party, but they didn't say much to each other. Most of the time it was just me, Mitch, and Alice talking. Michael hardly said a word. I swear I detected some kind of tension between them. At first I thought Mitch and Alice might not like him because he's Austrian, but he's not a Communist or anything like that. After a couple of drinks, we said goodbye to Mitch and Alice and took the 3rd Avenue bus downtown. That's when I asked Michael if there was anything going on with them, and he told me "no." My antennae tingled and I knew he wasn't telling the truth.

"Are you sure?" I asked him. "You seemed tense around them."

After a pause, Michael nodded and said, "When we were at that party, I overheard the man talking."

"Mitch?"

"He was saying insulting things about Eastern Europeans, that they're all Communists. Not everyone in that part of the world is a Communist. And there are many people living as Communists because they *have* to, not because they want to." He shrugged. "I didn't appreciate the things he said, that's all. I really don't know him."

I told Michael I was sorry for bringing them together again, but he took my *hand* and said, "Don't worry. It's all right. I am also very shy around people I don't know. You notice I don't say much?"

"Yes."

"I am shy. My English is not great."

"It's very good, Michael! Gosh, it's better than my German!"

I suppose the trepidation I felt was empathy for Michael simply being uncomfortable. That would make sense. The only problem with that scenario was that I felt most of the tension at the table coming from Mitch.

Once we got to the gym, I introduced him to Freddie, and we all sat in chairs on the roof.

The fireworks were amazing, as always. This time they meant so much more to me now that I'm involved in the election. I felt more patriotic or something. I got chills, yet it was a hot night. Michael held my hand the whole time. When the fireworks were over, I walked him outside to the front of the gym and we kissed again.

More fireworks!

JULY 10, 1960

It's Sunday and I'm home from a night out. A long night out. An all-night night out.

With Michael.

Yes, dear diary, you know what that means.

Yesterday was Saturday night and I managed to get away from headquarters for the evening. I told Michael I'd meet him somewhere if I could. We had dinner at the Roosevelt Grill in the Roosevelt Hotel on Madison Avenue. Fancy! It was very romantic, and Michael's eyes sparkled in the candlelight. I told him he shouldn't spend that kind of money, but he waved me off. Is he wealthy? I don't think so. I asked him where he lived, and he said, "Here and there, but tonight I have a room here."

Uh-oh, I thought. Very smooth. He'd planned it so we'd still have the rest of dinner to get through with something *unsaid* hovering over the table. And we both knew what that was. Needless to say, it created anticipation.

Well, that made me a little nervous, so I probably drank too much wine. At the end of dinner he asked me flat out if I'd like to share a bottle of champagne in his room.

I accepted. I couldn't help it. He was so handsome and exuded a certain strength and confidence I found very appealing. And I was a little drunk. And I—*wanted* it. So I followed him into the elevator and up to the 12th floor. His room was gorgeous, and the windows looked out over Midtown.

The champagne arrived and we each drank one glass on the couch. We had the second glass in the bedroom.

Once again, Michael didn't talk much. But, oh, my gosh, he didn't have to.

And that's all I have to say on the subject!

21
Martin
THE PRESENT

My mom is in the ICU of Northwest Community Hospital and so far she hasn't woken up. I'm worried sick, it's almost ten o'clock at night, and tomorrow is Thanksgiving.

I've tried calling Gina in New York, but she doesn't pick up. Her voice mail cheerily tells me, "Hi, this is Gina, leave a message!" The first time I simply told her to call me back. That was late this afternoon, after Maggie called me from the nursing home to let me know what had happened. I left work early and rushed to the hospital. Maggie told me she'd meet me there later, as she had to finish her shift and go back to her own office for a couple of hours. She said she already contacted Mom's primary care physician, Dr. Schneider.

I called Gina again just after seven and there was still no answer. That time I said her grandma was in the hospital and to please return the call. I just tried again, got the voice mail, and didn't leave a message. Where the hell was she? Probably out with friends, since it was the first night of their holiday. Juilliard had the rest of the week off, like everyone else. Who was she spending Thanksgiving with? She'd told me she'd be with "friends," but I didn't know them.

Dr. Schneider spoke to me in the ICU waiting room. He introduced me to Dr. Kitanishi, an Asian woman in her forties who'd be handling Mom's case. "Your mother has suffered a serious stroke and is in a coma," she told me. I swear I felt my stomach lurch when

I heard that. "But her vitals are strong and there's every indication she will emerge from the coma. We won't know what kind of damage there will be until she's awake. The CT scan revealed that she most likely had an arterial embolus that originated in the arterial tree. I don't think it came from her heart."

"Wait, wait," I said. "Better speak English."

"I'm sorry. An embolus is a particle of something—it could be fat, air, a tiny piece of tissue that got in the bloodstream, or a part of a thrombus that broke off. The embolus travels through the arteries and either hits the heart or the brain to cause the stroke."

"What's a thrombus?"

"A blood clot."

"Okay."

"Her records show your mother had a vasovagal syncope a couple of months ago."

"Uh, yeah, she fainted."

"That might have been an early symptom of a thrombus or embolus."

I had to sit down, so both doctors sat across from me. Dr. Kitanishi continued. "We're doing more tests, but it's quite possible the embolus has dissipated, which will be a good thing. If not, then we have to find it. There are several ways of destroying it, and we'll cross that bridge if and when we locate it. More importantly, we must find the source of the embolus. Where it came from."

I nodded like I was following her.

"Mr. Talbot, your mother has an old gunshot wound in her left shoulder as well as an old scar on her right shoulder that appears to have been made by a knife or other sharp object. Not only that, her body exhibits several scars and blemishes that must have resulted from an accident, I presume. Can you tell me how she got these wounds?"

There they were again, the tricky questions about Mom's health and past. Maggie asked them. Now Dr. Kitanishi. I immediately felt the familiar ball of anxiety in my chest. Whenever I came face-to-face with Mom's history and had to reconcile it with the present, I freaked out.

Naturally, I lied. "She never told me how she got them. I don't have a clue."

"She wasn't in the armed forces?"

"No." I smiled nervously. "The doctor at the nursing home asked me the same thing."

The woman stared at me. She must have been thinking—*how could her patient's son not know where such significant injuries came from?* Finally, she said, "Well, it's possible the embolus is a remnant of one of those old wounds."

"Can I see her?"

"You can have a peek, but she *is* in a coma and won't respond. After that, I suggest you go home and we'll call you if there's any change."

I had to ask. "Doctor—will she live?"

"I think so. Let's take it a day at a time, though. From what I can see, your mother is a very strong person. She must have kept very fit in her younger days, am I right?"

I nodded.

"That'll be in her favor. Do you have any other questions?"

Out of the corner of my eye, I saw Carol and Ross enter the waiting room. They approached as if they were part of the family, which I really didn't appreciate. Carol was *once* a part of the family, and Ross never was.

"Not right now," I answered the doctor. The three of us stood, and I shook hands with the two physicians. Then they left us alone.

"Martin, I'm so sorry," Carol said. "How is she?"

I told her what the doc said. Carol listened, her brow furrowed, as she nodded with concern. When I finished, Ross spoke up. He's a lawyer and apparently a very rich one, in his sixties, well dressed, and a little too pompous for my taste.

"Martin, my own mother went through the same thing and she got through it with flying colors. Lived another fifteen years."

I looked at him and said with plenty of sarcasm, "Gee, Ross, *thanks*. That really helps."

Carol jumped to defend him. "Martin, Ross just—"

I held up my hands. "It's okay. I'm sorry. I'm a little upset."

At that point, Maggie arrived. My savior. She was my excuse not to talk to Carol and her boyfriend. But it was also my chance to introduce her to my ex.

"Maggie, thank goodness you're here!"

"Sorry I'm a little late. The last patient didn't leave the office until six. Traffic was terrible getting here from Deerfield." She looked at Carol and Ross. "Hello."

"Maggie, this is Carol Wilton and Ross Maxwell. Carol is Gina's mother. This is Dr. Margaret McDaniel."

"Oh, I'm happy to meet you." Maggie shook hands with them. I watched Carol's face as she realized that the striking woman next to me was my new girlfriend. I believe she was surprised I could land someone so obviously out of my league. Ross appeared to be a bit knocked out by her, too.

"Maggie, we can go in and see Mom briefly." I repeated what I'd told my ex.

Maggie nodded and said, "It's what I thought." She wrapped her arms around me and gave me a warm, affectionate hug. "Don't worry, Martin. It may not be as serious as it looks." I happened to be facing Carol during the embrace and saw that she was still a little in shock.

When we parted, I addressed Carol. "I haven't heard from Gina. I left her a couple of messages. Do you know where she is?"

Carol regained her composure and answered, "She went to a friend's place in New Rochelle. It's not far from the city. She's spending the weekend there."

"Nice of her to tell me. She couldn't have left her phone behind, could she?"

"I doubt it. She's probably busy, doing something fun. I'm sure she'll call tomorrow if not later tonight."

"Okay. Come on, Maggie, let's go see Mom."

"Is there anything we can do?" Carol asked. "We rushed over here as soon as we heard."

Normally, I would have felt obligated to let her see Mom, too, or provide a meal or something. Not this time, not with Maggie at my side. "Thanks, Carol, why don't I let you know? I appreciate you coming, but there's nothing to be done at the moment." I gave her a sincere look and then walked away with Maggie. I heard Ross say, "Take care," and Carol add, "Call if you need us." I think they were a little miffed by the brush-off.

When we were inside ICU, Maggie said, "So that's Carol, huh?"

"That's Carol. And her *fiancé*."

"Weren't you a little rude?"

"Tough shit. I don't really feel like playing games with her and Moneybags right now."

Mom was alone, hooked up to a zillion monitors and machines. An oxygen mask covered her face. If it weren't for all the hospital paraphernalia, she'd look like she was peacefully sleeping. I approached the bed and stared at her face. What was going on inside that head? Did a person dream while in a coma? Could she hear us talk?

For several minutes, I didn't say a word. I just stood there and watched her breathe. Finally, though, I realized that my being there served no purpose. Tomorrow was Thanksgiving. I might as well go home.

"Good night, Mom. I'll see you tomorrow." I leaned over and kissed her forehead. "You get better, okay? I want you to get a good night's sleep and wake up soon, all right?"

The anxiety bubble in my chest nearly burst and I felt my eyes water. I turned to Maggie and hugged her again. Then we left.

*   *   *

We went to Maggie's apartment. The plan was that I'd stay the night, we'd go back to the hospital in the morning, and if there was still no change, we'd share Thanksgiving together. Maggie had all the food ready to go. Normally, I'd watch a football game or two in the afternoon, but that scheme was on hold.

She fixed us a couple of stiff drinks, even though she acknowledged I shouldn't consume alcohol while on antidepressants. "One won't hurt you, and I think you need it," she said. I did indeed.

We sat quietly on the couch after Maggie put on a Norah Jones CD. After a while, she spoke, "You know, Martin, it might be really helpful if we knew what caused those wounds your Mom has."

That again.

When I didn't answer, she continued, "Come on, Martin. Two gunshot injuries? Knife scars? What the hell did your mother do when she was young? You swear you don't know?"

I desperately wanted to tell her. The panic in my chest was a pressure cooker that could be relieved only by revealing the truth. That much I knew. Instead, I simply said I didn't know, and then tears ran down my face. Maggie took my hand and led me into the bedroom. She sat me down, squatted to remove my shoes, and then gently pushed me back to a horizontal position. She climbed on the bed next to me, and we stayed like that until we fell asleep.

Sometime later, we both opened our eyes and realized we were still in our clothes. I watched Maggie stand and get undressed. She then got under the covers and peeked out like a schoolgirl as I stood and removed my things. I slipped in beside her and relished her soft, warm skin. The kissing started, the hands roamed, and very soon we passionately became one. I felt my anxiety melt away.

It was then that I knew Maggie was the woman for me. And I'm pretty sure the feeling was mutual. Hearing her cry out my name as she reached a climax was heaven-sent music to my ears.

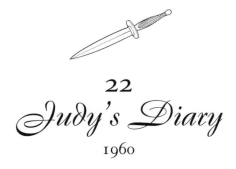

22
Judy's Diary
1960

JULY 11, 1960

The Democratic National Convention started today in Los Angeles. I wish I could've gone. It would have been so exciting. My fingers are crossed for Kennedy. His campaign has a lot of momentum, and most people here at headquarters think he'll get the nomination. He hasn't picked a running mate yet, and there're all kinds of speculation as to who it will be. Needless to say, it's going to be a busy week at my volunteer job.

Dear diary, I think I made a big mistake Saturday night with Michael. I looked back over what I wrote yesterday and now I don't feel as good about it. Yes, I had a nice time with him, it felt good and all that, but today I'm just not as enamored of him. Saturday night and most of the day yesterday I was in the afterglow, probably because it had been so long since I'd been with a man. There was Jimmy, of course, but I knew that wasn't going to turn into a romance. I know it sounds scandalous, but that was just a *physical* thing, something that happened because I must have lost my head for a moment. I believe sex before marriage is all right if you really like the guy. As for Michael, well, I'm not in love with him. I like him and I'll continue to see him. It's just that he's such an odd duck. I can't figure him out. Maybe Europeans are just—well, *different*. Fiorello was Italian, born in Sicily, but he grew up in America. I could relate to Fiorello, whereas Michael has been in the U.S. only three years or so.

All that aside, he didn't call me last night. You'd think a guy would phone a girl the next day after he'd slept with her. Geez, I sound like a loose woman.

I'm tired. It's not easy working the job at the gym and then going to HQ afterward, and I really don't want to think about Michael or Fiorello or even John F. Kennedy now. Good night and sweet dreams.

JULY 12, 1960

This evening I was caught doing Black Stiletto moves in the gym.

It was after hours (we close at 9:00) and I was in the middle of doing my workout, dressed in a leotard. The hanging bag serves as my opponent and I practice my *wushu* kicks and hand attacks on it, like I usually do. If I say so myself, I'm getting pretty good at my custom-designed Praying Mantis moves. I'm sure a Chinese *sifu* would disapprove of what I'm doing; it certainly isn't correct, but it's graceful and effective. I think. Of course, the hanging bag can't hit me back!

I remember clobbering the bag and thinking about how I miss Soichiro and his training, when I heard a noise behind me. I thought I was all alone in the place, so I whirled around to find none other than Clark! I haven't written about him in a while. The Negro teenager turned 17 recently and his body is becoming manly. With all the training Clark's doing, his muscles are getting bigger and he's improved with his boxing. Although he's a good school student and reads a lot, he says he wants to be a boxer. I've told him many times that it's good for him to do it for exercise and sport, but not for a profession. He's too *smart* to be a boxer.

At any rate, I was surprised to see him there. "What are you doing here, Clark? We're closed," I said, a little out of breath.

"I fell asleep in the locker room," he said. "I didn't mean to. I was so tired. I was up all night last night studying for an exam."

"Where did you fall asleep?"

"On the bench in front of my locker! I took a shower, dried off, and just felt like lying down for a minute. Before I knew it, it was late!" His face indicated he was more surprised by *me* than by what he'd done. "What was that you were doing? I've never seen that before!"

He was right. No one at the gym had witnessed my *wushu* practice. They all knew I boxed and did *karate*, but I've kept my Praying Mantis endeavors a secret.

"Oh, it's just some martial arts stuff I've been practicing," I told him.

"That wasn't *karate*, was it?"

"Uh, no, it's something I made up." That wasn't a total lie, at least.

"Wow, it looked *incredible*. Can you teach me that?"

"Clark, I don't really know it myself. I guess you could say I'm developing my own technique, but it's not perfected. I couldn't teach it to someone else."

"It looked perfected to me. It was really hard to follow your hands, they were moving so fast. You could really whup someone doing that!"

"You think so?"

"I know so!"

"Well, I hope I never have to. Come on, I'll unlock the door so you can get home. I don't know why you came to the gym if you didn't sleep last night. What was the test on?"

He told me it was geometry. I never had geometry before I turned my back on my education. Sometimes I wish I'd graduated from high school, but so far I'm doing all right without a diploma. I get by. Sure, it would be nice to have a million bucks and live on Fifth Avenue across from the Metropolitan Art Museum, but I don't. But I have a job I enjoy and I like my life as it is.

I think, ha ha.

After I let him out and locked the door behind him, I went back to the bag and continued my routine. It did feel good to get some positive feedback. I beat the living daylights out of that bag!

JULY 13, 1960

Two big things today, dear diary. *Big* things.

First, Kennedy got the nomination today! Hooray! He still doesn't have a running mate. The word at HQ was that he asked Symington to be the VP. Mitch predicted Symington wouldn't take it. I guess we'll find out tomorrow.

I'm taking off from work for the rest of the week. Jimmy doesn't mind. He likes having the hours. I'm happy to report that things are better between us. Does he still carry a torch for me? Probably. He gets a little moon-eyed when I'm around, but his behavior is appropriate. I helped spot him during his bench presses the other day, and he seemed all right with that.

The second big thing is what I really want to write about, and it's something that happened today at lunchtime. I'd left headquarters to get some coffee and something to eat, and I saw Michael on the street. He didn't notice me. I'd gone over to Madison Avenue, and there he was. He was leaning into the window of a black sedan at the curb, talking to the driver. I couldn't see the driver's face because I was behind the car, but I had a better view of a passenger in the front seat. I didn't recognize the man, but he reminded me of Michael. Another Eastern European? An Austrian? The driver appeared to be chewing out Michael for something. He kept jabbing his index finger at Michael, and I faintly heard angry words in another language. German? Russian? My acute hearing picked it up, but I didn't have a clue what it was. In hindsight, it did sound more like Russian.

I didn't want Michael to see me, so I stepped into a doorway of a building and watched from a better angle. The car was a 4-door

Packard Patrician. I had the presence of mind to memorize the license plate number—358 22X. I don't know what I'll do with that information, but at least I have it. Michael still blocked my view of the driver, but I could see the other man more clearly from my new position. He had wavy dark hair and thick eyebrows, like Michael, but he also had a mustache.

After a moment, the Packard's tires abruptly screeched on the pavement and the car sped away. Michael stood there watching it go, his back to me. I thought, *what the heck*, so I emerged from my hiding place and approached him.

"Michael!"

Startled, he swiftly turned around. I could tell by his expression that not only was he surprised to see me, he was also displeased.

"Fancy meeting you here," I said. "What are you doing? Want to join me for some lunch?"

He spoke nervously. "I was, uh, on my way to the pay phone to call you, Judy, but I didn't know if you were at the gym or at the Democrat headquarters." He pointed west. "It's just over there on Park, right?"

Liar. "Who was in the car?"

"What?"

"That black car just now. Who were you talking to?"

"Oh, just friends of mine."

I'd swear he was not pleased that I'd seen him leaning in that car window, but chose not to say anything about it.

"Yep. I took some days off since the convention is on." I pointed to a diner. "I'm going to get some lunch. Care to join me?"

He nodded and followed me inside. We sat in a booth and I tried to make small talk before the waitress took my order. He didn't say a word except to ask for a glass of water. He was tense and angry, but was doing his best not to show it.

"Anything wrong?" I asked.

"No."

"You seem upset about something."

"Oh, I, uh, forgot my wallet. I left it at the apartment. Now I have to go back."

"Where's your apartment?"

He immediately changed the subject. "Your Kennedy got the nomination."

"Yeah, isn't that great?"

"I think of you when I see something in the news about him."

Michael glanced at the door and lit a cigarette. There was no question about it. He was on edge and distracted. I tried a different tactic. "I enjoyed Saturday night," I said in my best coquettish voice, which, I have to admit, sounds goofy.

"I did, too," he replied.

That's all? I know some men tend to shy away from girls after they've gotten them into bed. It happened to me with that stupid Mack, the first guy I ever slept with. He didn't want anything to do with me after he succeeded in getting in my pants. Was the same thing happening here?

"Michael," I said, "I like you, but I want you to know I don't care for secrets. If you have something you need to tell me, please do."

"There are no secrets," he answered.

Liar.

"No? I'm a big girl, you can tell me."

"Don't you have secrets, too?" he asked, staring at me with those intense brown eyes. What the heck did he mean by that? For a moment I was speechless. Then, awkwardly, my food arrived and he stood. Right there in front of the waitress, he said, "Sorry, Judy, I can't see you anymore. Goodbye."

He didn't stay to see my reaction. Without another word, he left the diner! Can you believe it?

The waitress, a cigarette hanging out of her mouth, looked at me and said, "Honey, they ain't worth the trouble."

I was a little in shock. Humiliated and angry, too. "Well, how do you like *that*," I said. The waitress put my sandwich and fries on the table in front of me. "I'm tellin' ya, he ain't worth it. Coffee's on the house if you want it, honey."

That was nice of her. But can you believe that, dear diary? What kind of a brush-off was *that*? That was downright *mean*.

And besides being a total square, he's definitely hiding something.

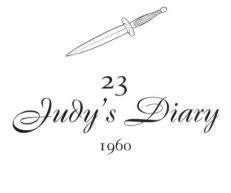

23
⒥udy's ⒟iary
1960

July 14, 1960

There must have been some wheeling and dealing in Los Angeles today, because Johnson accepted the vice presidential nomination after it was originally thought he would refuse it. Tomorrow Kennedy will assuredly accept his nomination and we'll be backing a Kennedy/Johnson ticket come this November! Hooray! I've decided I'll probably continue in my volunteer capacity and work for the Kennedy campaign. It's not clear at this point if we'll move to a different office.

I've collapsed in my room after a long and busy day and decided to write a bit. The radio is playing the funniest song. It's called "Itsy Bitsy Teenie Weenie Yellow Polka Dot Bikini." It's pretty dumb but I kind of like it, although I liked "Alley Oop" at first but I can't stand it now. I think I'll turn it off and just play the new Elvis record. It's called "It's Now or Never," and I love it. It's such a pretty song. The flip side is "A Mess of Blues." As soon as I heard it was out, I ran to the record store on Bleecker Street and bought it. The only word I can use to describe the feeling of getting a new Elvis record is—*bliss*.

I'm still puzzled by Michael's actions yesterday. I haven't heard from him, of course. Today Alice asked me how it was going with him, and I told her I wasn't sure about it. I didn't outright say it was over, I don't know why, but I asked her again if she or Mitch knew anything about him, and she replied that they first met Michael at the beatnik party, like me. She gave me Pam's phone number, of Ron and Pam, who hosted the party. I might call her and ask how they know him. Would that be rude? Truthfully, I'd forget that jerk if I didn't also think he's up to something.

I'll sleep on it.

JULY 16, 1960

It's a little after midnight and I'm just settling in for bed. I went out as the Stiletto tonight. It felt good to be stalking the streets again, but the outing was ultimately frustrating. I was looking for Michael, but, of course, that was like searching for a needle in a haystack.

Today I called Pam from HQ—Kopinski is her last name—and explained who I was and that I was a guest of Mitch and Alice at her party. The conversation was strange. It went like this:

Pam: "Oh, sure, I remember you. You're real tall."

Me: "Yeah. I wanted to ask you about a guy that was there. Michael Sokowitz?"

Pam: "Michael, was he the guy from Germany?"

Me: "Austria."

Pam: "Oh, right. Yeah, I remember him. What about him?"

Me: "How do you know him, if you don't mind my asking?"

Pam: "I beg your pardon?"

Me: "How do you know Michael?"

Pam: "I don't understand."

Me: "How come he was at your party?"

Pam: "I don't know. I thought he was friend of yours."

Me: "No, I met him for the first time at the party."

Pam: "He didn't come with Mitch and Alice? I was under the impression he was a friend of theirs."

Me: "No, Alice says that's not the case. What about your husband? Does he know Michael?"

Pam: "Who, Ron? He's not my husband. We just live together."

Me: "Oh, sorry."

Pam: "That's all right. I don't think Ron knows him either, 'cause I remember him asking me who the guy was."

Me: "So you don't have any idea how he was invited to your party?"

Pam: "I guess not, but that's not so strange. Several people there were friends of friends. The party was open to anyone, really."

I thanked her and hung up, more baffled than ever. Where did Michael come from, if Mitch and Alice and Pam and Ron didn't know him? He never gave me his address. I don't know where he lives. I don't have a phone number for him because I never thought to ask him for it. Michael always called me from a pay phone on the street, so it's unclear whether or not he even has a phone.

That's when I decided that tonight I'd go out as the Black Stiletto and try to find him. Dumb idea, right? A city with a couple million people in it, and I'm looking for one man without a clue where he'd be?

For the first hour or so, I was angry. Michael slept with me and then threw me away. Bastard. Was I some kind of American conquest for him? Does he do that to every girl he meets? I guess it's taught me a lesson. I shouldn't be so *amenable* with men I don't know well. My reputation is worth more than that.

So here I am, alone in my room. I suppose going out was good exercise for me anyway. The Stiletto hadn't made an appearance since I got that kid off the building. It also felt good because Kennedy accepted the party's nomination today in L.A. It was a cause to celebrate, and what better way to do that than to run across Manhattan rooftops, shimmy up and down telephone polls, and dart through pedestrians and traffic like some kind of Wonder Woman?

JULY 22, 1960

Gosh, I can't believe a week's gone by since I last wrote. My volunteer work has moved uptown to 48th and Park Avenue. It's a building

Kennedy once lived in or owns or something. Some rooms there will serve as the New York Kennedy/Johnson campaign headquarters. It's a farther commute on the bus, but it's exciting to be in Midtown for much of the day. I feel like a glamorous Madison Avenue secretary who works in an important firm! Who cares if I don't get paid? I'm happy to do it. Freddie thinks I'm nuts, but he doesn't mind as long as the gym isn't neglected. Jimmy's been a life saver in that regard.

Mr. Patton told us today that they're forming a "Citizens for Kennedy" group all over the country, and they're looking for volunteers to be "Kennedy Girls." He looked straight at me when he said it. Kennedy Girls will wear a uniform and appear with the senator when he's in town. Mrs. Kennedy is supposed to be designing the uniform. There will be Kennedy Girls in every major city.

Alice told me I should volunteer. I have to admit the chance of appearing with Kennedy is pretty tempting. I'd get to meet him!

I'm going to give it some serious thought.

JULY 28, 1960

Holy cow, almost another week has flown by.

I told Mr. Patton I wanted to be a Kennedy Girl, and he said I'm an "ideal choice." I was flattered. He said he'd let me know for sure in August once they've talked to all the girls who want to do it. I'm sure they only want young, attractive girls. Chip said they'd turn away all the "fat and ugly ones." I thought that was a mean thing to say and told him so, especially since he's pretty fat himself! But I guess he's right. It was funny, but *terrible*, when he teased Karen, telling her *she* should volunteer to be a Kennedy Girl. Karen turned red and snapped at him. We were all snickering behind her back, we couldn't help it, but I stuck up for her and said seriously, "I think Karen would make a great Kennedy Girl."

"*Thank* you, Judy," she said, and then left the room in a huff.

Alice asked me today if I'd heard from Michael. Until she said his name I hadn't really thought about him. I told her it was over weeks ago. She said, "Good riddance," and that I should be glad to be rid of him.

I have to agree.

In other news, Richard Nixon accepted the Republican Party's nomination today. Henry Cabot Lodge is his running mate.

The race is on!

24
Martin
The Present

Thanksgiving morning I got a call from the hospital. My mom regained consciousness. I can't describe what a relief it was to hear that. Maggie was glad to hear it, too. We had a quick breakfast and jumped in the car.

Once again I felt embarrassed about my behavior the night before. How many men cry in front of their girlfriends? No matter how often I told myself it wasn't a sign of weakness, I couldn't help but feel humiliated. Maggie was great, though. She didn't mention it. What was palpable were the sparks we'd experienced afterward, when we'd made love. It went unsaid, but I knew she was pleased with how that worked out. It's as if we finally found a rhythm that mutually suited us. Dare I say it? Something magical happened between us.

I asked her why she'd never married. She answered that she'd had someone serious once, back in med school, and that he broke her heart. Since then she dated irregularly and focused entirely on her work.

While driving, I came to the realization that Maggie was very, very good for me. I had to be careful and not blow it, but how could I continue the relationship without her knowing the truth about my mother? Whenever I thought about that obstacle, my chest tightened and my heart pounded. It took a concentrated effort to bring myself down from a full panic attack. *I hated it* that I had that problem. The medication wasn't working. It hadn't been a month, so it was probably too soon.

When we reached the hospital, the nurse paged the doctor on duty. Dr. Kitanishi wasn't there, of course. After a five minute wait, an Indian man in his forties appeared and introduced himself as Dr. Benji. He told us my mom woke up early, around six, but had not spoken. She was responsive to stimuli and drank water, but if asked a question she would ignore it. They had a catheter in her so they could manage her pee. She's under sedation to keep her from becoming agitated. Dr. Benji said she'll be going through more tests to see what kind of damage, if any, she'd sustained from the stroke. So far, though, she didn't appear to have lost any movement on either side of her body.

"How come she doesn't talk?" I asked.

The doctor held out his hands. "We don't know yet. It could possibly be that she can talk, but she just doesn't have anything to say."

Maggie and I were allowed to see her for a short visit. When Mom saw me, her eyes brightened a bit.

"Hi, Mom, happy Thanksgiving!" I said with as much cheer as I could muster. "It's turkey day, how about that?"

She smiled. Good.

"See, Judy, Martin, your son, is here," Maggie said. "And you know me, Dr. McDaniel, remember? How are you feeling, today?"

Mom smiled at her, too. Good.

"Can you say hello, Mom?"

When she didn't make the effort, I took hold of her hand. She squeezed it. Good.

"That's okay, Mom. You talk when you're ready. Maggie and I can only visit for a few minutes right now, but we're coming back this afternoon with some turkey for you." Dr. Benji had said she probably wouldn't be on solid food for a while, but I figured she wouldn't remember my promise.

Even though it was too early for her, I tried phoning Gina in New York. Again, I got voice mail, but I expected it. I told Mom, "I just tried to call Gina, but she's still asleep. It's a holiday for her. No school this weekend."

There was a flash of brightness in Mom's eyes. She knew who I meant, and I took that as a good sign. Gina really was the light of Mom's life.

All I could do was hope and pray my mother would be back at Woodlands soon.

Maggie started talking to her about how everyone misses her there, and I zoned out for a moment. I don't know why I thought of it then and there, but for some reason the conundrum of my mom's finances popped into my head. The mystery of how she supported us when I was growing up rushed back, and I felt a layer of uneasiness spread over my heart. Whenever I was young and asked her if she had a job, Mom replied, "My job is to take care of you." Once I was an adult, she told me we lived on an inheritance my father left us. At the time, I didn't think it was odd that she wouldn't discuss her money with me. I suppose that's reasonable. Most parents probably don't share financial matters with their children until, well, until they have to. Still, it was strange that I didn't have to do much in the way of paying bills for my mother. Her lawyer—Uncle Thomas— took care of a trust that paid the medical and nursing home costs not covered by Medicare. We never worried about money all that time I was a kid and lived at home. The "inheritance" had paid for our house, my college tuition, and our living expenses since my birth.

How much of a fucking inheritance did my father leave her? And where *was* it? Did Uncle Thomas know? Why the hell had I never pressed him—*or* my mom, when she was well—about all the Talbot family *puzzles* I stupidly ignored all my life? I've been a total idiot! If I'd taken a slightly more involved role in my mother's day-to-day existence, I might have learned her secret a long time ago.

"Who was my father, Mom?"

My God, I swear I didn't mean to say it aloud, but I did. I heard Maggie gasp beside me. My mom's eyes jerked toward me, this time with a look of pain.

"Martin," Maggie said softly. "Jesus—"

"I'm sorry," I said to Maggie but loud enough for my mom to hear. "I don't know why I said that, but it's been on my mind. I'm sorry, Mom." Suddenly I was choked up, so I left the room before I started crying again. I ran into Dr. Benji, who said our time with the patient was up. "We don't want her to get too excited."

I'm afraid it was too late for that, doc.

I felt terrible.

Maggie told me Mom handled my out-of-left-field question well enough. The confusion from the disease played a big role in her not responding negatively. It was quite probable she didn't remember who my father was. She wasn't upset after all. The doctor had entered and distracted her as soon as I'd left. Maggie said goodbye and departed as well.

On the way home in the car, Maggie commented, "I can't believe you asked her that."

"I can't believe it either," I said. "I swear, Maggie, it just came out. The thought was going through my brain, and I unintentionally vocalized it."

"I believe you, Martin, I really do." She laughed a little. "That was quite a faux pas."

That made me laugh, too. "I feel like one of the Three Stooges."

"Don't worry about it. She was fine when I left her. That said, I'd like to know who your father was, too. There are a lot of things about you and your mother I'd like to know, Martin. You're not wrong to wonder. I just can't get over the fact that you never did anything about it before she became ill."

"I know, I know. I'm a moron."

"Stop, no you're not. But sweetheart—if we're going to take this to the next level, we can't have secrets. Don't you agree?"

I looked at her, keeping one eye on the road. "I'm your sweetheart?"

"I don't cook Thanksgiving dinner for just anyone."

"Believe me, there's so much about my mother I don't know, and I'd like some answers." I left it at that, even though I withheld a gigantic, earthshaking secret that would change everything if revealed.

Everything.

While dinner was cooking, I tried calling Gina and got the voice mail again. I thought of phoning Carol and telling her about Mom's progress, but I didn't want to interrupt her Thanksgiving with *Ross*. I wondered if she had heard from Gina.

Savory smells drew me into the kitchen, where Maggie stood preparing a salad. The turkey had been slowly roasting in the oven all day. My stomach growled and I reached for the bottle of wine I had brought. "I'm gonna open this," I said, and Maggie told me to go ahead.

"Save enough to go with dinner, though."

"Where's the corkscrew?"

She pointed to a drawer near the fridge. I opened it and rummaged around until I found it. That's when I saw the business card stuck on the refrigerator with a magnet. It said, "Bill Ryan, Private Investigator." Phone number, e-mail address, and snail mail address.

"What's this?" I asked. "Why do you need a private investigator?"

Maggie looked up. "Oh, uh, Bill's a friend of mine. He started a new business and he gave me his card, that's all."

"But why is it on your fridge? You need his number handy?"

She put down her knife, moved to me, and took the card. She tore it in half and dropped the pieces in the garbage pail. "There," she said. "All gone."

"You didn't have to do that."

"It's all right. I wasn't sure which of your responses was worse—suspicion or jealousy—so I got rid of the whole thing."

"Maggie, geez."

She took the corkscrew and opened the wine. "It's all right, Martin. Let's have some wine. It's Thanksgiving."

As soon as the glasses were poured, my cell phone rang. Carol's ID came up on the screen. "Hi Carol," I answered. "Happy Thanksgiving."

"Martin!" She sounded distressed.

"What?"

"It's Gina!"

My heart stopped for a split second. "What?"

"Oh Lord, she's been *arrested* in New York!"

25
Judy's Diary
1960

Gee, I need to catch you up, dear diary. As always, I haven't been writing as much, even though we haven't been too busy yet at Kennedy/Johnson HQ. But that storm is coming soon. That's what we call it now—HQ.

I was chosen to be a Kennedy Girl. We're waiting on the uniforms to come in, and no one's really sure what we'll be doing yet. I've met two nice girls who were also picked. Betty O'Connor is a pretty brunette who works as a waitress at the Waldorf-Astoria Hotel. She's often at fancy banquets and has seen numerous celebrities and VIPs in person. Betty's my age and we hit it off from the very beginning. Louise Kelly is a blonde and is in her mid-twenties. All the guys like her because she has a big bust and she's gorgeous. I don't think she's particularly smart, though. The other day we were all talking about Francis Gary Powers, the pilot of the U-2 spy plane that was shot down over Russia in May. Powers is on trial for espionage in Moscow and could be sentenced to prison or even death. Louise thought Powers was a woman because his first name is "Francis." "They wouldn't execute a *woman*, would they?" she asked. She talks with a thick Brooklyn accent and is always noisily chewing gum. Mrs. Bernstein told her she'll have to spit out the gum when she's working as a Kennedy Girl. Most of the other girls think Louise is dumb and they roll their eyes when she says things like, "Wait, is the election *this* year?" But I like her. She's sweet and has a good heart. But Betty is becoming more of a close friend. I've been out with Betty at lunchtime, but I can't see myself spending time alone with Louise. She'd drive me crazy. On Wednesday night after a meeting, Betty and I went to see that new movie *Ocean's 11* with Frank Sinatra, Dean Martin, and Sammy Davis Jr. It just opened and there was a line around the block, but we got in. It was a "caper" story with a lot of suspense but it was pretty funny, too. I thoroughly enjoyed it.

Mr. Dudley and Mrs. Bernstein are in charge of the Girls. There are eight of us. We've had a couple of meetings, but nothing much happened. We were told to get white gloves. They're part of the uniform, but the campaign couldn't afford to pay for them. Betty winked at me and told me she knew where we could get some for nothing. She said to meet her at the Waldorf after I finished at the gym today, so I did.

What a beautiful hotel! I'd never been in it. It's pretty fancy, like the Plaza. The hotel is on Park Avenue between 49th and 50th. I met Betty at the employee entrance on 50th Street. We walked across a checkerboard floor to a place where she punched her card for work—she was just going on duty—above which a painted mural on the wall proclaimed, "History Building Bright Futures." We went up a few steps from there to an elevator. While we waited for it, Betty pointed out the hotel's loading docks right next to the bay. We rode the car to the 5th floor, where employees were running about like madmen. Betty explained this was where the men's and women's locker rooms, laundry facilities, and uniform room were located. They also had their own tailor who mended clothing on the spot. Down the hall was another place where they performed heavy cleaning on spots and stains. No one questioned my presence. They must have thought I was a new employee and Betty was showing me the ropes.

She took me in the uniform room and showed me stacks of white gloves in small, medium, and large sizes.

"Go ahead. Find a pair that fits," she said.

The mediums were tight, like my black leather Stiletto ones, so I chose those. I then followed Betty into the locker room, where other women were getting dressed for work. It wasn't much different from our locker room at the gym. I felt a little self-conscious, but Betty said not to worry about it. She was on duty in the Grand Ballroom that evening for a function, so she put on a white shirt, a dark vest, chocolate-brown pants, a matching jacket, and of course the white gloves. She looked elegant and spiffy.

Betty didn't have to start for a few minutes, so she gave me a brief tour of the hotel. We went down a set of stairs to the 4th floor and into a long hallway with groups of red curtains on one side. She pulled open one set and I gasped. We were looking down on the Grand Ballroom. A massive chandelier dominated the ceiling, and the room was decorated in a red-and-ivory color scheme. White tablecloths covered dozens of tables and there were flower arrangements on each one. Betty pointed to the "boxes" around the upper half of the ballroom, where some VIP guests sit. The entrances to those are on the 5th floor.

We went down to the 3rd floor and saw a very pretty space called the Basildon Room. The ceiling was painted in what she said was a scene from Dante's *Divine Comedy*. I'm not familiar with that, but the picture was spectacular. Next door was the Jade Room, which got its name from the green streaks running through marble pillars. I thought I was in a museum.

The last stop on the tour was the banquet kitchen on the 2nd floor. Betty said the kitchens take up three floors of the hotel! Well, the kitchen was gigantic. Different areas specialized in certain food items; for example, the soups and sauces were prepared in one section, the bakery was in another, meats and main courses were down the hall. Another mural sported the slogan: "The difficult immediately, the impossible takes a few minutes longer." Betty said that was truer than I could possibly think. All along the way, the other employees were very friendly. I even got to take a little pastry from a tray in the bakery section. Yum!

Betty had to start work then, so she took me down to the ground floor to say goodbye. Completely dazzled, I made my way home.

AUGUST 28, 1960

I'm still in shock by what happened last night, dear diary. I feel ashamed, angry, and frightened.

It's 5:00 on Sunday afternoon, and I haven't emerged from my room yet. Freddie knocked on the door, and I told him I wasn't feeling well. It was true. I've had no appetite all day.

The evening started with me getting drunk. I can't believe I did that—and *then I went out as the Black Stiletto*. What a stupid, brainless, idiotic, irresponsible, and *dangerous* thing to do! I could've been killed, and I may have seriously hurt a man, albeit not a very nice one.

The reason I got drunk? I was feeling sorry for myself. I know it's dumb because I really have no reason to feel bad. I have friends, I keep busy, I love what I do, and I'm proud of who I am. The fact of the matter, though, is that I'm lonely. Last night I particularly missed John and Fiorello. So I bought a bottle of vodka and made martinis. Freddie warned me not to drink more than two. I had five.

I don't think I'd ever been that drunk before. The evening proceeded to be a fragmented nightmare because I don't *remember* a lot of it! I recall being really looped in the kitchen, and Freddie telling me he was going to bed after watching Lawrence Welk. Then I was in my room, and it was spinning. I dropped on the bed and may have fallen asleep for a bit. The next thing I knew it was 10:30. I *thought* I didn't feel drunk anymore.

Then I got the bright idea to put on the outfit. The summer had not been a good one for the Black Stiletto; I'd gone out only a few times. I figured it was time to show her mask in public again.

What a mistake.

I remember the dash across the rooftops and going down the pole. As soon as my boots were on the sidewalk, though, I knew I wasn't in any shape to be the Black Stiletto. Besides having equilibrium problems, the alcohol had also deadened my otherwise heightened senses. No more amplified sound or intuitive lie detecting. Nevertheless, I didn't turn back and go home. I guess there's an ornery streak in me, and I let it take over.

There's a blank spot after that, for I suddenly found myself in the Bowery on the border of Chinatown. I had no idea how I'd gotten there. The only thing I can think is that my subconscious was operating my body. I realize that doesn't make sense. But apparently I crossed several streets and avenues, no doubt darted through pedestrians and traffic, and made it safely from 2nd Avenue to the Bowery without thinking about it.

But what *was* I thinking? I don't recall having the idea to go back to Chinatown, but there I was. Did my subconscious self guide me there? I felt a chill just facing that direction, and it was hot as heck outside. The Bowery is also a spooky place at night. There are a lot of bars, so the area is populated with bums and criminals. That's usually the first place I look when I go out as the Black Stiletto, so maybe I didn't have it in mind to return to Chinatown after all. I swear, though, I don't know what it is about that place that attracts me.

Nevertheless, I didn't enter Chinatown. I went south along the Bowery, and people were definitely surprised to see me. Some pointed and a few laughed. They didn't think I was the real thing. Someone said, "Is it Halloween?" To them I was just some stupid girl who dressed up in a Black Stiletto outfit. I suppose I wasn't moving as quickly as I usually do. I mostly give pedestrians just enough time to register that they've seen me, and then I'm out of there.

The sound of a glass or bottle breaking drew me to the wide-open door of a real dive, small, dark, smoky, and populated only by hardcore alcoholics. Inside two men were fighting around a single pool table. They were in their forties or fifties, but it's hard to tell with men who have been on the booze all their lives. They were shabbily dressed and drunk. Drunker than me.

One of them waved a broken bottle at his opponent. The bartender was on the phone, no doubt calling the police. It really did pop into my head that the two men could get hurt or injure the two other customers. I had good intentions when I ordered them, "Stop fighting, boys." But I didn't sound like myself. My voice cracked and was weak. The fighters, the bartender, and the two audience members turned to look at me. It was just like one of those scenes in a western when a stranger walks into the saloon.

Then they laughed. Forgetting their animosity toward each other, the two fighters became comrades in arms to belittle the Black Stiletto. Actually, they didn't think I was the real thing, either. One of them accused me of being a "naughty girl" and dressing up in a party costume.

Dear diary, I don't know what happened after that. Another blank. Maybe I started it, that's not clear to me, but I got into a fight I don't recall. The next moment I remember, I was on my back on top of the pool table. My face hurt. One of the fighting men was *on top of me*, attempting to pull off my mask. He was saying, "Let's see what she looks like!" Luckily, the mask is secured with a knot I'm good at loosening, but other people would find difficult. I started to fight him off, but the other man helped hold me down. The struggle was serious, and blood from my face wiped off on the man's shirt sleeves.

And then I flashed back to that horrible Halloween night in Odessa, Texas when I was thirteen. When Douglas raped me. Was I about to experience that indignity again, this time with two attackers and maybe more?

The men whooped and hollered.

"Let's see what she looks like!"

"I'll get her boots off!"

As I wrestled with them, I noticed that one of the customers had closed the joint's door and stood in front of it. The man on top of me, who stank of booze, sweat, and a latrine, almost had the ties of my mask undone. He pushed his lower body hard against mine, in between my legs. It hurt and it was revolting.

"The damn mask is tied on tight—"

"Cut it off!"

And, thank God, when the man said to "cut it off," I thought of something sharp, which led me to remember my knife. My stiletto was still in its sheath on my leg. The men must have been so drunk that they either didn't see it or thought it was fake. I reached down, grabbed hold of the hilt, drew the blade, and plunged it into the man's stomach. He screamed. That startled the other guy so much that he jumped back, allowing me to push the stabbed man off of me. I leaped to my feet and stood beside the pool table with the stiletto pointed at the others, blood dripping from its edge.

The wounded man clutched his belly and curled up as he groaned and moaned.

"What did you do, girl?" the other creep said.

I turned toward the door and waved my knife at the guy standing there. He flew away like a bug, allowing me to fling open the door and run outside.

Then, dear diary, it was another blank. My next moment of consciousness was as I walked east along 2nd Street. I had run up the Bowery and headed home without realizing it. I looked at my hand. There was blood on it, but the knife wasn't there. I frantically reached for the sheath, relieved to find the stiletto snug inside. I hadn't remembered putting it away.

What had I done? I had stabbed a man. I don't know how badly, but wasn't it in self-defense? Wasn't he trying to hurt me?

I told myself I'd had no choice. He wanted to unmask me. The other one was attempting to get my boots off. All the men in that bar wanted to abuse me. They wanted to rape the stupid college girl who dressed up as the Black Stiletto and recklessly showed up in the Bowery. They thought they'd teach her a lesson.

I had to stop them.

Didn't I?

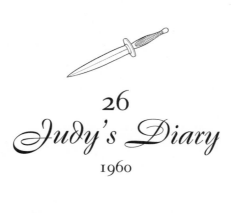

26
Judy's Diary
1960

Over the weekend huge crowds greeted Kennedy in Detroit. The press said they'd never seen anything like it. Both he and Johnson have begun the nationwide campaign, sometimes appearing together, but mostly separately. Mr. Dudley told me and the other girls that Kennedy will be in New York in October and that the Kennedy Girls will make their first appearance then as part of his entourage. I'm pretty excited about that! Will I get to meet him? Maybe even shake his hand? Gosh, what if he kissed my cheek or something? I understand he's been known to do that to ordinary citizens he meets. Will Jackie be with him? She's so gorgeous and elegant. I would like meeting her, too.

The Girls had to learn to sing a song. It's "High Hopes," the one Frank Sinatra did, only the words are different. Sinatra apparently sang it recently at one of Kennedy's stops, and now the head campaign office is adapting it to be *the* campaign song. We had to spend a couple of hours with a piano player named Choo Choo—yes, that's his name!—and practice it. My favorite part goes—

Oops, there goes the opposition–KERPLOP!
K–E–DOUBLE N–E–D–Y

Jack's the nation's favorite guy
Everyone wants to back–Jack
Jack is on the right track.
'Cause he's got high hopes
He's got high hopes

Pretty funny stuff. We kept laughing and kidding around while we practiced and Choo Choo yelled at us. We finally got our act together and did it well.

Kennedy and Nixon have agreed to do some debates on live television. There will definitely be three, and possibly four. Right now Nixon's in the hospital for an injured knee that got infected. I don't know how that happened, but the newspaper said he would be out soon to resume his campaign. You know how I can "read" people? When I see Nixon on TV, I just don't trust him. Besides, I think if he became president, we'd just have more of the same kinds of policies we had while Eisenhower was president. Kennedy talks about all sorts of progressive changes, especially an "equal rights amendment" to the Constitution. He's very tough on Communism, too. People wonder if the Soviets will come over to Cuba and set up a base close to our country. Kennedy won't let that happen.

My work at HQ has increased since the campaign got under way in earnest. Some volunteers have left, but they've been replaced by a lot of new faces. Mitch and Alice are still there, as are Karen and Chip. Betty doesn't spend much time at HQ because of her job at the Waldorf, but when I see her we usually have our lunch together or go out in the evening to one of the restaurants for a drink. It feels very strange to me to be visiting those places in an after-work setting where businessmen and women congregate. I hear them talking about the stock market and politics and sports. No one seems to discuss books or movies much the way Lucy and Peter and I always did. Mitch and Alice do. They're what you call "hip." That's a word the beatniks use if someone is "cool." I think I'm "cool," don't you, dear diary? I hope so. I don't want to be "square," which describes someone who isn't "with it." See? I'm learning all kinds of new vocabulary!

I haven't been the Black Stiletto since that awful night in the Bowery. The newspaper the next day reported that a woman "impersonating" the Stiletto seriously injured a man in a bar after a scuffle and then fled. The story said it was unclear why she was dressed in the costume or what she was doing there. It didn't mention that the men tried to rape the poor lady! The article made it sound like I'd asked for it. The bartender was quoted as saying "she wasn't the real Black Stiletto, because she was weak and drunk and stupid." Well, I may have been drunk and stupid, but I wasn't weak. Fine. Let them think it was someone else. I don't want the real Stiletto to take the rap for the knifing. I just hope it taught those bums a lesson and not to try to take advantage of a girl like that. A related story reminded citizens that the Black Stiletto was a wanted vigilante. The police commissioner issued a statement warning women not to dress up as the character, even on Halloween. Apparently there were already Black Stiletto costumes in the stores. I hope they sell out! Wouldn't it be "cool" if I got a piece of the sales?

Well, I'm trying to avoid drinking now. I might have a glass of wine with dinner, but I'm not touching the hard stuff for a while. I learned my lesson. If I feel blue like I did that night, I go down to the gym and spend a half hour punching the bags. It really does relieve tension. I can let out my frustration on the speed bag or I kick the heck out of the hanging bag. And I still work on the *wushu* movements. The Praying Mantis techniques that I know, combined with my expertise in *karate* and boxing, have given me a totally new way of defending myself. One night I showed Freddie what I could do and he was amazed. When he asked, I admitted I'd had a few lessons in Chinatown last winter, but I mostly make up stuff now. He helped me a little by correcting my stance prior to a kick that was a combination of a *Yoko-geri* side kick and the Praying Mantis one I'd seen at the tournament. It was a matter of turning my torso a little more into the kick. Once Freddie showed me the difference, it worked much better.

Maybe it's time for the Stiletto to make a reappearance.

SEPTEMBER 9, 1960

You're not going to believe this!
I saw Billy today!
He was at the Kennedy/Johnson campaign HQ! I nearly swallowed my chewing gum when I saw him. It's a good thing I caught myself, because I almost shouted, "Billy!" But I didn't say a word because Billy doesn't know Judy Cooper. He never met me. Billy only knows the Black Stiletto. I nearly gave myself away, dear diary!

Apparently there are a lot of high schools in the city who are offering extra credit in social studies for students who volunteer to work the campaign of their choice. Billy's school in Chinatown is doing the same. He was one of two kids, the other being a girl named Lily.

I tried to avoid them. I was afraid Billy would recognize my voice or maybe my eyes. But I was jumping up and down inside because I now knew he was alive and safe and still in the city.

It's 9:00 now and I'm putting on the Stiletto outfit to go out. I plan to return to Chinatown to see if Billy and his mother are back in their old apartment above the restaurant. I know it's a risky thing to do, but I have to know. Wish me luck!

LATER

It's nearly 11:00. I didn't stay out long because the trip was useless and I ran into a little trouble.

I had no problems making my way through the streets to Chinatown and finally to Elizabeth Street. The building I used to hide in—the one under construction—was finished, so there was nowhere to perch. I was in full view of the pedestrians, who pointed, gawked, and spoke to each other in their language.

Nevertheless, I boldly approached the restaurant and saw it was now called "Dim Sum." I don't know what that meant. The lights were on and Chinese people sat at tables eating dinner. The place had been redecorated. I didn't see Billy or his mother inside, so I figured the Tong had indeed taken it over and turned the place into another establishment.

From there I went inside the door that led to apartments upstairs and scanned the mailboxes in the foyer. The one that was once Billy's now had the name "Ming" written above it. So they were truly somewhere else.

I really wanted to learn where Billy lived now, but there was no way I could do it unless I followed him home from the campaign HQ. *Judy Cooper* could do it. He wanted me to stay away from him, but I can't help it. He became a friend and he put his neck on the line to teach me *wushu*. I owe him.

But it was time to scram. I'd overstayed my welcome, so I headed north on Elizabeth at a fast pace. Then I heard a piercing whistle behind me; someone had put his fingers to his mouth and blew one of those loud birdcalls.

A voice shouted, "Hey, lady!"

I turned to see six young thugs purposefully striding toward me in the middle of the street. They were armed with what appeared to be meat cleavers!

So my appearance in Chinatown had not gone unnoticed by the Flying Dragons. Dear diary, I had a big decision to make. Should I stop, face them, and possibly get into another dangerous brawl? Or was it better to simply get out of there before anyone got hurt? I knew I could outrun them. Would they see it as cowardice?

That's when another shrieking whistle resounded in *front* of me at the top of Elizabeth. Four more hoodlums had emerged from the shadows. They also held hatchets—and machetes.

My choice was made for me. I didn't want to get pinned in again, so I bolted forward. Four was easier to get by than six. I drew the stiletto, held it in front of me, ready to strike, and ran full-steam ahead. The young Tong members in my way rushed at me, weapons wielded. We met in the middle of the street and almost collided— except I cannily slipped between two of them as I sliced the air back and forth with my blade. One of them swung his hatchet at me but I blocked the blow with my left forearm. It hurt like the dickens, but at least I prevented him from driving a sharp wedge into my skull! I didn't stop to fight, I just kept going. I made it to Canal and veered right. The boys ran after me, hot on my tail, but my hours of training in the gym proved too much for them. I shot out onto Bowery directly in front of traffic. Cars honked and tires screeched, but I wasn't hit. A taxi squealed to a halt in front of me, impeding my route. I leaped, grabbed the top of the car, scampered over it, and dropped to the other side. That stopped the gang members' pursuit. It was as if they didn't want to venture off of their turf. I made it to Chrystie, which, of course, turns into 2nd Avenue farther north.

Before I knew it, I was safe in the gym's vicinity. I made sure I hadn't been followed, and then slithered up the telephone pole to the roof.

It was a close call, but I wondered if I'd *ever* be able to visit Chinatown as the Stiletto again.

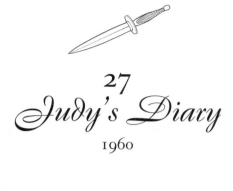

27
Judy's Diary
1960

I know a little more about Billy, and I've stumbled upon a new mystery.

Today at HQ, Billy was working in the envelope-stuffing area with Lily, while I was helping to organize the literature we hand out on the streets. We keep a radio on in the office, and the station played "It's Now or Never" (it's still number 1!). That gave me the courage to introduce myself to him. I casually got up, went to their table, and asked, "How's it going over here?"

Lily answered, "Fine."

I held out my hand to her first. "Hi, I don't think we've met. I'm Judy." She shook my hand and told me her name. Then I did the same to Billy. He smiled at me, shook my hand, and said, "I'm Billy Lee."

Even though I knew the answer, I asked, "How did you come to volunteer for Kennedy?"

Billy explained about their high school extra credit in social studies. In an attempt to find out where he lived, I asked, "Where do y'all live? Do you have to travel far to get here?"

Lily answered, "We live in Chinatown. It's downtown on the East Side, below Canal Street."

"I know where Chinatown is, I've been there. I love the food!"

Billy looked at me funny. "Where are you from? You have an accent," he said.

I thought, *uh-oh*. I cleared my throat and said, "Uh, yeah, I'm from Texas. I don't think I'll ever shake the accent. I sound like a hick."

Lily laughed and said, "What about me? My English not so good." She nodded at her friend. "Billy sound American."

"I *am* American," he said. "Born and raised here."

It was true—Billy's speech was like any other boy in New York. Lily, on the other hand, did have an accent and spoke slowly.

"Your English is just fine, Lily," I told her, but Billy was still looking at me as if he was searching for something on my face. Did he recognize my voice? I thought I'd better cut off the conversation. "Well, I'm glad to meet you two. I should get back to work. I have a million stacks of pamphlets waiting for me to sort."

When I reached my desk, I glanced back at them. Billy was still staring at me. Maybe it wasn't such a good idea to talk to him. Freddie once told me that I sound a little different when I'm the Black Stiletto. My accent is still there when I speak, but my voice assumes a more commanding, self-confident quality than I have as Judy Cooper. I certainly don't *try* to sound different, and I don't hear it myself. Maybe it has something to do with what wearing the outfit does to me. I *feel* like another person.

When their work was over, Billy and Lily got up to leave. As soon as they did, I made an excuse to Mr. Patton that I had to quit early. Since it's a volunteer job, hours are flexible unless we're in the middle of something with a deadline. He said to go on and not worry about it. So I grabbed my purse and headed outside to Park Avenue. I spied Billy and Lily turning the corner to walk east. They were most likely headed for the subway to take them downtown.

So I followed them. I put on sunglasses and blended in with the clumps of people moving along the sidewalk. The kids were a block ahead of me, but I could see them clearly. At one point, Billy took Lily's hand. Aha! So she was his girlfriend! I thought that was sweet. She seemed like a nice girl.

Sure enough, they turned north on Lexington and approached the 51st Street subway entrance. As soon as they were down the stairs, I descended as well. They had already gone through the turnstile. I had to buy tokens. The tricky part would be waiting on the platform for the train without them seeing me, so I remained on my side of the turnstile for a few minutes. I pulled a book out of my purse—I'm reading *To Kill a Mockingbird* by Harper Lee—so I dug into a chapter while I waited (everybody's talking about this book at HQ!). Eventually, I heard the train coming, so I slipped my token in the turnstile and went through. With a quick glance to the right, I saw Billy and Lily sitting on a bench together. I turned my back and walked to the opposite end of the platform just as the train roared in. I got on and noted the kids stepping into the third or fourth car.

Once we were on our way, I moved forward from one car to the next until I was directly behind theirs. I could see them through the windows. They sat on a seat together, holding hands. They looked so cute. Instead of sitting, I stood and held on to the pole so I could watch them.

It took a while, but the train finally rolled in to the Canal Street station. I made sure Billy and Lily got up to exit, so when the doors opened I stepped out to the platform. They were behind me, so I quickly turned my back to them and rushed to the stairs like I was in a hurry. By the time they reached street level, I was already waiting, out of sight.

Keeping my distance, I followed the couple west on Canal until they turned south on Mulberry. I stood on the corner next to a phone booth to blend in. They stopped in front of a brownstone and spoke for a minute. I kept thinking he would kiss her, but I guess Chinese teenagers don't do that so young. Maybe I'm wrong. What do I

know? At any rate, it was obvious that was her home and Billy had
walked with her there. Once she had entered the building, he continued south toward Bayard. I continued shadowing my prey. He
never looked back once, and I had nothing to fear being in Chinatown because I was Judy Cooper, not the Stiletto.

He turned east on Bayard and ultimately went south on Mott
Street. I followed Billy almost to Pell, when he stopped and entered
a building on the east side. I waited a minute and then approached.
It was a ratty, dilapidated structure, desperately in need of repair. I
stepped inside the street door and looked at the mailboxes. Sure
enough, number six said "Lee" in English and in Chinese characters.
I guessed the apartment was on the second floor, so I crossed Mott
and stood on the other sidewalk. Lights were on in both second floor
windows. A fire escape ran down the front of the building. After a
moment, I saw Billy's mother cross behind a pane.

I knew which apartment was theirs.

Satisfied with myself, I headed home. I walked up Mott to Bayard and then took a right. And then, dear diary, I saw something
that gave me goose bumps.

The swarthy passenger from the black Packard I'd seen Michael
leaning into, just before our breakup. I can't believe I recognized
him, but he came out of a convenience store just in front of me and
crossed the street. Then—another shock. He got into the passenger
side of a black Packard that was parked against the curb along with
other cars. I knew it was the same one because of the license plate:
358 22X. I remembered it. And this time Michael was in the driver's
seat. They drove away without seeing me.

Did they live in Chinatown? In one of the buildings there on Bayard Street?

I probably should forget all about it, because I have no interest
in seeing Michael again. But you know me, dear diary, and I know
myself. I've got more curiosity than a hundred cats.

I had another mystery to solve!

SEPTEMBER 11, 1960

The Black Stiletto was nearly blown away this evening, dear diary! And I don't mean by a gun, but by Mother Nature!

The weather started getting stormy while I was at HQ. The radio announcer said Hurricane Donna was headed toward New York, but I really didn't pay much attention to it. I was more excited by other news—Mr. Dudley told us that the Kennedy Girls would make an "emergency" appearance in *three days*! Kennedy will be in town and they want us to do something with him. I don't know what it is yet, but supposedly our costumes will be here in the nick of time. Gosh, I hope mine fits. I'm the tallest girl in the bunch.

When I got home, it was pouring down rain, but stupid me, I was too suspicious and curious about Michael and that other guy and that Packard on Bayard Street to stay put. I put on the Stiletto outfit and went out my bedroom window, just like usual. I could tell the wind was stronger than usual during a typical rainstorm, but I didn't let that stop me. Sure, I got wet, but that's nothing new. The leather on my outfit repels water, and I don't get soaked to the bone. Well, normally I don't.

As I crossed the roofs to the telephone pole, I knew it wasn't going to be an easy night out. The wind was *strong*. But I made it to the street and began the trek to Chinatown. There were still cars on the roads, but most people had gone inside. The few pedestrians I saw ran about with broken umbrellas, unsuccessfully tried to flag down taxis, and huddled in doorways. Dear diary, it was difficult to move against the wind and rain, but I eventually got to Bayard Street.

The Packard was still parked in the same spot. I looked in the windows but couldn't see a darned thing because of the rain. It just kept getting worse. That's when I knew I'd made a terrible mistake. What the heck was I doing? What did I hope to accomplish? I guess in the back of my mind I thought I might catch Michael or his passenger buddy or maybe the first driver whose face I never saw getting in the car, or maybe I'd see where they lived. What were the chances of that happening? About a million to one!

So I turned around and headed home, but within minutes the storm had doubled in intensity. It was a *hurricane* and I was in the middle of it! Cars pulled over to the curbs to wait it out, that's how bad it was. Debris blew all around me—trash, tree branches, pieces of metal—it was *dangerous*! Just crossing Bowery took a superhuman effort. The resistance against my body may as well have been a brick wall. I fell down twice and slid in what was essentially a *river* flowing down the street. Managing to pull myself up, I crawled to the other side and rested in a doorway. I considered staying there, but it was obvious the hurricane was just growing worse. The sky was black with clouds. Street lights went out. I heard windows breaking. And then I saw an empty *bicycle* flying through the air. It crashed against a parked taxi.

I had to get home. There was no way I could stay outside. There were no other pedestrians *anywhere*. I swear the wind was strong enough to pick up a human and fling him like a bug. I've never seen anything like it.

Hugging the fronts of buildings, I slowly moved north along Bowery, clutching anything I could to anchor myself. Dear diary, it was even hard to *breathe*! It felt like I was inhaling nothing but water. I couldn't see three feet in front of me. It was a good thing I knew the direction, for I may as well have been blind.

At Grand Street or Broome Street—I don't know which one!—I turned east. Bowery had acted like a tunnel for the storm because of its width. The wind wasn't as bad on the east-west streets, but it was still a monster. Then I got to Chrystie. The eastern side of the street is a park, Sara Roosevelt Park, and it's full of trees. Those trees were bent at an *angle* and served as sources for projectiles of loose branches and garbage. Like Bowery, Chrystie was a north-south street and therefore also served as a funnel for the storm. But it was my only way home. Once again, I faced inward and clung to edges of storefronts in order to move forward.

Crossing Houston Street was a challenge. I've never been on rapids before, but that's what it was like. A torrent of water rushed westward from the East River. It came up to my thighs! The only thing I could do was get into it, fight the force, and struggle to the other side. At one point I lost my footing and the water carried me like a log for several yards until I managed to upright myself and dig my boots into the street below. I trudged forward until I was safely across Houston. Only two short blocks to go.

When I got to 1st Street, something hit me on the side of the head. I have no idea what it was. It hurt and stunned me for a few seconds, but I believe my leather hood protected me from the worst of the blow. I stopped to get my bearings in a doorway on the east side of 2nd Avenue. It wasn't far now. But how the heck was I going to climb the stupid telephone pole, traipse across the roofs, and climb in my window? There was no way I could do that.

So I did the only thing possible. When I got to the Second Avenue Gym, I buzzed for Freddie. I banged on the front door. I shouted for him. I pushed the buzzer button again. I banged again. Over and over. *Finally,* I saw the lights go on inside. Freddie, my savior, appeared, with a look of shock on his face. He opened the door and I practically *fell* inside, panting and, it turned out, bleeding from a small cut on my head.

Dear diary, Freddie was *so* mad. Instead of saying, "Judy, how are you?" he yelled at me. "What the *hell* are you doing? You stupid, stupid girl!"

He helped me up and I started crying. I hadn't realized how scared I was out in the storm until that moment. I guess he brought the reality of my foolishness home. I told him I was sorry, that I'd made a mistake, but he kept berating me.

"You could have been killed! And what are you doing coming in the front door in your goddamned costume? You could've been seen!"

"Freddie, there's no one on the street. No one saw me."

"You crazy girl, I was *worried* about you!" He helped me pull off my mask and walked me upstairs. "I knocked on your door to say, 'look out the window, can you believe this?' and you were *gone*! I was afraid you'd get blown away to kingdom come!"

"Or Oz," I tried to joke.

"It's not funny! Don't you *ever, ever* do that again!"

I apologized again as he sat me down and doctored the wound on my head. It wasn't much, but there was a little hole in my hood. I'll have to sew it up.

Finally, Freddie gave me a hug and said he was glad I was all right. I kissed his cheek and we made up, and then I went to my room to peel off my wet outfit and get into a warm bed.

Hurricane Donna is still raging as I write this, but I assume we'll all still be here tomorrow. I hope.

Good night.

28
Judy's Diary
1960

Hurricane Donna did a lot of damage, especially in Long Island. In the city it wasn't as bad as we thought it would be. Everything was wet for a day, there were some broken windows, and a lot of garbage was in the streets. Electric power was out for a while and just came on today. Freddie and I had to use candles in the apartment last night, and most businesses were closed yesterday and today. We kept the gym open, but hardly anyone showed up. Clark came for his training session, so that kept me busy for a couple of hours. Because work was so light, Freddie gave me the rest of the day off. I think he felt bad about yelling at me the other night.

I took a walk outside to survey the destruction. Of course, I found myself walking to Chinatown, but as Judy Cooper I didn't have anything to fear. Shops and restaurants were starting to open. Naturally, I passed through Bayard Street. The black Packard was parked in the same block, although the driver would have to move it sometime that day for street cleaning. I loitered in some of the shops around there on the chance that I might see one of the guys get in the car. There was a restaurant open across the street, so I went in, sat at a table by the window, and had hot and sour soup, an egg roll, and beef with broccoli. No one ever showed up to move the car. After I ate, I gave up and went home.

Why the heck do I care? Why am I so suspicious? I know why—it's because the reason Michael stopped seeing me had something to do with his conversation with the driver that day.

Oh well. I better get some rest for the big day tomorrow. Judy Cooper, Kennedy Girl, will make her debut!

SEPTEMBER 14, 1960

Oh, my gosh, dear diary, *what a day!*

I met John F. Kennedy!!

I swear, if he wasn't married, I'd be all over him. He is so handsome and charming. He even *spoke* to me! I was so flustered I probably sounded like an idiot, but for a few minutes I was in heaven.

The day started at HQ. All the Kennedy Girls arrived at 9:00 to put on the costumes. They're cute sleeveless cotton dresses with fitted waists and A-line skirts that just cover the knee. They have a red-and-white striped ticking, so with the navy cummerbunds inscribed with "Kennedy" in white letters, we look like walking American flags. We also got white "straw" hats made out of Styrofoam. They also have navy bands. We supplied our own white gloves, of course, but the campaign gave us fake white pearl necklaces that were surprisingly pretty. Shoes were totally up to us as long as they were high heels. Once we were all dressed, Mr. Patton and Mr. Dudley took photographs. I have to admit that Louise looked stunning. Even though she's a little short on smarts, she could win a beauty pageant hands down. Betty looked great, and she told me I did, too. When I gazed in the mirror, I thought, "Hmm. Not bad at all," if I do say so myself.

Kennedy was set to arrive at LaGuardia Airport between 12 and 1:00. He was coming in from St. Louis. We were sent to meet him at the Commodore Hotel at Lexington and 42nd Street. The Women's Division of the Democratic State Committee was sponsoring a luncheon there. People had to pay a lot of money for tickets, and there were around 4,000 attendees, mostly women. The Kennedy Girls got to attend for free.

The anticipation in the banquet room as we waited for Kennedy was excruciating. My heart was beating like a sparrow's. I kept whispering to Betty, "When's he going to be here? When's he going to be here?" She told me I sounded like a lovesick schoolgirl, ha ha.

Finally, he arrived, and oh, my gosh, it was like seeing a movie star in person. He was all smiles and looked wonderful in a sporty fall suit. Everyone stood, applauded, and cheered when he entered. He sat at a table with the head of the committee and other people on his campaign team. The Kennedy Girls had their own table nearby. I was so close to him I could've thrown a roll at him! After the senator ate, Mr. Dudley gave us the signal, and the Girls stood and formed a line behind the podium. Someone introduced Kennedy, he stood, and approached the podium, but first he gave us a big smile, and said, "Hi, girls!" Everyone applauded and laughed. Then we sat while he gave a brief speech.

I have to say I felt really good about myself at that moment.

Around 2:45, Mr. Dudley and Mrs. Bernstein hustled us into a van with just enough seats for them and the eight girls. HQ had rented it for the day. We were let out at City Center on W. 55th Street for a senior citizens' rally on medical care. The street was *packed* with old people! Mr. Dudley said there were at least 4000 of them, all carrying "Kennedy/Johnson" signs and cheering. Once again, the eight Girls stood in a line behind Kennedy when he addressed the crowd. He gave us that trademark smile of his and introduced us as *his* Kennedy Girls and said, "Aren't they wonderful?" We waved and blew kisses at the crowd.

We were done there around 4:15 p.m. After his talk, they rushed the senator into a limousine and he was off to the Waldorf-Astoria for a private fund-raising reception in the Jansen Suite, thrown by Bill Brandt, the Democratic state campaign chairman.

As we were about to leave City Center, some sweet old guy at the rally asked me out to dinner. A little fellow next to him said, "Don't pay attention to Mort, come have a drink with *me*!" Then a couple of other seniors chimed in. They were *all* flirting with the Girls. It was pretty funny. I said, "Maybe next time, Mort," and then we piled into the van.

It took a while to get to the Waldorf because there was a big crowd of people outside hoping to see the senator. We didn't get to go to the reception. It was for VIPs only, so we were told to wait in the Waldorf lobby. Mitch, Alice, Chip, Karen, and a few other workers showed up because there was another big rally scheduled at 5:00, sponsored by Citizens for Kennedy. All the volunteers in the New York campaign office were helping put it on.

Just before the rally, though, Kennedy came down to the lobby from the reception and stepped outside to Park Avenue—and by then there were *thousands* of people on the street! It was incredible. In just thirty minutes the number had increased tenfold. The Girls did an impromptu appearance, too. Mr. Dudley quickly rounded us up and herded us out the doors to stand behind the senator as he waved to the crowd.

Then it was time to go to the Grand Ballroom, where the rally was being held. Chip said there were 5,000 people packed inside. This time the Girls were on stage with Choo Choo and a piano behind the podium. We were going to sing "High Hopes" when the senator was finished with yet another speech.

Well, dear diary, I was listening to his talk and looking out into the audience—when I nearly jumped out of my skin. I saw *Michael* in the crowd on the floor. At least I thought I did. It sure looked like him. He was standing about a third of the way back from the stage. The strange thing was that he wasn't focused on Kennedy the way everyone else was. Instead, he was gazing up at the boxes on the sides of the ballroom. Michael seemed more interested in the room itself than in Kennedy's speech.

Before I knew it, the senator was done and Choo Choo started playing the song's intro. We all started to sing and the crowd joined in. I forgot about Michael and just enjoyed myself as we did our number. When we hit the end, the crowd went wild. We felt like the Rockettes! As everyone applauded and cheered, I focused on the crowd where Michael had been, but he was gone. I scanned the room and thought I'd lost him, but then I spotted him near the exits on the side. He wasn't applauding or cheering. He just stood there with that expressionless face of his, staring intently at Kennedy. Of course, I was in no position to get off the stage and go talk to him, not that I wanted to. But what was he doing there? How did he get an invitation?

My puzzlement was interrupted when Kennedy turned to us and blew kisses again, so I averted my eyes from Michael as the Girls smiled, waved, and blew kisses back at the senator. When I got the chance to look again, Michael was gone.

Well, I *think* it was him. Now I'm not so sure, but at the time I really thought so. It shook me up a little. Betty asked me if I was all right, and I told her I saw someone I knew. She could tell I wasn't happy about it, so she asked, "An old boyfriend who didn't appreciate how terrific you are?"

"Something like that," I answered.

"I've had a few of those, too."

At 6:00 p.m. the Girls moved to the beautiful Jade Room for a private fund-raising dinner given by Adlai Stevenson. About 150 to 175 people attended, all supposedly with very deep pockets. We were very lucky to be invited, 'cause none of the other campaign workers got to go. Our job was to greet people as they came in. I thought it was very nice of Stevenson to host a dinner for Kennedy, since they were rivals earlier in the year. Actually, Kennedy and the Girls didn't eat, because there was *another* dinner planned at 8:00 p.m. that we were going to.

Then we got a big surprise. After former Senator Herbert Lehman and the governor of Connecticut, Abraham Ribicoff, entered the room, none other than Eleanor Roosevelt came in. She looked lovely. Gosh, I think she's at least 75 years old. I shook her hand and she said, "How do you do?" After *her* came *Harry Truman*! Oh, my gosh! I didn't know he was going to be there. I got to shake his hand and say hello, too. He was much smaller than I expected, but he wore those unmistakable Truman eyeglasses. He must be in his 70s, too.

And then and then and then—*I met Kennedy!* He came through the line and spoke to each and every Girl and asked our names. When he got to me he held out his hand and said in that adorable Boston accent, "Hello there, and what's *your* name?" I took his hand and shook it, but I was in shock and couldn't speak! Betty discreetly nudged me, and then I managed to answer, "Judy Cooper, sir. I'm so pleased to meet you."

"And I'm very pleased to meet you, too." And *then* he asked, "Where are you from, Judy?"

That threw me again and for a moment I just stared into his gorgeous blue eyes. He blinked and that brought me back down to earth. "Texas," I said.

He nodded and said, "I thought I recognized the accent! I've been there several times. I enjoy visiting Dallas." Then he moved on to the next girl. Lord, my heart was beating like crazy. I felt as if I'd touched royalty. I never wanted to wash my hand again.

I was smitten, right then and there.

The rest of the dinner was a blur. Before I knew it, we were ushered outside to the van again to go back to the Commodore Hotel for the 8:00 dinner. It was sponsored by the Liberal Party, and the purpose was for Kennedy to accept their nomination for president. George Meany, the president of the American Federation of Labor and the Congress of Industrial Organizations, was the bigwig there. By the time we sat at the table, I was starving. I think I'd gone through my supply of adrenaline during the day and felt a little weak. Or perhaps it was just Kennedy's touch that did it, ha ha.

The senator delivered a wonderful speech. It was all about being a liberal. I don't remember his exact words, but he put it very succinctly. He said a liberal is someone who looks ahead and welcomes new ideas, and, most importantly, cares about the welfare of the people. Kennedy got a rousing ovation when he said, "If that is what they mean by a liberal, then I'm proud to say I'm a liberal."

After all the speeches and hoopla, the Girls lined up again to say goodbye to the senator. Kennedy was off to New Jersey in the morning, so we wouldn't see him again for a while. When he got to me, I swear he gave me a more appreciative look than the other girls got. And he remembered my name!

"I hope I'll see you again, Miss Cooper."

I don't know what I said, but it was something that made no sense, like, "Thank you me too I do too." Geez! I felt like a dunce. But after he'd gone, Betty said to me, "Better watch out, Judy, I hear he likes the ladies."

I waved her off and said, "Go on, he's married."

But, hey, if he likes *me*, then I guess he's got good taste!

29
Maggie
THE PRESENT

Martin and his ex-wife, Carol, flew to New York on the Friday after Thanksgiving, two days ago, to deal with their daughter's situation. I spoke to Martin last night and found out Gina was arrested for stalking, or harassing, a man and he had filed a complaint against her. I'm not clear on the details, but Martin and Carol had to hire a lawyer. I know Gina had some problems recently with an assault and attempted rape. Martin said she's obsessed with finding the man who did it. Apparently, the man she was harassing was one of the suspects. Poor Martin. He has a lot on his plate right now with his mother in the hospital. I haven't met Gina yet, but it sounds like she could use some better psychological counseling than she's getting. Martin tells me she's a good kid and never got in trouble before. Considering she was a fine student in high school and is attending Juilliard, that must be true. Nevertheless, it sounds like she has some issues.

Bill Ryan called me yesterday with news that continues to puzzle me. Apparently, Judy and Martin moved to Illinois from Odessa, Texas. There are records of a Judy Talbot in that town for several months in late 1962. Bill's trying to work in reverse from that, tracing their movements all the way back to Los Angeles. We have to assume Martin's telling the truth that he was born in L.A., and that they must have traveled from California to Texas in 1962. I wonder why she would pick up and move with an infant in arms?

Bill says a lot of Judy or Judith Talbots lived in the Los Angeles area during that time. It would be extremely difficult for him to find out if any of them was her. Again he reiterated how he would have to spend time there and that would get expensive.

More interesting was Bill's discovery that no soldier named Richard Talbot died in the Vietnam War prior to 1962. Granted, the records are not 100 percent reliable, and we don't know if Richard Talbot was in the army, navy, air force, or was a Marine. American involvement in that war in the early part of the decade was minimal. Officially, our troops were only "military advisors" then, but by 1963 we had around sixteen thousand men stationed in South Vietnam. Less than a hundred had been killed. Were the odds such that Richard was one of them?

I decided to snoop around in Martin's apartment. That's a terrible thing to do, I know, but I need answers. I justified my actions by telling myself I indeed want the relationship with Martin to work out. Yes, I'm falling in love with him, and I know he feels the same way about me. He'd given me a key to his place. "I trust you," he'd said with a wink. I'm sure he was joking that I would never steal anything. I don't think he meant that I was free to go through his closets and chests of drawers, so I felt guilty doing it.

Well, tough. My peace of mind was more important.

His house in Buffalo Grove is in a quiet neighborhood. It's actually one-half of a duplex, which is perfect for a single man living alone. I started with the front closet—nothing but coats and clothing—and then went through drawers in the kitchen. Nothing of interest there. The Kennedy/Johnson 1960 campaign button was still on the coffee table. I wonder if it's worth something as an antique?

The house has two bedrooms, one where he sleeps (and me, too, when I'm there), and another that serves as his office of sorts. I chose the latter to investigate next. The desk drawers revealed nothing but personal records dealing with Martin's house, car, health insurance, and Gina's school. Two file cabinets contained his work-related stuff—tax returns and other material from his job as an accountant.

But as I went through the bottom drawer of one cabinet, I noticed some give behind the hanging manila folders. At first I thought the entire drawer was full, but it wasn't. Some object took up the back half of the space. I pulled out the folders so I could get to it and found a metal strongbox.

I removed it and held it in both hands. There were things in it, for they rattled when I shook the box, and it was heavy enough to indicate weighty items were inside. Unfortunately, it was locked. I thought breaking the lock would be crossing the line, not that I hadn't already. Even so, I replaced the strongbox and closed the drawer.

That foolish and selfish venture was a disappointing waste of time. I felt even guiltier once I had finished snooping. To ease my conscience a little, I found a notepad on Martin's desk and wrote, "I miss your kisses," and signed it. I tore off the page, went into the bedroom, and placed the note on the bed, where he'd find it when he got home.

At least that was a sincere sentiment.

30
Judy's Diary
1960

SEPTEMBER 15, 1960

It's Thursday and I worked at the gym today. After the whirlwind
with Kennedy yesterday, I'm exhausted. I was so worked up from
all the excitement that I didn't sleep well last night. John F. Kennedy
spoke to me! And I met Harry Truman and Eleanor Roosevelt! Un-
believable. I wonder what my brothers back in Odessa would think
of that. John is probably still in the army, making a career of it. I suppose Frank still works at that hardware store.

Michael's appearance at the rally still bothers me. Now I'm not
so sure if it was really him, but I'm going on the assumption that it
was. This evening after dinner I took a walk to Chinatown and Bayard Street.

The black Packard was gone.

The whole thing is more of a mystery than ever.

SEPTEMBER 26, 1960

Tonight was the first television debate between Kennedy and Nixon.
We all think the debates will have a big influence on the election. I
watched it with Alice and Mitch at their apartment. They'd turned
their fire escape platform into a terrace by placing plants and stuff
there. Some of us stood outside on the "terrace" to smoke cigarettes

(not me!) and talk politics. Other folks from HQ were there, including Betty and Chip.

The candidates were in a studio in Chicago and the debate was broadcast live. It was pretty exciting. Before it started, Mitch had the TV on the NBC channel so we could see a new campaign advertisement that Kennedy's national headquarters created. We knew exactly when it would air. It was real cute. It had lots of pictures of the senator accompanied by a catchy song that went, "Kennedy, Kennedy, Kennedy, Kennedy, Ken-ne-dy for me—a man who's old enough to know and young enough to do—"

At debate time, Mitch changed the channel to CBS. I thought Kennedy looked great. Nixon, on the other hand, looked sick. None of us in the room thought he came off well at all. After the debate, Chip said, "Well, I think there's no question who won *that* round." We all agreed.

OCTOBER 1, 1960

Tonight the Black Stiletto caught a liquor store robber red-handed.

Since I hadn't seen any action in a while, I decided to put on the outfit and go out. I avoided Chinatown altogether and headed just a few blocks uptown. It was a little after 9:30 and there were still plenty of people outside. Within a half hour of hitting the street, I came upon a crime in progress at Brown's Liquors at 2nd Avenue and 9th Street. There was a creepy-looking guy pacing the sidewalk in front of the store when I went past. He was mumbling to himself like some homeless New Yorkers tend to do. He didn't notice me, which is strange because *everyone* turns to look at me when I dash by. I figured he was what he appeared to be—homeless and crazy—so I started to move on. But suddenly I heard a woman shriek, "He's got a gun!" I turned around and saw that the guy had entered the shop and two old women had poured out the door. One of them shouted, "Someone call the police!" So I ran back and asked if they were hurt in any way. I'm afraid I may have frightened them more than the man with the gun. They gasped at me and moved down 2nd Avenue as fast as their little legs could take them.

"I'm one of the good guys!" I yelled at them, but then I turned my attention to the liquor store. Sure enough, through the window I saw the creepy guy pointing a handgun at the man behind the counter. The shopkeeper's hands were raised. That's when I *knew* the gunman was off his rocker. No one in his right mind, not even a crook, would hold up someone in plain view of the storefront window at that time of night. Anyone could see him.

I burst through the door, charged the robber, and tackled him. We both fell to the floor. The gun went off loudly and I heard a bottle shatter. I grabbed his gun arm and easily knocked the weapon out of his hand. The man started crying, "No, no, not the needle! Not the needle! Please, no!" I had no idea what he was going on about, but I subdued him and tied his hands behind his back with my rope. By then, the proprietor had called the cops.

"Poor Eric," the shopkeeper said. "I was waiting for the day he'd flip his lid. Thanks."

"You know this guy?" I asked.

The man nodded as he started to clean up the mess of spilled booze. "That's Eric. He's a drunk. Comes in here every day for a bottle. I've noticed his behavior getting pretty screwy lately. Tonight he wanted a bottle of whiskey for free."

"You could have been killed."

The man shrugged. "I run a liquor store. It's a hazard that comes with the job. That's why I keep Esther." He pulled a *shotgun* out from under the counter. "I just didn't have the chance to grab old Esther here and show him my gun was bigger than his. I'm pretty sure Eric would've backed down."

I heard sirens approaching. Eric sat on the floor sobbing and muttering about the needle. "What's he talking about?"

"Hell if I know. You better go on. Thanks again. Now I can tell everyone I met the Black Stiletto." He held out a hand, I shook it, and then scrammed out of there before the cops arrived. To tell the truth, I thought that storekeeper was almost as nutty as the robber. Who names their shotgun "Esther"?

I figured that was enough excitement for one night, so I went home.

OCTOBER 5, 1960

I saw Michael today, dear diary.

It happened at Nixon's rally at Rockefeller Center. The candidate was in town today, and several of us from HQ got permission to leave the job and go over and hear him speak. After his poor performance on the TV debate, Nixon put out a statement that he was feeling ill and that CBS's lighting in the studio unfairly favored Kennedy. CBS denied the charge.

I was surprised to see such a large crowd. Nixon had as many supporters as Kennedy did when he was here in September. That shows you how naïve I can be. I honestly thought most everyone in New York was for Kennedy. That's certainly not the case. At any rate, none of us were impressed with Nixon's speech.

After he finished and everyone was cheering and applauding, I saw Michael standing in the crowd. He was maybe thirty feet away from me and was in the middle of a sea of people, but my keen sense of sight zoomed right in on him. This time I was sure it was him. Once again, he wasn't applauding or cheering. He just stood staring at the platform they'd set up for Nixon.

Well, I decided to confront him. I excused myself from Alice and started moving through the throng. When I got closer, Michael turned and saw me. I swear a look of *hatred* passed over his eyes, and then he ran. He shot through the horde, rudely knocking people aside. I wanted to pursue him, but the assembly moved forward toward the stage in an attempt to shake hands with the candidate. Nixon had boldly stepped down from the stage and was personally greeting his supporters. There was no way I could get through the pack without hurting someone, so I gave up the chase. I lost sight of

Michael and found myself unintentionally moving with the swarm. I didn't particularly care to shake Nixon's hand, so I struggled to go against the grain and force my way back to Alice and the others.

"Where did you go?" she asked with concern.

"I saw Michael. I was going to talk to him, but he ran when he saw me."

She made a face like she was disgusted. "Really?"

"Why would he do that? There's something very fishy about him," I said.

Alice shook her head. "Forget about him, Judy. Seriously." She seemed angrier about it than I was.

"Why do you care?" I asked her as we walked back to HQ.

"I just don't want to see you get hurt, that's all."

I told her I'm beyond being hurt by Michael. She didn't say another word until we reached the office on Park Avenue. I asked if anything was wrong and she nearly snapped at me.

Sheesh!

OCTOBER 7, 1960

Tonight was the second televised debate. This one was held in Washington, D.C. Once again there was a group gathered in Alice and Mitch's wonderful apartment. Mitch wasn't there at the beginning. He arrived a little late and looked harried. He greeted everyone and then took Alice into the kitchen so they could speak quietly together. When she returned, I asked her, "Everything all right?"

"Sure," she said. "Mitch got stuck in the subway for nearly an hour and he's mad about it." As soon as the words left her mouth, I knew they weren't true. Alice had made it up. Obviously she didn't want to tell me where Mitch had been, and I suppose it was none of my business. When he joined us, he had a drink and cigarette in hand, and was obviously in a foul mood.

The debate seemed more evenly matched this time. Nixon looked better. Alice said he wasn't wearing makeup during the first debate, but this time he was. We thought Kennedy held his own, but it felt like Nixon may have had the upper hand this time.

OCTOBER 10, 1960

I found out today that I'll be a Kennedy Girl again on Wednesday. The senator arrived in the city today and is staying at the Biltmore Hotel. We got new outfits to wear for the cooler weather. They couldn't be more different than the first ones—straight blue skirts with a slit in the back, and white wool jackets with blue piping. Louise said she thought we all looked like sailors, and I had to agree, but the red scarves we tie around our necks and the same phony white straw hats help to dispel that image. I don't think it's as cute as the first outfit, but we still look pretty sharp. Choo Choo taught us a couple of new songs: "Walking Down to Washington" and "Happy Days Are Here Again." And of course we practiced "High Hopes" again and again.

I'm tired and want to hit the sack. It's going to be a busy couple of days.

OCTOBER 12, 1960

Michael Sokowitz is a Communist spy! I'm sure of it. I don't have any proof, but I would bet every penny in my pocket—which isn't a lot—that it's true. And I don't know what to do about it.

Geez, what a day. It started with all the Kennedy Girls getting dressed at HQ and then going to the Waldorf-Astoria at 11:00 a.m. for a luncheon given by the National Council of Women. It was wonderful to see Kennedy again. He beamed when he saw us in the new outfits, and during his talk he said that Jackie had given her approval of our costumes' design. We sang our songs, waved our hats as if we were in a chorus line, and were then hustled out of the building to the van.

Next stop was the Park-Sheraton Hotel, where Kennedy would

address the National Conference on Constitutional Rights. Where do they come up with all these organizations? While we were in transit, Betty said it was ironic that Kennedy and Khrushchev (it took a few tries learning how to spell that one!) were in town on the same day. That surprised me.

"You didn't know? He's staying at the Waldorf!"

I asked her if she'd seen him, and she said no.

Our appearance at the Park-Sheraton was short and sweet. We sang "High Hopes" and then we were out of there. I don't know how Kennedy had time to say anything to the conference attendees, but he did. We weren't there for his speech; instead, we were already on our way to the Columbus Day Parade on 5th Avenue. At 12:30, HQ wanted us in place at Kennedy's reviewing stand at 64th Street. The senator arrived just after we did. He looked a bit stressed, but he put on a big smile and we waved at the people as floats rolled by and high school marching bands performed patriotic songs.

Our duties were done after that. We had the option to ride in the van back to HQ, but traffic was so bad that most of us just wanted to walk. After changing clothes, I walked alone over to the Waldorf to see what was going on. Someone at HQ said that Khrushchev was at the United Nations that morning and had pounded his shoe on the table! Later on there was a picture of him in the evening paper. He really did it! How uncouth can he be? But at the time I was curious and wandered over to the hotel. A lot of official-looking cars swarmed the front of the building. Police were out in droves keeping onlookers and reporters back. I stood on the other side of Park Avenue. Thanks to my excellent vision, I could clearly see the doors.

My timing was perfect. A limousine pulled up and the cops made special arrangements for it to come through and park right in front. Then I saw him. Nikita Khrushchev, in the flesh, got out of the car and entered the hotel as reporters' cameras flashed. Some people in the crowd booed him! The Russian ignored them and slipped inside without saying a word to anyone. In a way, I thought I was witnessing history being made.

I waited a little while longer, and then the crowd started to disperse. I figured the show was over. Police remained, though, and checked out anyone who wanted to enter the hotel. I can't imagine what it would be like to be a regular guest on a day like today.

Well, just as I made up my mind to catch the bus downtown, I saw Michael. He was walking on the hotel side of Park Avenue and heading from the south toward the police barricades. He flashed something at the cops—his ID?—and *entered the hotel*. That's when it hit me. Michael was a Commie spy. He had to be. Why would he be going into the same hotel as Khrushchev and his entourage? Michael certainly wasn't *staying* there, was he?

Maybe that's why Michael attended Kennedy's and Nixon's rallies. The Soviet Union believes that both candidates are strongly anti-Communist and will interfere with the USSR's future plans for Cuba. That's a big issue in the campaign—what is the U.S. going to do about Cuba, now that it's a Communist country?

Was Michael gathering intelligence for the Soviets? Was that why he stopped seeing me? Was that why he's such a cold bastard who treated me like dirt?

I could be imagining things, dear diary, but somehow my intuition on the matter felt exactly right.

31
Judy's Diary
1960

I have a lot to think about, dear diary. I learned some things about Michael today.

I didn't have to be at HQ until noon, so I went to Bayard Street this morning. The black Packard was parked on the street again, except in another spot. My heart started to race when I saw it because that car emanates something sinister. I've felt it from the first time I saw it.

The convenience store across the street from the car was open and doing brisk business. I stepped over and the Chinese man behind the counter grinned and welcomed me in English. I bought a pastry and a small carton of milk and then stood and ate it in his vicinity.

"Nice day, yes?" the man said.

"Very nice," I answered. "I like this neighborhood." I really didn't, but I wanted to break the ice with him.

"You live in neighborhood?" he asked.

"No, no. I have friends in the area." I held out my hand. "I'm Sally."

The man grinned as if he'd never had a friend before. "Joe," he said. He timidly shook my hand.

"Nice to meet you, Joe. Is that a Chinese name?"

The man actually got my joke and laughed. "Joe," he said again, and then nodded furiously.

I nodded at the sedan, which we could see through the window. "Say, Joe, do you know who owns that car?"

"Black car?"

"Yes."

Joe's English was pretty good. I hadn't encountered too many shop owners in Chinatown that spoke it particularly well. Nodding, he said, "He come in here sometime."

"He have a mustache and little beard?"

"What?"

I mimed painting my upper lip and chin. "Hair. Mustache."

"Oh, yes, yes." Joe then looked past me out the window. "There he now."

I turned to see none other than Michael emerging from the steps leading to a basement apartment, walking over to the Packard, unlocking it, and getting in the driver's seat.

"Go catch," Joe said. "There still time."

"No, I don't need to see him. Old boyfriend." I shook my head at the proprietor and made a yukky face. My new friend laughed and nodded as if he completely understood.

Michael started the car, pulled out, and drove away.

I finished my roll and milk, threw the remains in the trash, and waved at the Chinese man. "Bye, Joe. I'll see you later."

"Thank you, good day, Sally!" Big grin.

I crossed the street and slowly approached the basement apartment steps. It was broad daylight. People were everywhere. I had to look like I knew exactly what I was doing, so I purposefully went down the steps while I "searched" my purse for the keys to the door. At the bottom of the stairs, I was basically hidden from view. I knew basement apartments usually had a window in front that looked into a bedroom or living room, and this one was no different. The inside curtains were open. I slowly approached the window and peered inside.

It was a bedroom, and I could see on the right side of the room. A man lay asleep, and I recognized him as the passenger of the Packard when I first saw it. Dark hair. Mustache. Resembled Michael in a way. Who was he? And who was the sedan's driver that day, the one whose face I never saw?

I got out of there quickly, once again bounding up the steps to the street and walking to the corner as if I lived there. As I rode the bus uptown, I thought about what I should do. Was this something for the Black Stiletto? Perhaps. Probably. But there was always the FBI. John would listen to me, but I didn't really want to talk to him. I could call the public number and give an anonymous tip, but I'm sure no one would believe me. What would I tell them? I can just hear the response: "There's a guy named Michael but maybe that's not his real name and you think he's a Communist spy? Why?" And I wouldn't be able to answer. "My female intuition?" I'd say and they'd get a few laughs out of that. There was the license plate and the car. I could give them the number and say it was stolen or something. But would that really do any good?

Nope. It looked like it was going to be a job for the Black Stiletto after all.

When I got to HQ, something happened that was a gift from providence. Pure luck. Coincidence. I was in Mr. Dudley's office delivering a bunch of paperwork, and I noticed the top page of the stack in my arms was a report concerning Kennedy's use of government vehicles in New York. It listed a bunch of cars and their license plates, and it struck me that all of the numbers ended with the letter X. 337 24X. 594 65X. All like that. And they reminded me of the Packard's license number: 358 22X. So I asked Mr. Dudley, "What is the significance of the X on these license plate numbers?"

He looked up from his desk and said, "That means it's registered to the government, or an embassy, or individual diplomats. Why?"

"Just curious. There's a car that parks on my block with one of those."

Before I left the room, I memorized the phone number listed for the company that provided the cars to Kennedy. When I got to a spot where I could talk quietly on the phone, I called the number. When a nice man answered, I told him I was with the Kennedy campaign and wanted to find out about a car with a specific license plate that the senator may have used before and left something behind in it. The guy on the phone bought it, so I gave him Michael's license plate number. After a moment, my new friend came back and said that it was impossible for Kennedy to have had the car. It's been registered to the *Soviet Embassy* for three years.

I went back into the workroom. Alice did a double take at me and asked, "What's wrong with you?"

"What?"

"You look like you've seen a ghost."

"I think Michael is a Communist spy," I blurted. I don't know why I said that, but it came out. It didn't matter—I trusted Alice.

She looked at me like I was nuts, but at first I think the idea scared her. She jumped a little when I said it. "How do you know that, Judy?" she asked me skeptically.

"I don't know," I stupidly answered. "Just a feeling."

"I thought you were going to forget about him."

"I have."

"That's not what it sounds like."

After work I went home and watched the third debate on TV with Freddie. The two candidates were in New York, broadcasting from ABC Studios over on W. 66th Street. I think it went well. Freddie said he thought Nixon won it, but I disagreed. But then again, I'd probably say Kennedy won even if he hadn't.

But I know this time he did!

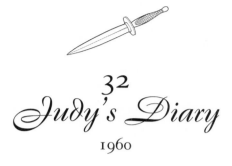

32
Judy's Diary
1960

I put on the Stiletto outfit tonight and went to Chinatown to spy on Michael's apartment. It was a little after 10:00, so shops and restaurants were closing and the number of people on the street had somewhat diminished. When I got there, I crouched in the shadows of the convenience store doorway across the street and watched the building. The lights were on in the apartment, but the Packard was gone.

Nothing was going to happen if I stayed where I was, so I crossed the street and slinked down the steps to the basement level. I started to peep through the window but had to jerk my head back—both Michael and the other man were in the room. I moved back into the darkness so I could take in the scene without being noticed. The other man was on the phone. Michael sat on the bed watching him. Through the window I could faintly hear the guy's voice. It sounded to me like he was speaking Russian. Michael slowly flexed his fingers in and out, making fists and relaxing them. Maybe he was cracking his knuckles. The other man appeared to me that he was more of an intense fellow than Michael; in fact, just by looking at him I could discern he was a very dangerous man. There was a blunt coldness about him, as if he had no emotions whatsoever. He also had very cruel eyes. I've always thought that one's eyes can tell a lot about a person. Was he related to Michael? It was possible, for they did have similar features.

The man hung up and the two men conversed, although the other man did most of the talking. Michael listened without looking at his roommate and continued to crack his knuckles. It went on like that for about five minutes, and then the Russian left the room. Michael grabbed a jacket and put it on. *Uh-oh*, they were leaving.

I had to hide. They'd be opening the door any second. I scampered up the steps and looked both ways down the street. Luckily, the nearest pedestrians had their backs to me, but others were heading toward me from the opposite direction. The only way I could go was up, so I swung my rope with the pulley hook and caught the fire escape railing. I climbed the rope hand over hand until I was on the second floor platform, safely hidden in the shadows.

Dear diary, after a moment the black Packard pulled up and stopped in front of the building. I heard the apartment door below open and a few seconds later slam shut. Michael and the other man appeared on the sidewalk and walked toward the car. I was directly above them. Because of the angle, I couldn't see the driver, again! However, I did see that this time a woman rode in the passenger seat. A decidedly feminine arm and hand with painted fingernails rested over the open window, but I was behind the car and couldn't see the woman's face. Michael and his roommate got in the backseat and the sedan drove away.

That was my chance. I jumped down from the fire escape and landed lightly on my feet. A quick look around, confirming that no one saw me. I snaked below to the apartment door and retrieved my lockpicks from the pouch on my belt. Getting inside wasn't difficult. I had the door open in less than a minute. A hall led to the living room and kitchen, and a door to the left went to the front bedroom by the window.

It was obvious two bachelors lived there. The place was a mess. Newspapers were strewn all over the living room, along with empty coffee cups and dirty dishes. Some of the papers were New York dailies, but most of what I saw appeared to be written in Russian. The kitchen was a pigsty. Yuck. I figured the bedroom would be where I'd find anything interesting, so that's where I concentrated my efforts.

There were two twin beds and a desk. Clothes were scattered about. Michael was usually well dressed and well groomed, so it was surprising to see how he lived. I went to the desk and rifled through papers and folders on the top. I found a lot of presidential campaign literature from both parties. Kennedy and Nixon. Inside the top drawer were some documents written in Russian and a checkbook. The checks were from a New York bank. The register was blank, so there was no way to know how much money was in their account.

Stuck inside the checkbook was an opened but unaddressed envelope from the Waldorf-Astoria. The hotel's name was embossed on the top left corner. Inside were two tickets for the Alfred E. Smith dinner set for October 19, five days from now. I knew all about that. Kennedy and Nixon were both attending the event. I wasn't sure yet if the Kennedy Girls would be on duty that night, but I had things to do for the campaign during the day. How did Michael get two tickets to this prestigious dinner?

There was nothing else in the desk, so I moved to the closet. Among the clothes hanging there were two Waldorf-Astoria bellhop uniforms. I recognized them from the few times I've been to the hotel.

Three brown attaché-like cases sat on a top shelf; two were small and one was large and long. I took down a small one, opened it, and gasped.

A handgun sat inside. "Smith & Wesson" was engraved on the side of the barrel. I don't know anything about guns, but I'm pretty sure it was what they call a semi-automatic because it had one of those clip things—a magazine—to hold the bullets. I carefully put back the case and checked out the other small one, which held an identical weapon. The longer case contained a rifle with a high-powered scope. I'd swear it was a sniper rifle. Don't all sniper rifles have those telescopic sights on them?

Before I could register what I'd found, I heard footsteps on the steps outside the window. Two pairs of shoes. The men were back!

I frantically threw the case back on the shelf, stepped inside the closet, and shut the door. At the same time, I heard the front door of the apartment unlock and open. Voices. I recognized Michael's. They were speaking Russian.

Please don't come in the bedroom! I screamed in my head.

Yes, I was scared. If they caught me, it could blow everything. They'd know someone was onto their plans, whatever they were. They'd kill me and then disappear. No one would ever know they existed. On the other hand, if they didn't kill me and I managed to subdue them, we might never know what they intended to do.

The men went straight to the living room. I heard someone turn on the tap in the kitchen. I cautiously opened the closet door just enough for me peer out. All clear. I stepped out of the closet and quietly moved to the bedroom door. I stole a glance into the hall. The other man stood in the living room with his back to me. I couldn't see Michael, but I knew he was in the kitchen. *Now or never.* I swiftly moved to the front door, but something in the closet where I'd hidden fell and made a loud noise. I figured it was one of those gun cases—I must not have placed it on the shelf securely.

"Hey!"

I heard the other man running toward me as I fumbled with the lock on the door. Just as I was able to swing it open, a pair of strong arms wrapped around my torso, pulled me away, and slammed me against the wall. He shouted in Russian, grabbed me again, this time with my arms pinned inside his, and then he turned me to face Michael, who had just appeared in the hall. I struggled, but the guy held me like a vice. Michael drew a knife and came at me. Luckily, the Russian didn't have control of my legs, so I delivered a *Mae-*

geri—a front kick—and knocked the weapon out of Michael's hand. Then the judo training came in handy. I squatted, pulling the Russian's weight down and over my back, and threw him clumsily over my shoulder. He landed hard but he managed to grab my leg as I attempted to regain my balance. I tumbled down on top of him. Michael then rushed in and kicked my head, causing a lightning bolt of pain behind my eyes, so I rolled off the Russian just to avoid another blow. Luckily, my back was to the wall; I used it for leverage to kick with both legs. I repeatedly slammed my boots into the Russian's side, forcing him to move and get up.

There wasn't a lot of room in that narrow hallway. By the time I'd sprung to my feet, Michael was on me, swinging his fists. I blocked him easily and successfully slipped a hard right hook through his defenses. Frankly, I was more afraid of the Russian. *He* was the better fighter, and he weighed more. The man started swinging powerfully strong punches at me, which I barely managed to block. There wasn't enough space for me to perform *karate* kicks, so I reverted to the Praying Mantis *wushu* improvisations I had created. My arms and fists flew at the men, taking them by surprise. As my blows connected to their faces and chests, they retreated toward the living room. I advanced, keeping the rhythm and force of my attack constant. Finally, they stepped far enough back that there was a wide gap between us.

I drew the stiletto and jabbed the air in front of me. They looked at me in shock. The men didn't know what I had just done. Michael rubbed his chin. The Russian's nose was bleeding.

"Stay back. I'm leaving," I announced.

They didn't move. I stepped backward to the front door, got it open, and ran outside—up the steps to the street, and *whoosh*, I sprinted off toward Bowery and home.

Once I was safely in my room and had removed my outfit, I examined my face and head. The side of my skull hurt where Michael had kicked me, but I didn't have any visible damage.

We couldn't have a Kennedy Girl with ugly bruises or marks on her face, now could we?

OCTOBER 15, 1960

I didn't work at HQ today and stayed at the gym. During my lunch hour, I walked over to Bayard Street—in street clothes, of course—and checked out Michael's apartment again.

The black Packard wasn't there. Taking a big chance, I moved a little down the steps to the apartment door so I could see in the window. No one was inside. The bedroom was completely clean. All the clothes I'd seen littering the place had disappeared. The closet door was open, and the space was empty.

Michael and the Russian had moved out.

I figured they did it because the Black Stiletto had discovered them. But then the big question now was where did they go?

Frustrated, I went back to the gym and tried to forget about them. But of course, I couldn't.

OCTOBER 17, 1960

Yesterday I made another trip to Bayard Street, but the basement apartment was still vacant. I had to admit I'd lost Michael and his Russian roommate. They could be anywhere in the city, plotting who knows what. My only consolation was that they probably didn't know I'd found their tickets to the dinner on the 19th.

That's where I'd find them.

Something happened today at HQ that shook me a little. I was stuffing envelopes in the back room with Billy and Lily. They spoke Chinese to each other, but I distinctly heard Billy say "Black Stiletto" in English. That startled me, so I asked, "Did you just mention the Black Stiletto?"

He grinned and said, "Sorry, Judy, it's rude for us to speak Chinese. We will try to speak English."

"No, that's all right, I don't mind that. But I thought I heard—"

"I was telling Lily that some people said they saw the Black Stiletto in Chinatown a couple of nights ago."

I pretended to be interested. "Is that so? Did you see her?"

"No, but I've seen her before."

"You have?"

"She's been to Chinatown a few times. I met her and talked to her."

I put on my best I-don't-believe-it face. "Oh, get out of town," I said. "You have not."

"I have. I really have."

"He has," Lily said. "Billy tell me all about it."

I continued to stuff envelopes. "Hmpf," I muttered as if I took the story with a grain of salt. "So what's she like?"

"Well," Billy said, "Miss Cooper, she's a lot like you."

My blood froze, but I recovered quickly and continued stuffing. "And how is that?" I asked.

"She's as tall as you," he said. "And her voice—I don't know, you remind me of her, that's all." He blushed and looked back at his work.

"Well," I answered, "I guess I'll take that as a compliment," and then I found an excuse to leave the room!

33
Martin
The Present

I can't believe I'm back in New York City again, not even two months since the last time I was here. And, by golly, I'm here again with Carol and we're trying to act like parents to our reckless and very troubled daughter. At least, that's the way I see it. And no matter what I say, Carol disagrees with me, and then Gina disagrees with both of us. It's been nothing but a fun-filled fight-fest since Carol and I got here.

It started off badly and went downhill from there. I admit I was angry with Gina even before I found out what she'd done. All we knew was that she'd been arrested for harassing a man. No details. So I didn't start off in the right frame of mind. Carol and I had visions of Gina sitting in a cell with the general population of gang-bangers, drunks, and drug addicts, so the flight to New York was tense and unpleasant. Our cab ride to the hotel was completely silent. And then I made the mistake of saying, "I wish she would have listened to me when I told her she should take the semester off and come home."

Carol blew up at me. She accused me of assuming Gina was guilty without knowing any of the facts. Then out of left field she let me have it because—and this was a surprise to me—I allegedly "make her feel guilty" when she sees me because she thinks I'm upset she's marrying Ross.

The rest of our stay in Manhattan was a lovely nightmare.

My old friend Detective Ken Jordan met us at the 20th Precinct station on W. 82nd Street. I think Jordan was surprised to see us again so soon, too. It turned out Gina was seen following a man on the Upper West Side near Juilliard on several occasions. Finally, the man, an artist living in the area, confronted her. Apparently Gina acted like she was going to physically attack him and they had harsh words. The artist complained. Since there are pretty strict stalking laws these days, the cops picked Gina up. It didn't help that the man she was "harassing" was one of the cleared suspects in her assault case.

Gina was fine, they'd put her in a single cell and made sure she was comfortable for the night. They fed her well and, according to my daughter, were very nice to her. So she was none the worse for wear, other than she got to sleep overnight in a sparsely decorated hotel room. However, we had to pay $5,000 in bail and hire an expensive lawyer. It pissed me off that *Ross* was the one who put up the money, although I could have done some maneuvering and come up with most of the sum. It would have hurt the pocketbook, though. The bail-bond route would have been the way to go, but Ross had the money, so he paid cash and Carol brought it with her on the plane. Then, after we'd gone through all that hassle, the artist— whose name is Gilbert Trejano—dropped the charges as long as a restraining order was put in place against Gina. She's not allowed to go near Trejano's residence. Another piece of fallout was the possibility Juilliard could suspend her.

A consolation to all this was that Jordan was privately taking Gina's accusation against Trejano seriously. "We'll be looking a lot more closely at Mr. Trejano," Jordan told us. "Just keep her away from him. Her class is in his neighborhood, but that's the only place on the block she's allowed to go."

"Wait a minute, what class?" I asked. "Her classes are at Juilliard."

"Her martial arts class." When Jordan saw the blank expressions on our faces, he said, "I take it you didn't know Gina was taking self-defense lessons?"

Uh, no.

When we got her home to her dorm room in Meredith Willson Residence Hall, Gina's roommates greeted her supportively and then split, wisely leaving us alone for a while.

"He's the one who did it," Gina said. "I'm sure of it."

"But honey, you didn't pick him in the lineup," I answered.

"That's because I never saw his face that night!"

"Has he spoken to you?"

"Only when we had the fight."

"Then why do you think it's him?"

"I don't know! It's the way he moves or something. I can't explain it."

Carol spoke up. "Let's try and forget about it now, all right? It's over. He's not going to press charges. Ross got his money back."

"And that makes it all better?" I asked. "I'm seriously concerned here. Gina, this is unacceptable behavior, you know that, don't you?"

"Dad, please."

"Dad, please? That's all you have to say?"

Carol interrupted, "Martin, leave her alone, she just got out of *jail*!"

"I'm just trying to understand what happened here, Carol. Our daughter committed a *crime* and, yeah, that's right, *she just got out of jail*! Did you *ever* think our daughter would *ever* spend a night in jail? That's not the Gina we *know*, is it?"

"No, of course not! But—"

"*Stop it!*" Gina screamed. "*Just stop it!*" And then she ran into her bedroom and shut the door. We could hear her bawling. Carol glared at me. "Way to go, Martin." *What?* What did *I* do? Carol knocked on the door and asked to be let in, but Gina wouldn't see her. Fine. So it's my fault.

Well, I'm *sorry*, but it doesn't take a numbskull to see that Gina needs some help. The assault damaged her psychologically and it's altered her conduct. That's why she should come back to Illinois and make a fresh start at school next year. But no one will listen to me. Gina won't have it, and Carol backs her up. Carol seems to think Gina has the strength to carry on and is somehow justified in her actions. "Her anger is to be expected," Carol says, "given what happened to her." I agree with her, I'm angry about the assault, too, and I am fully aware that it's far more personal for Gina. But a different Gina looks out at me through those beautiful eyes of hers. The anger is changing her; I can see it and I can feel it, but I don't recognize it. I also understand human emotion plays a big role in what's going on; with the anger comes the desire for revenge. And that's where Gina has to draw the line, because it's *wrong.*

And what the fuck is she doing taking martial arts classes?

I told Carol I was going across the street to one of the restaurants to have a drink. She didn't stop me. She probably wanted one, too, but was damned if she was going to accompany me. I didn't want her to anyway. I wanted to drown my sorrows in peace.

By the bottom of the second martini, I knew the reason I was freaking out was because my daughter reminded me of what my mother used to do when she was Gina's age.

Hello panic attack.

Carol and I flew home the next day. What else could we do? Neither of us wanted to sit around Gina's dorm room or our respective hotel rooms and argue with each other. Gina promised us she'd stay away from Trejano and that she'd learned her lesson. We didn't discuss the martial arts class. The possibility of Gina coming home for a semester wasn't brought up again either. She would continue to see her therapist. Hopefully the unfortunate incident would go away.

My anger had abated and now all I felt was love and concern for my daughter.

My ex-wife and I barely said a word during the flight. I could tell she was just as concerned about Gina as I was. The difference between us is Carol was always an optimist, whereas I'll forever be a pessimist.

I did find the courage to say to Carol, "I don't know what's given you the impression that I'm upset about you getting married again, but I wish you happiness. I hope we can be friends. And I'll make an effort with Ross, too."

She appreciated that, took my hand, and squeezed it.

34
Judy's Diary
1960

Actually, it's a couple hours before dawn on October 20. I'm shell-shocked by what happened last night at the Waldorf-Astoria. I'd better start at the beginning and write it all down before I try to get a few hours' sleep.

I was a Kennedy Girl again in the senator's motorcade that went down lower Broadway yesterday. Now *that* was exciting! All of the Girls were present, and Jackie Kennedy was there with her husband as well. She's *very* pregnant, but she looked radiant. She wore an oyster-white coat, a matching beret, and white gloves. She told me and some of the other Girls this was her last public appearance in the campaign. From here on out she was going to rest and take care of that bundle in the oven. Kennedy greeted us warmly. He looked at me and said, "Miss Cooper, right?" I can't believe he remembered my name. He must meet hundreds of people every day.

The weather was threatening rain. The sky was dark and cloudy, but luckily it held off until later. We started at the Biltmore Hotel on E. 43rd Street and went down in our van to the Battery, where the motorcade was lined up. *Thousands* of people had already gathered along Broadway, where a ticker-tape parade was planned. It was going to be a busy day. Kennedy had several events scheduled, culminating in the Alfred E. Smith dinner that night at the Waldorf. The one I was worried about.

The parade started close to noon and it took nearly a half hour for us to move from Bowling Green to City Hall on Broadway, a trip that normally would take ten minutes. There was a marching band, the Girls walked beside the Kennedys' convertible, and we all waved at the multitudes as we were showered by confetti, torn paper, and ticker tape. *That* was the rain! We sang "High Hopes" and "Marching Down to Washington" as the band played along. We stopped briefly at Trinity Church, where Kennedy made a short speech. It was amazing that people shut up long enough to listen. Mr. Dudley said a million people had turned out for the parade. Mayor Wagner was waiting for us on the steps of City Hall. Once we arrived and assumed our places on the steps, the mayor spoke first. He announced that this was the greatest reception anyone had ever received in lower Manhattan. Kennedy thanked the mayor for inviting him and his wife to receive the city's official greeting.

He gave a wonderful speech. I can't remember it all, of course, but a few things stuck out. I'm paraphrasing, but he said, "From Wall Street to the remotest part of the land, the American people will choose progress. They're tired of standing still. In 1960, the people will say 'yes' to progress. I'm running against Mr. Nixon, who is campaigning in these most dangerous times in the country's history on the slogan that 'you never had it so good.' I don't believe it is good enough!"

The crowd roared with appreciation.

From there we were rushed to Rockefeller Plaza and Café Française, where we had lunch. The food was delicious, but the Girls were relegated to a table by ourselves and we couldn't talk to the senator or his wife. Our duties were over for the day after that, because Kennedy was going to Yonkers after he ate, then back to Manhattan to speak at the Employees Union Hall, and then to HQ itself in the late afternoon. The dinner at the Waldorf was set for 8:00 that night. Betty told me she was working the ballroom as a waitress, so she'd get to see not only Jack and Jackie Kennedy again, but Richard Nixon and his wife, too. Some other bigwigs from the campaign HQ had tickets: Mr. Dudley and Mr. Patton, of course, and a few volunteers who got to work the event. I knew Alice and Mitch would be there, but because of my stint as a Kennedy Girl, I didn't get picked.

The rain finally broke through after lunch. I heard that poor Senator Kennedy had to stand bare-headed in the downpour in Yonkers while he addressed the people there. As for me, I went back to HQ to retrieve my backpack (my Stiletto outfit was stored inside). I considered going home, but I was simply too worried about the dinner. Michael and his Russian roommate would be there, I knew they would, and they had guns. There was no question in my mind that something bad was going to happen. What were they planning? I had to find out and, more importantly, I had to stop them.

It was around 4:00 when I got to the Waldorf. The front doors were naturally under heavy security, so I went to the employee entrance on 50th. Surprisingly, I walked right in. I told the security man I was looking for Betty O'Connor, and that we were both Kennedy Girls for the campaign. He believed me and figured I was part of the dinner festivities. I took the elevator up to the fifth floor and the employee locker rooms, and sure enough, I found Betty getting dressed in her uniform.

"What are you doing here, Judy?"

"Betty, don't ask me how I know, but I think the senator is in danger. Maybe everyone is, I don't really know."

"What are you talking about?"

I tried to explain that some Russian spies had infiltrated the dinner and planned to cause some trouble. She laughed a little and said that was the craziest thing she'd heard in a long time. "It's a little early for cocktails, Judy!" she teased. I told her I was serious, but she said, "Judy, the senator has Secret Service people and bodyguards. So does Nixon. The Grand Ballroom is probably the safest place in the world right now. Look, come with me."

She led me downstairs to the third floor and the entrance to the

ballroom. It was beautifully decorated. Gorgeous white cloths covered the dozens of tables that spread across the floor. The dinner and
glassware sparkled from the light of the chandeliers. Betty explained
how both Kennedy and Nixon would be at the head table and they'd
be surrounded by security. I was starting to feel a little better about
the situation, when none other than Billy entered the place! He carried programs to be distributed at every table.

"Judy! Betty!"

"Hi, Billy," I said. "Are you working the dinner?"

He nodded. "Mr. Patton asked me specifically."

"Where's Lily?"

"She couldn't do it. It's just me and some of the others." He
named some folks I knew.

Betty excused herself. "Kids, I have to get to work. Talk to you
later."

"Have fun tonight!" I called after her. I turned back to Billy and
asked, "Have you seen Alice or Mitch?"

"Yes, they're around." He pointed to a box high on the right wall.
"I've seen him up there. I don't know where Alice is. They'll be at
one of the tables down here. They have tickets."

"Why would he be up there?" I asked. "They didn't sell tickets
to the balcony or box seats, it's a dinner."

He shrugged his shoulders. "I don't know."

"Thanks, Billy. I'm going to look for him."

"See you later, Judy."

Entrances to the boxes were on the fifth floor. The balcony level
was the fourth floor. Either position would be an ideal place for a
man with a *sniper rifle* to hide. I left the ballroom and took the elevator to the fifth, where bellhops and hotel staff were hustling about,
but I didn't see Mitch or Alice. Just as a precaution, I looked in each
of the boxes on that side of the ballroom. There were red velvet curtains on each one, for privacy, and a lovely small chandelier hung
over four cushioned chairs that looked out over the floor.

As I turned to leave, I saw Mitch coming up the hallway along the box entrances. He was dressed in an elegant tuxedo.

"Judy!" He was obviously surprised to see me.

"Oh, hi, Mitch, I was looking for you."

"What for?"

I led him into the box where we could speak quietly. "Mitch," I said, "don't ask me how, but I have reason to believe that Michael—remember Michael?—and another man are Communist spies and they're going to be here tonight to hurt the senator."

Mitch wrinkled his brow. "Judy, that's a pretty far-fetched story. Where did you hear this?"

"I can't say, Mitch, you just have to trust me."

"I don't understand how you can know that."

"It's true, Mitch, really. Are you going to help me? Or should I go to the police by myself?"

He shook his head and said, "No, come on, let's go talk to the Secret Service guys. I know them. You can tell them what you told me. They're probably going to think you're nuts, but I'll vouch for you."

"Thanks, Mitch."

So I followed him out of the box, into the hallway, and up a little red ramp and through a door. We were next to a stairway that went down to the fourth floor, so we descended, turned left, and then stood behind the scenes in the employees-only area. I recognized it from when Betty took me on the tour. We walked down a short hall to the staff elevator. Mitch pressed the button to call the car.

"We have to go up to the room they made their headquarters," he explained.

"You sure know your way around the hotel," I said. "Did Betty help you out?"

"Betty? Oh, yeah, sure, she did give Alice and me a tour."

The elevator came, we stepped in, and he pressed the button for floor 27. At that point my instincts started to go haywire. *27th floor?*

"What were you doing on the fifth floor?" I asked Mitch.

"I was looking for Alice."

I wondered, *why would Alice be on the fifth floor?*—and then the doors opened. Mitch stepped out. I remained.

"Come on," he said.

"Where are we going?"

"I told you. Room 2730. That's where my Secret Service contact is."

It didn't feel right. Being near Mitch produced those pesky danger signals I get sometimes. Nevertheless, I followed him down the hall to the room in question. When he took out a key to unlock the door, I really knew something was definitely out of whack. Why would Mitch have a key to the Secret Service's room?

I backed away. Mitch asked, "Where are you going?"

"I, uh, think I left something downstairs," I muttered and then I *ran* back to the elevator.

"Judy! Come back!"

The doors had closed and the car had already gone down. I had no idea where the stairs were. Mitch walked back toward me, calling my name. I pressed the call button a dozen times, as if that would speed it along.

"Judy, what's wrong?"

Come on, I urged the elevator.

Mitch was nearly upon me when the doors finally opened and out stepped a bellboy. But *no, he wasn't a real bellboy*, he was the Russian, Michael's roommate! Wearing one of the uniforms I'd seen at the basement apartment! I reacted with a gasp, turned to run, but Mitch caught me in his arms.

"Ivan!" he spat.

The Russian moved in behind me and I felt the hard barrel of a gun in the small of my back.

"What's she doing here?" the man asked in a thick Russian accent.

"Snooping," Mitch answered.

"Has she talked to the police?"

Mitch looked at me. "Have you, Judy? Have you told *anyone* what you told me?"

Mitch? I couldn't believe it. *Mitch was one of them?*

I left Betty out. "No," I lied. "I swear."

All sorts of scenarios went through my head. Should I use my Stiletto prowess and take on these two men in my street clothes? It would certainly give me away. On the other hand, I could play the helpless victim, Judy Cooper, and try to find out what the heck was going on.

"Let's go to the room," Mitch said. He wagged a finger at me. "Not a sound, Judy, or Ivan will blow a hole in your spine."

The pair walked me down to Room 2730. Mitch once again removed his key and unlocked the door. They shoved me inside a large suite consisting of a sitting room and a separate bedroom. While Mitch locked up, the man called Ivan gestured with the gun for me to stand still. At that moment, *Michael* entered from the bedroom. And *he* was dressed in the other bellhop uniform from their apartment.

"What the hell?" he said. Then he snapped questions in Russian at the other two. Both Ivan and *Mitch* answered in Russian as well, and then Mitch switched to English.

"Your old girlfriend was snooping. She knows something. We have to keep her here."

"What does she know?"

"Enough. And it's all your fault."

Ivan took my backpack but thankfully didn't look inside it, then he indicated with the gun and said, "Go in there." Dear diary, I nervously walked in the bedroom, where they made me sit on the bed. Michael retrieved a roll of duct tape from an open suitcase. There was no way I could resort to a fight without Ivan shooting me at close range, so I had to submit to Michael taping first my wrists together in front of me, and then my ankles. Once that was done, Ivan threw my backpack in a corner, put away the handgun, and grabbed a brown liquid-filled medicine bottle and a washcloth from the bathroom. I took a moment to take in the surroundings.

Ivan opened the bottle, and I immediately smelled something sweet. He poured a little on the washcloth, screwed the cap back on the bottle, and then approached me with the rag. Michael held me down as I struggled. Ivan placed the cloth over my mouth and nose, forcing me to hold my breath. I didn't want to inhale that stuff, for I realized what it was. *Chloroform*!

I kicked, I wrestled, I tried to scream—but it was no use. Eventually, my breath gave out. Those flowery fumes went into my lungs, and then everything faded like you were turning down the volume on the radio until it all went black.

35
Judy's Diary
1960

OCTOBER 19, 1960

I woke up groggy and disoriented. At first I didn't know where I was. My ears were ringing and sounds were muffled. I had blurry vision, but it slowly sharpened to reveal the elegantly furnished room. I was lying on a soft, large bed. Then I remembered—the hotel suite in the Waldorf. They had drugged me.

Dear diary, I felt nauseous and wanted to throw up. My hands and ankles were still taped together. When I turned my body to the side, the room spun and my stomach lurched. The chloroform or whatever it was Ivan used to put me to sleep did not agree with me at *all*.

A clock on the nightstand read 7:13. The dinner was about to begin in the Grand Ballroom.

My hearing eventually improved and muted sounds became a man's and woman's heated conversation in the other room. I was confused why I couldn't understand what they were saying, and then I realized they were speaking Spanish. But I recognized the voices. Mitch and Alice. And then I heard a door open and shut. A third voice spoke English in a heavy accent. It was Ivan, the Russian.

"Michael is in place. He takes the shot at exactly nine o'clock."

Alice continued to speak in Spanish.

"Speak English, damn you!" Apparently, it was the only language that all three of them had in common.

"I was telling her we have to get to our table," Mitch said. "Kennedy and Nixon have already been escorted into the ballroom, right?"

"Right. What were you arguing about?"

"Judy."

"What about her?"

"What we're going to do with her."

Alice spoke up. "We can't just kill her."

"Why not?" Mitch asked. "She knows too much. She knows who we are. When all this is done, we have to get rid of her."

"That's absolutely correct," Ivan said. "Alice, you know it's what we have to do. We'll keep her asleep. She won't know a thing."

"All right, I understand. It's just a pity, that's all."

"The bigger concern is Michael," Mitch said.

Ivan snarled, "He is a womanizer and a fool. His recklessness is what brought the girl into this. We have our orders."

"What are you saying?" Alice asked.

Mitch answered. "Michael's a prima donna. He thinks too highly of himself and believes he has impunity. He wasn't supposed to fraternize with the population, but he couldn't help it. You've seen how difficult he is to control. He followed us to that party where he met Judy. His orders were to stay incognito, but he started a relationship with her."

Ivan continued, "That was careless and unprofessional. He might have blown the operation."

"But we ordered him to stop seeing her, and he did," Alice said.

"It doesn't matter. What's done is done," Ivan retorted.

So that was it, dear diary. It was Mitch who had been driving the Packard that day when I saw Michael on the street. Michael gave me the brush-off right after that. And when I saw the car again on Bayard Street, it was Mitch and Alice who picked up Michael and Ivan. They were all in it together.

"Come on, you two, get ready," Ivan ordered. "I'm going to check on Michael."

Mitch said something in Spanish to Alice, and then I heard the door open and shut. After a moment, Alice walked into the bedroom.

"You're awake," she said.

I had to be Innocent Judy, so I asked, "Alice, what's going on? Why did they do this to me?"

"Judy, you stuck your nose where it didn't belong," she answered sternly. This wasn't the Alice Graves I knew from HQ. Now she was quite cold and spoke as if she hated me. I could also sense she was scared. "Pardon me while I get ready for the dinner."

She started to change her clothing to a fancy black formal gown. "I feel sick."

"That's the effects of the chloroform. It'll pass."

"And then you'll kill me?" She didn't answer. Instead, she sat on the bed beside me. "Are you going to tell me anything? At least tell me *why* you're doing this. Who *are* you?"

"My real name is Alice Garcia. Mitch's real name is Perez. We're Cuban Americans working for the Soviet government. We joined the Kennedy campaign to keep track of the senator's movements. The Soviets needed someone on the inside, and that was us."

"And Michael? And the other man?"

She stood, stripped to her underwear, went in the bathroom, and spoke to me from there as she worked on her makeup. "Ivan is a Soviet facilitator. He's the boss of the operation, you could say. Michael is a KGB assassin. He is one of the best snipers in the Soviet Union."

Suddenly, the full impact of what she was saying hit me. They were going to kill Kennedy. Tears welled in my eyes.

"You can't kill the senator," I whispered.

Alice came out of the bathroom and finished putting on the dress. "We can and we will."

"Why? That's what Khrushchev wants?"

She laughed a little. "I don't know if Khrushchev even knows of the plan. Maybe he does, maybe he doesn't."

I winced when I heard her words. "But it makes no sense!"

"We don't question orders or fail them, otherwise we die. And who wants to? We get a sizable fee and transportation out of the country."

I had to get out. I had to stop it. I struggled against the tape but I couldn't break it.

She sat on the bed again. "Stop it, Judy. It's useless."

"You won't get away with it!"

"Yes we will. Michael's instructions are to kill Kennedy first, and then, if he can, shoot Nixon as well. They'll die at their tables during dinner. And even if they catch any of us, we are equipped with cyanide tablets, and we will use them. We'll be long gone when the hotel staff finds your body here in the room in the morning, along with—I'm sorry, Judy, this isn't my idea. It's already gone horribly wrong."

They were going to kill Michael and leave him with me. There was no telling what kind of scenario the cops would think had occurred. As Alice finished getting dressed, I thought about what their motive could possibly be. Kennedy is very anti-Cuba. If he's elected president, the Soviet Union's plans for Cuba would be jeopardized. Were they trying to throw chaos into the presidential race? I didn't know for sure and I might never know. It was all so crazy.

There was a knock on the bedroom door. "Come in," Alice said. Mitch entered.

"It's time," he said.

Alice left me on the bed, and went in the bathroom. She returned with the chloroform bottle and the rag. I could smell the dreaded chemical from several feet away, and it made my stomach turn.

"I'm going to be sick!" I managed to say. Then I *did* throw up, right there on the bed.

Both Alice and Mitch cursed, I think, in Spanish. She put down the bottle and rag, and grabbed a trash can. Alice shoved it at my face, just in time to catch another heave. Yuck. I hate throwing up.

She held the can there until the spasms subsided, and then she took it and emptied the contents into the toilet.

I had to get up. I had to fight her. I had to escape.

"Leave her!" Mitch commanded.

I was just too out of it to do anything. My head felt like lead, all I wanted was to drop it on the pillow. I didn't care if there was a foul mess on the bed beside me.

I seem to remember a feeble struggle as Alice and Mitch appeared above me with the chloroform rag. My last thought, I recall, was that they were going to kill me in my sleep. Then I was gone again.

I took a break from writing to take a shower. That felt good.

So—I did wake up, still alone in the hotel room. I didn't know if it was minutes or hours later. Alice wasn't in the bedroom.

The vomit had dried a little, so that was an indication that *some* time had past. It still stank. My stomach was doing somersaults, so I managed to roll away from it and face the other side.

The clock read 8:49.

Oh my God, dear diary, I realized I had very little time to save the senator and vice-president, and this brought on a rush of adrenaline. It must have helped me somehow, for I immediately felt better.

I tried breathing deeply, the way Soichiro had taught me. Closed my eyes. Attempted to clear my head. Breathed.

At 8:51, I rose, swung my bound feet to the floor and searched the room.

I stood and hopped across the floor. It felt good to move. I managed to get to my knees and then sit beside my backpack. I picked it up with my two bound hands and placed it in my lap. It was awkward, but I unzipped it and dug out my outfit, piece by piece. At first I thought I could use my stiletto to cut the tape, but I found it difficult to grasp the hilt with my hands twisted and bound. Ivan had taped me wrist-to-wrist with the top hand face up, the bottom one face down. Believe me, it's nearly impossible to grasp something with your hands in that position. I had to resort to the smaller knife I kept in my boot. The folded, knee-high boots were at the bottom of the backpack, so I wrestled them out and retrieved my six-inch wrist dagger. It was just the right size to "wedge" the hilt in between the backs of my hands. The knife was more or less gripped as firmly as I could get it.

I pulled up my knees and sawed away on the tape around my ankles. As soon as my legs were free, I got up and went to the door with my wrists still taped together. With one hand I slowly turned the knob and cracked the door a sliver. I was alone. Good.

Moving to the bed, I sat Indian-style, now that I could, and managed to draw the stiletto and place it between the soles of my feet. The stockings were slicker than I'd wished, but I didn't have time to try and take them off. Holding the knife firmly, I sliced and stabbed the tape around my wrists until I could pull my hands apart.

I quickly dressed as the Black Stiletto. By the time I left the suite it must have been a minute or two before nine.

36
Martin

Coming back to Chicagoland didn't hold much of a promise of things getting better. As soon as I got home midday, I hopped in my car and drove to the hospital to see Mom. On the way, I phoned Maggie to tell her I was back. She didn't answer, so I left a message. When I got to Northwest Community, Mom was asleep, but I had a chance to speak with Dr. Benji.

The news wasn't too good. He said Mom had improved because she speaks now, but he fears she's reached a plateau and may or may not regain all of the abilities she had before the stroke. In other words, it's possible that the Alzeheimer's symptoms will now get worse. Right now she is quite disoriented, so Dr. Benji wants to keep her in ICU for a while longer. Her heart is fine, but it's best that Mom not get too excited. Oddly, the doctor said, she doesn't seem too distressed about being in the hospital, as many Alzeheimer's patients— and my mom—have experienced. They often don't understand what's going on, so they become anxious or angry and sometimes even violent.

Mom was awake after I talked to the doctor. A nurse named Victoria was in the room with her and seemed to be handling her well. "Oh, look who's here, Judy," she said as I approached the bed. Mom looked bewildered, not focusing on anything in particular. I thought maybe it was because she'd just woken up, but her lack of being in the moment lingered through the entire visit. Usually, even if she doesn't remember who I am, she smiles when she sees me because she knows I'm someone she loves. This time she didn't even do that. The only way I can describe it is the "blankness," the thing that Alzheimer's inflicts on a victim, was more prominent. Nevertheless, I sat and talked to her. I told her about my trip to New York and that Carol and I had gone to see Gina, but I didn't say why. She'd respond now and then with a "Really?" or a "That's nice," and was at the very least listening to me. Whether or not she comprehended it, I couldn't say, but I stayed there all afternoon anyway.

On the way to Maggie's place, I felt pretty bummed. The visit with Mom was disheartening and it made me sad. I can't help but think that she might not be around much longer, and I'm not sure how I'm going to react to that.

We had Chinese take-out for dinner. I brought a bottle of wine. Maggie seemed a little nervous when I got there, so I asked her about it and she said she was just tired and that it had been a stressful few days without me around. She looked pretty and it was nice to feel her arms around me and get a kiss. I told her about my mother, and she said the right things and tried to make me feel better about the situation.

She had put Christmas decorations up and there was a tree with lights and baubles and an angel on top. "Hey, when did you have time to do all this?" I asked.

"While you were in New York, of course."

"But I would've helped you. You should've waited."

"It gave me something to do over the weekend. And I wanted it to be a surprise when you got home."

My mood improved as we watched TV and ate in her living room. I told Maggie about the trip to New York and my concerns about Gina. I also mentioned that I made peace with Carol. Her wedding is next week.

"I hope you'll go with me," I said.

"I'd be delighted," she answered. "I was afraid you'd never ask."

"I wasn't so sure *I* was going, but I guess I am. Gina will be home for it, too. It'll be a lot less disturbing with you there, Maggie."

She raised an eyebrow at me. "Why should it be disturbing, as long as you're in love with me and not still in love with her?"

"What? No, no way," I said. "Still in love with Carol? Are you kidding? No, no, no, no, no. You're the love of my life right *now*." I meant it, too.

World Entertainment Television came on the TV, and my old friend Sandy Lee was the anchor/host, as usual. There were the same old inane stories about the Hollywood in-crowd, who was dating who, why so-and-so had to go to jail, and other gossip about stuff I didn't care anything about.

Then, out of the blue, Sandy Lee said, "Stay tuned for a story about the Black Stiletto and her time in Los Angeles, right after this message." That got my attention. In fact, it startled me so much I spilled wine all over my shirt. I had to run into the kitchen and splash cold water on it. It was stained but I didn't care. I got back to my seat in time for the story. Luckily, Maggie was more concerned about my shirt and made me take it off. She took it to the laundry room while I watched the program.

Sandy Lee interviewed a retired policeman from L.A. who said he encountered the Stiletto during a bank robbery. His name was Scott Garriott, and he was a beat cop in the late fifties, sixties, and seventies. He retired in the eighties and was now pushing ninety. The man seemed to have his wits about him, though, for he described my mother quite accurately.

"She was tall and athletic and had pretty brown eyes," he said. "It was 1961, and I was in the patrol car with my partner Danny Delgado. It was in September; I remember it plain as day. We were heading back to the precinct 'cause our shift was nearly over. Suddenly we got a radio call about a robbery in progress at the Security Pacific Bank off of Hollywood Boulevard. Danny and I were the first officers on the scene, and we surprised the bank robbers. One of the tellers must have triggered the silent alarm. Danny and I didn't wait for backup. There were four altogether, armed and disguised; two had the employees and a few customers held hostage while the other two went to work in the back. They wore Halloween masks of movie monsters, you know, Dracula, Frankenstein, the Wolf Man.

"We burst inside and Danny got shot. I took cover behind a counter and fired my weapon at one of the robbers. But one hoodlum grabbed a civilian and held a gun to her head, so there was nothing I could do. Danny was wounded and needed medical attention, so I tossed my gun to the crooks and raised my hands like they ordered me to do.

"Suddenly, who shows up? The Black Stiletto. I have no idea where she came from, but there she was in the bank, dodging bullets and fighting the perps. I couldn't believe it. I'd heard she was in Los Angeles, but I didn't believe it until I saw her with my own eyes. But the robbers got away in a van that screeched up to the front door to pick them up. The Black Stiletto vanished, too. The robbers got something out of a safety deposit box, but didn't take any money. Maybe they didn't rob the bank of its cash because the Stiletto showed up. The thing is, I'm not so sure the Stiletto wasn't involved in the robbery. Was she in cahoots with the gang? It's possible. Her intrusion might have been simply a diversion, allowing the crooks to get away."

Well, I didn't believe that theory. It was crazy. Mom would never help bank robbers. She was probably trying to stop the heist and her actions were misinterpreted.

The bank robbers were never caught.

You know, I've always wondered how and why my mother moved from New York to L.A. Will that be revealed in the next diary? I have to get on the ball and finish reading the third one and go on to the next. Maybe there will be a clue as to who Richard Talbot really was.

Watching that TV story and thinking about my father's identity triggered something. All of a sudden I didn't feel so good. I felt another panic attack coming on, and I didn't want to be in front of Maggie when it happened. I went and found her in the laundry room. I took my shirt from her, wet, and put it on.

"I have to go," I said.

"Martin! Your shirt's wet!"

"I don't care, I have to go. I'll take it off when I get home."

"Martin, what's going on?"

"Nothing, I just need to go. I'm sorry, Maggie. Please—"

"But why?" Maggie asked. "You've been drinking, you can't drive."

"Sure I can."

"Martin, what's wrong?"

"I don't feel so good."

"Then you can't go."

"I'm going." I abruptly went to the front door, and put my jacket on over the wet shirt.

"Martin, *what* are you *hiding* from me?" Maggie demanded.

"*Nothing!*" I shouted. Maggie recoiled at my anger, and I immediately said, "I'm sorry. Maggie, I'm sorry. I didn't mean to yell at you."

"Martin, it's all right. I'm on your side, for God's sake."

I didn't know what to do, so I copped out. "I have to leave. Sorry, Maggie. I'll talk to you tomorrow."

So I left.

Crap, I'm a fucking cripple. And it's all my mom's fault.

37
Judy's Diary
1960

OCTOBER 19, 1960

I took the elevator to the fourth floor. When the doors opened, I cautiously looked out into the employee area and made sure no one was about. I dashed to the stairs, ran up to the fifth floor, and stood at the entrance to the hallway where the ballroom boxes were located. Carefully peering around the corner, I spotted Ivan standing outside a box. The curtains were closed. I figured Michael was inside with his sniper rifle, preparing to assassinate Kennedy and Nixon. Ivan was dressed in the same bellhop uniform I saw him in earlier. A hotel cart sat nearby, the kind bellhops use to roll luggage around. Folded cloth tablecloths and napkins currently rested on its bed. I figured they had used the cart as cover when moving about the hotel. No one would suspect a couple of bellhops rolling tableware through the building.

Ivan appeared to be waiting for something, so I took that to indicate the shooting hadn't occurred yet. I thought perhaps I could make a difference in how the evening turned out after all.

Without a plan of action in mind, I took off in a run, 50-yard-dash style, toward the Commie agent. I was so fast he didn't see what was coming until it was too late. Ivan's eyes widened in horror as he focused on the speeding locomotive that was the Black Stiletto headed right for him. He reached inside his brown jacket and drew a handgun, probably one of the Smith & Wessons I had seen before, but before he could properly aim the weapon, I collided into him. He managed to twist and deflect my momentum, but I spun and delivered a *Mawashi-geri* roundhouse kick by twisting my hips in a circular motion so the ball of my foot swung inward at a right angle to Ivan's body. My boot smashed into his gun hand, knocking the semi-automatic into the air. I didn't give him time to react. I immediately regained my footing and released a barrage of my special Praying Mantis fist chops, striking him relentlessly on the face, shoulders, chest, and neck, over and over. Needless to say, he went down, but he shook away the stars that must have been spinning around his head and lunged for the weapon that lay five feet away. I kicked the Smith & Wesson across the hall to the other side, out of his immediate reach. Then, with my other leg, I kicked Ivan directly in the face.

At that point, Michael stuck his head out through the curtains. "Wha—?" he muttered, and his eyes popped when he saw me.

"Get back in there!" Ivan commanded. "Do the job now! Now!"

I turned to grab Michael to keep him from completing his mission, but Ivan tackled me. We both tumbled to the carpet with him on top. He pummeled me with both fists as Michael disappeared into the box. For a moment I was stunned. Ivan ceased the onslaught, got off of me, and crawled across the hall to the gun. As soon as I realized what he was doing, I rolled over and performed a six-foot leap across the hallway to catch him. But he surprised me by using both hands to lasso a strip of wire around my head. He pulled it tightly and *oh my* God, dear diary, I was suddenly choking to death. The leather mask did little to protect me; all it did was prevent the wire from cutting into my skin, which wouldn't have been pretty either. Ivan had attacked me with a garrote, an instrument that killers often employed to strangle or decapitate their victims. Fiorello told me all about them.

While gripping the wire around my throat, Ivan stood and

pulled me up with him. I was in great pain and couldn't breathe—but I'd instinctively drawn my stiletto. What was my choice? Stop Ivan from killing me, or stop Michael from murdering Kennedy?

I flung the knife across the hall, where it bisected the red velvet curtains in front of the theatre box. I didn't see it happen, but the soft thud of the blade hitting its target was music to my ears. Nevertheless, after a few seconds, Michael emerged from the box and started moving awkwardly down the hall toward the exit. My stiletto stuck out of his back. He was making a run for it.

That left the Russian, and I knew I had only seconds to turn the tide before I blacked out. Ivan was strong and powerful, but I was lithe and swift. I performed a back kick and struck his left leg. He grunted, so I knew it hurt him. I did it again, harder. But darn it, the Russian just wouldn't submit to the pain. I aimed for the knee itself but simply ran out of steam. The hallway became dark. I was out of oxygen. A panic set in. I was dying.

And then I thought I was aware of something dark and *fast* broadside us. We both fell and Ivan released the garrote's tension! Gasping for breath, I rolled forward, carrying the blasted wire with me to keep it out of his hands. With sweet air filling my lungs, I looked up and saw what had happened.

Billy stood in a traditional *wushu* stance and faced Ivan, who was still recovering from whatever attack my young Chinese friend had used on the Russian. As soon as Ivan focused on his assailant, Billy advanced and struck him several times with Praying Mantis slaps and punches. I got to my feet and coughed, still trying to open my windpipe, and watched Billy let Ivan have it. As I got my breath back, I wondered if anyone could hear us down below in the ballroom. So far the fight had been surprisingly silent. Did I dare call out for help? What would I do if Secret Service agents or police stormed the hallway? I'm not sure I wanted that to happen.

I snapped back to Billy and Ivan—just as the Soviet agent punched Billy hard, knocking the boy down. In the tiny second it took for me to react and attack, Ivan spied the gun laying a mere couple of feet from his shoe. His eyes met mine. I knew, and he knew I knew, that he could pick up the gun before I was able to stop him. And that's exactly what happened. The man crouched, snatched the pistol, and aimed at me just as I propelled myself at him. He may have succeeded in retrieving his weapon, but I bowled him over before he could fire. I clutched his wrist with both hands, attempting to squeeze him so hard that he'd drop the handgun; however, he managed to twist his hand anyway and point the barrel at my head. I moved my right hand off the wrist and snapped it onto his hand. Then the struggle became a tug-of-war with the gun, only we were pushing and not pulling. With every ounce of vigor I could muster, I threw my body into it, gaining a bit of leverage by digging into the carpet with the heels of my boots. Out of the corner of my eye, I saw Billy get up and shake his head. I couldn't rely on my friend to save my rear end this time, so I concentrated on overcoming Ivan's uncanny strength.

The hand and gun moved an inch toward the Russian's side of the arc. Then it slid two inches in my direction. And so on, back and forth, just like arm wrestling. I grunted and he gritted his teeth. Our eyes met and I felt the hatred pour out of them. I had ruined his big plan. No matter what happened now, the plot to kill Kennedy was kaput.

And then there was a muffled *thump* as the Smith & Wesson jolted in our hands. It was loud, but it wasn't as noisy as a gunshot. I didn't know what had happened, but Ivan was obviously in distress. The look on his face went from surprise to that of sheer terror. His white shirt blossomed with blood red that spread over his chest. He died right there in my arms, face-to-face and locked in combat.

The Smith & Wesson dropped to the carpet, and that's when I noticed the barrel was different. There was a thick cylinder on the end that I hadn't previously noticed.

Billy helped me get to my feet, the gun in my hand. "Are you all right?"

"Yeah. How about you?"

"I'm fine."

"What are you doing here?" I asked.

"I came up to listen to Kennedy's speech from one of the empty boxes."

"Well, you got here in the nick of time, Billy. Thank you."

"You're welcome. Now we're even!" He grinned broadly, very proud of himself.

"You did great, Billy." I looked at the handgun. "This wasn't very loud."

He indicated the barrel. "It has a silencer."

"What?"

"That's a sound suppressor on the barrel."

"Oh, is that what it is?"

The sound of applause in the Grand Ballroom snapped me back into the situation at hand. I quickly moved to the box and parted the curtains. The sniper rifle was on the floor. I took the opportunity to glance down at the crowd below. Kennedy and Nixon sat at their respective spaces, apparently oblivious to what had just happened two floors above them. Even the Secret Service men had no clue. They hadn't heard nor seen us.

I picked up the rifle and left the box. Billy waited for instructions and I indicated Ivan. "We have to get him out of here," I said. "The less the public knows about this, the better." Billy pointed at the bell-hop cart. I nodded. "Good idea."

Billy helped me lift Ivan and place his body on the cart, and then we covered it with a tablecloth. I threw the sniper rifle and Smith & Wesson underneath, too.

Dear diary, I can't believe what Billy and I did. We managed to roll that cart through the hall, up the ramp, and then *carry* it down the stairs to the fourth floor, where we skirted around the corner to the employee elevator, and called the car. Not a single person saw us. The only explanation I could figure was that the entire staff was busy doing something else. After all, a major celebrity-filled banquet attended by a senator from Massachusetts, the vice president of the United States, and many other VIPs was going on in the hotel ballroom. The route we had taken was indeed off the beaten track and used only by employees in between shifts. Nevertheless, we were very lucky.

"Thank you, Billy," I said. "I want you to leave now. Please don't say anything to anyone, all right?"

"You don't want me to go to the police?"

"No. We can't get involved in this, believe me."

"You sure you're all right?"

I looked down at my outfit. Ivan's blood had soiled much of my jacket.

"Yes. Now please, Billy, you must go."

"Okay."

"Thank you."

"Okay."

The elevator came. I rolled the cart into it and Billy took off. I thought I might know where Michael had gone. Once I was on the 27th floor, I squatted, lifted the tablecloth, and reached into Ivan's trouser pocket to retrieve the key to the suite. I found it and then silently unlocked the door. I fully expected to find Mitch and Alice and Michael in the room, guns in hand and ready to blast me away, but I swung open the door anyway.

Michael lay face down in the middle of the living room. He had collapsed from the knife wound, and the stiletto was still sticking out of his back. Blood was all over the carpet. The bedroom door was closed, so I crept to it and carefully opened it.

Empty.

I went back to the door and rolled the cart inside.

The first thing I did was remove my stiletto, and then I washed the blood off of it and my outfit the best I could. Then I thought about where I was and what I'd done. The Black Stiletto was alone in a hotel suite with two dead Russian agents. I knew the police and

FBI would eventually have a hand in the case, so I mulled over what story I could tell them by arranging a crime scene. It wouldn't be the real scenario, but perhaps they'd buy it.

When I was done, I removed my mask and put it in the backpack, slipped my trench coat on over my outfit, and left the hotel suite. I took the passenger elevator to the ground floor. With the dinner still going on in the ballroom, or perhaps just finishing, I walked out of the hotel as if nothing had ever happened.

Luckily, I knew where I'd find Mitch and Alice. They'd discover my handiwork in the hotel suite and then run home, where the Stiletto would be waiting for the treasonous couple.

38
Judy's Diary
1960

Outside their apartment building on E. 52nd Street, I stepped into shadows, put on my mask, and crammed the trenchcoat in my backpack. I was the Stiletto again. I knew which fire escape "terrace" was Mitch and Alice's—the sixth and top floor. I could easily pick out the silhouettes of the plants, for there was a light on in the window. And, guess what—the black Packard was parked several spots down on 52nd.

I carefully considered what I was going to do; the trick was climbing the fire escape without being seen by pedestrians. The time was between 9 and 9:30 so, alas, there were plenty of people about. I didn't want the Black Stiletto associated in *any way* with what had gone on so far. The police would surely talk to people at HQ, and I, Judy, would be interviewed. Something might inadvertently connect me with the Stiletto. I also believe it would have been bad publicity for my alter ego, even if I did save the day.

Luckily, there was a lull in sidewalk traffic. The nearest persons were at the other end of the block, headed my way. I ran across the street, stood below the fire escape, swung my rope and hook, and pulled down the ladder. I was up in the darkness of the fourth-floor platform by the time the pedestrians passed underneath. From there, I slowly ascended to the top floor and looked in the window. I remembered the "terrace" was outside Mitch and Alice's bedroom.

I was surprised to see Alice lying on the bed, still dressed in her gown. An open suitcase sat next to her, but I couldn't see what was in it. It appeared that Mitch and Alice had left the dinner early and were getting out of town, but why the heck was Alice taking a nap?

I tried the window and it was unlatched. I slid the pane up and stepped inside. Only after I approached the bed did I realize what had truly happened. Alice's eyes were open, staring blankly ahead. White foamy stuff was all over her mouth and she'd drooled it onto the bed. I guess she wasn't kidding when she told me about the poison tablets. She was gone, and I felt a little sad. After all, we *had* been friends. I'd actually *liked* her. I liked her *and* Mitch! But they fooled me. And for that I was angry.

Another shock awaited me when I glanced at the open suitcase. It was full of money, stacks of high-denomination American bills. The payment Alice had eluded to?

I looked up to see Mitch standing in the doorway. I must have been too jolted by my discoveries on the bed not to have heard him. *Of course* he pointed a gun at me. The reflexes kicked in, for I leaped to the side just as he fired the weapon. The gunshot was loud and would certainly attract the police, but he missed me. I performed a forward roll on the floor at the end of the bed and came up on the other side, close enough to grab Mitch's gun arm, drop onto my back, and throw him over my head. The gun sailed across the room. I quickly got to my feet, drew the stiletto, and pointed it at him as he cowered on the floor.

"Please don't!" he stammered.

He was scared to death, and not necessarily of me.

"Going somewhere?" I asked.

Mitch nodded.

"Leaving the country?"

He nodded again.

"What happened to Alice?"

"When nine o'clock came and went and nothing happened, we got up from our table and left. We knew something had gone wrong. Alice was too frightened. She—insisted—"

"Why didn't you kill yourself, too?"

Mitch's mouth trembled and his eyes darted around the room. "I was afraid," he answered. "Please—Judy—let me go."

Judy? He called me Judy!

"It is you, isn't it?" he said. "I thought you might be her."

That certainly made things more difficult. I didn't want to tie him up, leave him for the cops, and have him tell them that the Black Stiletto, alias Judy Cooper, caught him. What was I going to do with him? I didn't want to *kill* him in cold blood, I could never do that.

"You still have your pill?" I asked him.

He nodded.

"Don't you think that's preferable to prison?"

Mitch shook his head. "Prison is preferable to what happens to us when we fail."

With that, he abruptly jumped up and darted to the window. I bolted after him and caught his leg just as he scampered onto the fire escape platform. Mitch kicked me hard, loosening my grip, and he got away. I crawled out the window and followed him up the fire escape stairs to the roof—but before he reached it, one of the bolts that attached the top of the ladder to the edge of the building broke free. Bits of brick and concrete showered us as Mitch lost his grip and footing. He fell. I had the temerity to reach out and catch his arm, but his weight pulled me down. I plummeted to the sixth-floor platform. Mitch, however, hit the guardrail and bounced the other direction into thin air. There was nothing I could do. He screamed all the way down. When I brought myself to look, I saw his body splayed on the sidewalk below.

Heaven help me, but I didn't feel any sorrow for Mitch or Alice, and I was relieved my secret died with the traitors.

I quickly moved back into the bedroom, but I didn't shut the window. I had to fashion another crime scene of my own invention and get the heck out of there. Police sirens in the distance grew nearer, and I had no doubt they were headed to 52nd Street. I unmasked myself and threw on the trenchcoat. Before leaving the bedroom, though, I shut the suitcase full of money, latched it, and carried it away. It was heavy, but I could manage.

The elevator was empty. When I got to the ground floor, some people had already gathered outside around Mitch's corpse. "What happened?" I asked innocently.

"Guy jumped," a man said.

"Oh my God!"

"Do you live in the building?"

"No, I was visiting a friend. I'm on my way to the train station." The man paid me no mind after that, so I walked away.

I'm home now and it's nearly dawn. I'm going to try and catch a few hours' sleep before I have to show up at the gym. I'm anxious to count the money in the suitcase, but I'm just too tired. I hid it under my bed for later, and now I'm getting between the sheets.

Like I said—I was a little shell-shocked by what happened tonight, but I feel better having written it down. Good night.

OCTOBER 21, 1960

Tonight I watched the fourth debate between Kennedy and Nixon over at Lucy and Peter's apartment. It went very well and I believe Kennedy was the winner. I also now have a very good feeling about the election. I think Kennedy will win. Seeing the two candidates on television over the four debates has helped bring them into everyone's living room, so to speak, and we all feel as if we're making a much more personal choice.

At any rate, I'm happy they're both alive.

Yesterday the newspapers had some pieces about my handiwork. One article reported that two Russian men dressed as Waldorf-Astoria bellhops had killed each other in a suite. One was stabbed and the other one shot himself. Apparently they had diplomatic ties to the Soviet Mission to the United Nations, so the FBI and CIA were looking into whether or not their presence had anything to do with the presidential candidates' appearances at the Alfred E. Smith dinner elsewhere in the building. The mission denied any knowledge of the men, of course.

An unrelated article reported that a Cuban-American couple had also committed suicide in an eastside Midtown apartment. The woman, Alice Graves, was poisoned, while the man, Mitch Perry, jumped from his sixth-floor fire escape. Police were still looking into the possibility that Perry had murdered his wife before leaping to his death. Perry was described as a successful stockbroker, so the motivation was a mystery.

There was no mention of the Black Stiletto.

Police came to talk to Mr. Dudley and Mr. Patton at HQ today. Because Mitch and Alice were volunteers for the Kennedy campaign, the cops were covering all the bases. They didn't talk to any of us. So far they hadn't linked the couple to Michael or Ivan, and I doubt they will.

I think I've figured out what was supposed to happen at the Waldorf that night. Ivan had booked a suite on the 27th floor as a base of operations. Mitch probably brought the sniper rifle in its case to the hotel along with other luggage. The dinner tickets were actually for Mitch and Alice, not Ivan and Michael. Ivan and Michael dressed as hotel bellhops in order to get around the hotel with impunity. At the right time, Michael would have gone to the ballroom box, opened the case, assembled the rifle, shot Kennedy and Nixon, and then rushed to the stairwell with the case. He'd stash it in room 2730. He and Ivan, still dressed as bellhops, would have then innocently left the hotel amidst all the chaos, departed the city, and disappeared. Mitch and Alice would spend the night in the suite, check out in the morning, and leave with the rifle case among their luggage. Their attending the dinner was the perfect alibi.

Unless I'm wrong, the history books won't contain any references to the attempt on John F. Kennedy and Richard Nixon's lives on October 19, 1960. No one has a clue it even occurred except the Commies, and they won't be talking, ha ha.

Oh, and guess what, dear diary? There was $20,000 in that suitcase. I have no idea where the money came from, but it's mine now! Ya-hoo!

39
Maggie
THE PRESENT

A couple of nights ago I got very upset with Martin. He walked out of the house for no reason. His behavior was totally bizarre—he put on a wet shirt I was cleaning for him and then he left. All right, he was distressed about something, but he wouldn't tell me what it was. Something on the television set him off, I think. I realize he got some bad news about his mother at the hospital, so that could be a big part of it. But if he doesn't talk to me and be honest about what is bothering him, then how can we move forward?

Bill Ryan called me today at the office, so I returned the call during my lunch break.

"Judy's and Martin's Social Security numbers were registered in Odessa, Texas, in 1962," he said.

"Martin was a newborn, so that's understandable," I thought out loud. "But why her?"

"Maybe she lost her card and had to reregister. Maybe she never had one. Or—"

"Or maybe she changed her identity?"

"That's always a possibility. The new card was in her married name—Talbot—so that part of the equation is still a mystery."

Indeed it was.

I'm afraid I believe Judy was some kind of criminal in Los Angeles. The evidence is too compelling. How could Martin not know about those gunshot wounds? It just doesn't make sense.

I've decided I must confront Martin with my suspicion and tell him that if he doesn't reveal what he's hiding from me, then I'll have to call off our relationship. I don't want to go through that again. Lies and deceit destroyed the one other serious love affair I ever had. There's a *shadow* that covers Martin and his mother, and I need to know what it is. It's all I think about, because, well, I think I really do love him. I don't want to push Martin away, but I know from experience that it's what must happen if I don't get some answers.

But first we have to go to his ex-wife's wedding. Oh, boy.

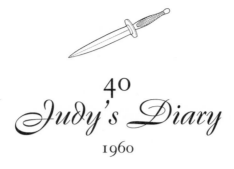

40
Judy's Diary
1960

NOVEMBER 5, 1960

Yesterday was my birthday. I'm twenty-three. My friends at HQ surprised me with a cake. Last night, Freddie took me to dinner at Gage & Tollner's, down on Fulton Street. That was where I first met Fiorello, so it brought back poignant memories. The dinner was exquisite, though, and Freddie thanked me for "looking out for him" all year. He was very sweet. I got a little teary-eyed.

I didn't hear from Lucy. Did she forget?

Oh, well, these birthdays are starting to get overrated.

My last Kennedy Girl assignment was today, Saturday, at the New York Coliseum at Columbus Circle. Kennedy held a rally there, and it was also his last big event in the city before the election on Tuesday. Nixon had a rally in the same location on Wednesday, but I didn't go. I was too busy playing my new Elvis record, "Are You Lonesome Tonight?" over and over. I had to stop when Freddie threatened to slit his wrists if he heard it one more time, ha ha.

Betty, Louise, and the rest of the Girls were all present today, and we sang "High Hopes," "Marching Down to Washington," and "Happy Days Are Here Again," just like we always do. The rally was very crowded. I heard over a million people attended the senator's rally in Chicago yesterday. There may very well have been that many supporters at the Coliseum today.

Kennedy thanked each girl personally for our help. Once again, he called me "Miss Cooper." I'm amazed that he can remember my name. I wished him luck and I told him I know he will win.

"Do I have a guardian angel watching over me?" he asked with a twinkle in his eye.

"More than you know," I answered.

He shook my hand and went on to the next girl. *Sigh*.

I will miss being a Kennedy Girl. Luckily, we get to keep our uniforms. Betty joked that they'll be worth money someday.

One thing bothers me about today, though. Billy was supposed to be there and he wasn't. He and Lily had important volunteer jobs. I asked Lily where he was, and she averted her eyes and said, "He sick." I asked, "Is he okay?" and she wouldn't answer. In fact, she looked like she might cry! That's when I knew she wasn't telling me the truth. Something was very wrong.

I decided to pay a visit to Chinatown tomorrow.

NOVEMBER 6, 1960

Tonight I took the chance of dressing as the Stiletto and venturing back into dangerous waters. It had been a while since I'd shown my mask in Chinatown, and I didn't know what to expect. I knew where Billy and his mother lived on Mott Street and unfortunately, that was in Flying Dragons and Hip Sing Tong territory. Hopefully I could get in and out as quickly as possible without attracting much attention.

I waited until 10:00, after businesses and restaurants were closed and less people populated the streets. The sidewalks were never completely empty, though. I'm sure I was seen by someone as I darted from one shadow to the next and made my way from Canal to Mott. The building where Billy lived seemed to be in more disrepair, and scaffolding now stood in front of it. That actually made my job easier; I didn't have to bother with the fire escape and it concealed my presence outside their window. I climbed to the second-floor platform and peered inside.

It appeared to be a studio apartment—one room—that contained the bedroom, kitchen, and living area all in one space. I saw one bed and what I thought was an army cot. Billy lay in that one, and, Lord, his face was bruised and swollen. He had been badly beaten. His mother sat in a chair beside him with a book in her hands.

Even though she disliked me, I tapped on the window. The woman looked up and made an angry face. She stood, jabbered at me in Chinese, and gestured for me to go away. I put my hands together in prayer fashion and mouthed "Please, let me in," but she would have none of it. Then Billy opened his eyes, saw me, and said something to his mother. She argued with him for a moment, but apparently he won out. She came over and opened the window. I slipped inside.

"Thank you," I said to her, and then I knelt by Billy's cot. Only then did I see bloody bandages around his torso. "Billy, what happened?"

Dear diary, he could barely talk and was in a tremendous amount of pain. From the way he was breathing, I guessed he had some broken ribs and maybe even a punctured lung, which could be quite serious.

Even so, he looked at me and smiled. "I'm glad . . . to see you."

"Billy," I repeated. "What happened? Who did this to you?"

"Flying Dragons. Who else?"

"What happened?"

He spoke slowly with great effort. "We owe them ten thousand dollars. They wanted me to join instead. I refused. How could I join the gang that killed my father? I stood up to them and they…they …"

I shushed him and examined his injuries. He had a *knife wound* in his chest, and his mother had tried to patch it up with a bunch of rags. His face was battered and he couldn't move his right arm. When I touched it he winced, indicating it was broken.

"My God, Billy, you need to be in the hospital!"

He shook his head. "We don't have moneyfor hospital."

"*I'll* give you money. They should treat you anyway, silly. They're not going to turn you away." I looked around the room. "Do you have a phone?"

Again, he shook his head.

"I'm going outside to call an ambulance." I dug into my back-pack and pulled out all the money I had on me—$35. But there was plenty more at home. I thrust it into his mother's hands. "For hospi-tal," I told her, but she looked at it as if it was gold. I turned back to Billy and said, "I'll bring back more money tomorrow night. Tell your mother to expect me around this same time. What's the nearest hospital?"

Billy was fading fast. "Beekman Downtown." he managed to murmur before passing out.

I left, found a pay phone on the corner, and called for the ambu-lance. I hid in the shadows and waited until it arrived, and then watched as the medics brought Billy down on a stretcher. I'm afraid I shed a few tears as they drove away.

Then I went home.

NOVEMBER 7, 1960

Beekman Downtown Hospital is located near City Hall. After work at the gym, I took the bus in my street clothes to check on Billy. When I asked to see him, the dumb nurse asked, "Are you a relative? Oh, of course you're not." I explained I was a friend, but she wouldn't let me in the room. All she could tell me was that he was stable, whatever that meant. However, as I was leaving, I saw Lily in the hallway and managed to catch her.

"Oh, hi, Judy. You here to see Billy?"

"They won't let me. How is he?"

"I can take you. They let me. But he asleep now. His mother here, too. She no like visitors."

"I understand. Tell me, do you know what his injuries are?"

She explained in her broken English that Billy had been stabbed, he had two broken ribs, a slightly punctured lung, a broken right arm, and numerous contusions on his face and body. The Flying Dragons had taken him close to death but purposefully left him alive so he would always remember what they perceived to be a snub.

That made me hate the Tongs more than ever.

Tonight at the appointed time, as the Stiletto, I brought Billy's mother $5000 of the money from Mitch's suitcase. This time she seemed eager to see me, ready for the handout. I didn't mind. I'm sure she'd never seen that much money at once in her entire life. I told her, "For Billy. For Billy." She nodded as if she understood, but then she immediately sat and started counting the bills. I didn't wait to be asked to have a cup of tea, so I left the way I came in—through the window.

Gosh, tomorrow's Election Day. All that hard work I did for Senator Kennedy is going to pay off.

At least I hope so!

November 9, 1960

It's three in the morning, dear diary, and I just got home from a victory celebration at HQ! JOHN F. KENNEDY IS THE NEXT PRESIDENT OF THE UNITED STATES! Holy cow, it was so *close!* I don't think an Alfred Hitchcock movie would ever be as suspenseful as tonight was. Kennedy and Nixon were neck and neck throughout the day, and the senator eventually won by just a hair. I was surprised it was so close. That just shows how blinded I was by working on Kennedy's campaign. I knew Nixon had a lot of supporters in the country, but I didn't think he'd actually give Kennedy such a run for his money. Wow.

Well, we threw a party at HQ. We had champagne. A *lot* of champagne. Everyone was there—Mr. Dudley and Mr. Patton and Chip and Betty and Louise and Karen and Mrs. Bernstein and a lot of my other friends and the rest of the Kennedy Girls. Of course, Billy wasn't there, and neither was Lily. A few people mentioned Mitch and Alice, but they remained a mystery to the rest of the team. There had been no more in the papers about them, nor about Michael and Ivan. That chapter of 1960 was closed.

I was very, very happy, but on the way home in the cab—it was so late that I splurged, and besides, I can afford it now—I did get a little sad. I couldn't help thinking about how the year started with someone I care about in the hospital—Freddie—and now it looks like 1960 will end with another person I care about in the hospital.

I'm not much for prayer, but I did say one tonight for Billy.

41
Judy's Diary
1960

The first thing I did tonight was pack a suitcase.

Then I went out as the Stiletto, with the suitcase, around 9:30. It was nippy and windy, so not many people were on the streets in Chinatown. The restaurants were shutting down and shop proprietors were locking up for the night. At my destination, I hoped to find the friendly Chinese convenience store owner who could speak English. I knew he'd still be open.

Joe was there, all right, and he sure didn't grin at the Stiletto like he smiled at Judy Cooper! I must have scared him something awful. He held up his hands and almost started to cry; he thought I was going to rob him.

"No, no, Joe, Joe, I'm a friend. Calm down," I kept saying over his protests. Finally it hit him that I was calling him by name.

"Joe?" he asked.

"Yes, *Joe*. How are you doing?" I held out my hand and waited. Joe couldn't believe what was happening. He cautiously reached out, and I vigorously shook his hand. "I'm happy to meet you, I hear you have a great store here."

That made him grin.

"Oh, thank you very much! Thank you very much!"

I bought a bottle of Coke, opened it, drank it right there in the store, and chatted with Joe. Customers came in and out, gasped and stared, but went about their business. Joe took their money and then eagerly rejoined the conversation. Finally, when we were alone and best of buddies, I said, "Say, Joe, do you know much about the Tongs?"

That spooked him a bit. He furiously shook his head. "No, no, don't know Tongs, no, no."

But I knew he was lying. It was as plain as his cute smile. I liked Joe. I have no idea how old he is, but he must be at least fifty.

"Oh, come on, Joe, I was told you have good information." I slipped him a $20 bill. "I need to know where I can find the Flying Dragons."

Oh, my gosh, his eyes grew really big when I said that. He held the twenty in his hands and stared at it as if he was trying to decide if the money was worth the risk of getting his throat cut by the Tong. It didn't take long. Joe pocketed the bill, leaned over the counter, and then spoke very softly. I didn't think Joe was *capable* of speaking softly, but he did. He told me of a bar on Pell Street that Tommy Cheng and his "friends" frequented. Their headquarters was probably a back room or adjoining space. That made sense to me, since I knew the Dragons were allied with the Hip Sing Tong, whose building and offices were on the same street in plain sight.

"Thank you, Joe." I pinched his cheek with my gloved hand, and then left the store.

So with purpose I sprinted down Mott to Pell. There were fewer people out, but I still got double-takes and stares and pointing fingers. The word would travel fast. The Black Stiletto was back in Chinatown. This time, though, I reached the Flying Dragons before the news did.

The bar in question wasn't marked. It was just a door with a number and a bunch of Chinese writing on it. It was the ground floor of a brick building that had seen better days, and there was a window, through which I could see the neon lettering of beer brands and more Chinese characters.

Butterflies flittered in my stomach. I knew I was taking a big risk. I could get hurt bad, or worse. I could hear Freddie yelling at me, saying I was crazy. I was walking into the lion's den wearing a big sign that said "Fresh Meat," ha ha. Fine, it *was* something truly dangerous. But something had to be done, dear diary. I was tired of those punks terrorizing my friends, and I was tired of feeling intimidated in Chinatown.

I walked into the bar. It wasn't a large place; in fact, it was downright intimate. The joint was lit only by colored lights, neon and otherwise. All conversation stopped. I expected to hear weird Chinese music over the radio, but it was plain American rock 'n' roll. Chubby Checker screamed about doing "The Twist." I figured that was what was about to happen.

Every face turned toward me. Chinese. Young and male. Cigarettes or toothpicks hanging out of their mouths. Cold hatred emanating from their eyes. No one moved. They were frozen in position—bent over a pool table, leaning against the bar, or sitting in booths with rotting, torn vinyl.

"I want to see Tommy Cheng," I announced. "Business."

Silence. Several of them glanced back and forth at each other.

My vision zeroed in on one guy I knew—my old friend Pock Face. He was in one of the booths, and I swear he was snarling at me.

"Is someone going to answer me? Where can I find Tommy Cheng?"

A fellow in Pock Face's booth, sitting with his back to me, slowly stood and turned. He was in his twenties, had an Elvis-style haircut, and a scar above his left eye. The suit he wore was perhaps a size too large, but he definitely managed to project that superiority thing all gangsters seem to have, no matter what their race or culture might be.

"I'm Tommy Cheng," he said in English with little accent. Before I could speak again, he pulled a switchblade and flicked it open, and that was the cue for every Tong member in the joint to draw a weapon. The bar's colored lights reflected off their shiny metal surfaces, and I found myself staring at a dozen handguns, knives, and meat cleavers.

I dropped the suitcase and held my hands out to show I wasn't armed. "Whoa, fellas, hold on. I'm here to negotiate something. I want to talk business." I addressed Cheng and said, "How does $10,000 sound to you?"

They all remained silent.

"Doesn't anyone speak English? Mr. Cheng? Are you the leader of the Flying Dragons or not?"

Cheng took two steps forward and made a big show of displaying his switchblade again, and then with a flourish he closed it and put it in his pocket. The others didn't follow his lead, though.

"What do you want?" he asked.

I nodded at Pock Face. "I want to challenge him to a tournament fight. Right here. Right now." Pock Face seemed to like that idea. He licked his lips and revealed rotten teeth.

"Why?" Cheng asked.

"He and I have unfinished business. Here's the deal. If he wins, I give you $10,000 in cash and the Lee family's debt is paid off. You and your Tong will no longer bother Mrs. Lee or her son. If I win, the same terms apply to the Lee family, but you don't get the money."

Cheng looked at Pock Face and they both started to laugh. "Are you serious?" the leader asked me.

"Dead serious. But here are the rules—we do it like a tournament. Anything goes, but no one dies. We're not fighting to the death."

Cheng's eyes went to the suitcase on the floor. "What's in the bag?"

"The money, of course. May I show you?"

He nodded. I picked up the suitcase and placed it on a table. When I opened it to reveal stacks of bills, every hoodlum in the joint murmured approval. I shut the bag and placed it on the bar. "I'll leave it right here. If I win, I take it with me. If I lose, you keep it. Are we agreed?"

"Why do you care about the Lee family?" Cheng asked. "This is not your business, Black Stiletto. This is not your neighborhood. They are not your people."

"They are my friends, and that's all you need to know," I said. "What do you say?" I jerked my head at Pock Face. "Unless he's too scared to fight me."

My nemesis barked Chinese at Cheng. They exchanged more words and then Cheng stepped closer. "Very well," he said.

I held out my hand. "You agree to stop harassing the Lees, no matter who the victor is? You'll leave them alone?"

"Yes." We shook hands.

"All right then. Let's have ourselves a fight."

Everyone in the bar got up and moved out of the way. The darned pool table took up much of the space, but there was approximately a six-foot-by-eight-foot area in front of the bar that was just a little smaller than what they used for bouts in the *wushu* tournaments. It would do.

We didn't remove our shoes. The stiletto was still sheathed on my leg. No one said weapons weren't allowed, but I wasn't going to draw the knife unless I had to. Pock Face entered the "ring" empty-handed, but I didn't put it past him to have a concealed weapon. I knew from experience he carried a switchblade and a gun. Even though we agreed no one would die, I'd have been stupid to assume he would abide by the rule.

Tommy Cheng appropriated the role of judge, of course. He designated underlings to serve as time and scorekeepers. The bartender provided the timekeeper with a metal pan to bang at the beginning and end of a round. The rest of the Tong circled the space. Someone drew boundaries of the competition area on the wooden floor with a piece of pool chalk. There wasn't much room to maneuver. The fight would be up close and very personal.

Pock Face entered the ring and we performed the palm-to-fist salute to Cheng and each other, followed by a bow. Then the timekeeper slapped the pan and the first round began.

Pock Face wasted no time. He advanced toward me with speed and launched into a barrage of Praying Mantis slaps and punches. For the first half minute, all I could do was block blows, but the killer broke through several times and hit me. He was racking up points like crazy. Cheng indicated to the scorekeeper each time Pock Face won a point.

I'm sure the gang thought I was losing. They cheered for Pock Face and laughed at me. As the round progressed, my opponent pushed me farther back toward the boundary and then delivered a crushing blow to my chin that caused me to step outside the ring. Two points for Pock Face. He got cocky then, and made a face of triumph at his friends—and that's when I leaped back in and delivered a *yoko-geri karate* side kick and knocked the killer down. He rolled out of the ring, so that was four points for me. Pock Face got to his feet quickly, and we were at it again. This time, though, it was *me* who was the dominant force. I clobbered him with an onslaught of *karate*, American boxing, and my invented *wushu* tactics that under normal circumstances wouldn't have been allowed in a real tournament. But this was no ordinary competition. The maneuvers took my opponent by surprise, like they did the last time we met, and he was unable to block most of my attacks.

The timekeeper slapped the pan. The two minutes had flown by. I went back to my side of the ring and took a few deep breaths. Pock Face did the same, but someone handed him a glass of water. No one was that kind to me.

The second round started and my opponent attempted to gain the upper hand, but I wouldn't let him. My unusual fighting methods fooled him again as I slammed him with a *mawashi-geri* roundhouse kick followed by my modified *wushu* attacks. For a moment he attempted to block me, wavering on his feet, as I pummeled him with slaps and punches. I sensed that he would fall over if I simply *blew* at him; but to make sure, I stepped back and let him have a hard *mae-geri* front kick. Pock Face went down, stunned. But the round wasn't over yet. The scorekeeper counted in Chinese while my opponent attempted to get up. He got to his knees and then to his feet, but he was definitely waning. Pock Face indicated he was ready to continue the fight and beckoned me forward. I obliged him and rushed at the guy, but he was ready with a kick I didn't expect. His shoe crashed into my jaw, knocking me sideways and out of the ring.

Round two ended, but I was ahead. I had to be, if Cheng was scoring us honestly. We each had a brief rest, and then the final bout started.

As we approached each other, I detected a glint in Pock Face's eyes that wasn't there before. The old instincts told me he had something up his sleeve, so I immediately jumped backward—just as his right hand swung an open switchblade in an arc right where my belly had been a second before. He continued to lunge with the knife until I stepped out of the ring. I thought he'd stop and move back, but he kept coming. The match was obviously no longer a tournament competition with rules. Pock Face was playing for keeps.

The gang members parted when he pursued me out of the circle, and I found myself backed up against the pool table. My opponent bolted toward me, the knife a deadly spearhead. Resting my elbows and forearms on the edge of the pool table, I lifted my lower body and kicked out with both legs. I struck Pock Face's blade hand, but his grip remained firm. My follow-through was a backward somersault; I landed on my feet on top of the table. Several pool balls were scattered over the playing area, so I kicked one at my attacker. He dodged it and kept coming, slashing the air in front of him in a wild attempt to cut me.

Fine. Two could play with knives.

I drew the stiletto, jumped off the table, and changed the odds. It had been some time since I'd been in an honest-to-gosh knife fight, so I had to recall the tricks and strategies Fiorello had taught me.

For a moment I thought the other Tong members would join in the fray and I'd have to battle them all, but they respectfully kept their distance. This was Pock Face's war, and they were going to let him prove his mettle.

The table was between us, so I let him come around for a thrust. He was all too eager, so I kicked him in the face with as much strength as I could muster. Pock Face stepped back. His expression told me he wasn't quite sure what had hit him. I didn't stop there. Moving forward, I jabbed his knife arm with the stiletto. The blade punctured his sleeve and drew blood. He shrieked, but managed to hold on to the weapon. I lunged at him in order to hit him with my left fist, but he recovered from my previous kick and sliced my upper arm. The blade cut through the leather and I felt it break skin. It smarted like the dickens, but he was unable to halt my momentum. My fist didn't hit its target, but my entire body banged into his and we both fell to the floor. My first instinct was to put all my effort into disarming him, so I spear handed his forearm with the same strong blow I used to break 2 by 4s in Soichiro's studio. Pock Face yelped and dropped the knife. I probably shattered the bone.

He was on his back and I stood over him. I shoved my boot into his chest and held him down, and then I stuck the point of my stiletto under his chin.

"Do you yield?" I growled.

My opponent just stared at me with hate. He spit at me, and his glob of phlegm hit my mask and mouth. Yuck. Well, that really angered me. The guy cheated, he didn't play by the rules, and he was a murderer. He'd tried to kill me and he left Billy without a father. He was one bad man.

So I sliced off his ear.

He screamed bloody murder and rolled over to protect himself, but he still bled all over the floor. I got up and prepared to defend myself against the other Tongs. Tommy Cheng stood nearby with a heavy frown on his face, but he held up a hand to prevent anyone from attacking me.

"You said no one dies," the leader said.

"Tell that to *him*. He tried to kill me, you saw it. He deserves to die. He killed Mr. Lee and his brother." I tossed the bloody ear on the floor in front of Cheng. "But that's the only penance I'll take from him."

I wiped the edge of my stiletto on the pool table felt and sheathed it. I then walked over to the suitcase full of money and picked it up. I looked at Cheng. "I'd say I won, right?"

The punk hesitated. I stared him down until he finally nodded.

"And you'll leave the Lees alone? The mother and her son? Their debt is canceled?"

Once again, Cheng nodded.

"If you break that promise, I'll be back for *you*."

I left the bar and went home. The cut on my arm was superficial and didn't need stitches. Freddie was already asleep, thank goodness, so I cleaned the wound and bandaged myself.

Writing down this stuff sure acts as some kind of catharsis for me. When I started the diary entry, I felt anxious and my heart was pounding. Now I'm more relaxed. And I'm alive.

I'm going to have a glass of wine, a shower, and then go to bed.

42
Martin
The Present

It's ten days before Christmas and Gina is home from New York. She's staying with Carol, of course. It's good that Gina is there to help with the wedding, which will take place tonight at Ross's house in Lincolnshire. He has a pretty big place because he's a rich lawyer and all, so Carol will sell her house and move in with him.

Mom is still in the hospital, but the doctors think she'll be able to go back to Woodlands before Christmas. I was proud of Gina. She cheered up Mom immensely. Mom really brightened up when she saw her granddaughter. They actually had a conversation that made sense. It was a little one-sided with Gina doing all the talking, but Mom had appropriate responses and seemed genuinely interested in what Gina had to say. Gina told her about school and classes and teachers and boys. Apparently she had a date recently with a guy who also goes to Juilliard. I found that encouraging, not so much that I want Gina to get involved in a serious relationship, but rather I think it's good for her to get out socially. She's just now starting to show signs of normalcy since all the trouble. One interesting part of their talk had to do with Gina's martial arts lessons. She told my mom about them, that she was taking *krav maga* classes and learning how to defend herself. *Krav maga* is an Israeli fighting system that can be pretty rough from what I know. Gina was trying to explain what it was to Mom, so she asked, "Do you know what *karate* is?" and my Mom actually answered, "Yes, I do." Then Mom formed her hand spearlike and made a chopping gesture in the air! Gina laughed and said, "That's right, Grandma! You could be a black belt!" And then my mom said very seriously, "I have a black belt." Gina was either humoring her or she thought Mom might have been talking about regular clothing, so my daughter laughed and said, "You do, Grandma? That's pretty cool."

I thought it best to change the subject, so I prompted Gina to talk about her mother's wedding plans. When she could comprehend who *I* was, Mom had no problem remembering that Carol and I were divorced since it happened long before she got sick. I think, though, she's picked up on the fact that Maggie and I are an item. Whenever we're together in the hospital room, Mom perks up and seems to enjoy our company more when we're together than if I'm alone.

Gina and Maggie took to each other well. I was afraid Maggie had preconceived notions that Gina was some kind of problem child since she'd been arrested. But Maggie understood the trauma Gina had gone through and excused her on all counts. Gina later told me that I'd picked a "winner."

Maggie and I had an awkward reconciliation after my idiotic behavior the other night. I realized that the reason I freaked out after seeing that TV story on my mom was because I desperately wanted to tell Maggie about the Black Stiletto. I had to leave the house because I was afraid I'd blurt it out. I called my doc the next day to say I didn't feel the antidepressants were working. He said to give it a little more time, a couple of weeks, and then he'd reevaluate everything and either increase the dosage or change the medication. He said that finding the right "cocktail" can sometimes take months, mainly because you don't know if something works until you've been taking it for four or five weeks. Great.

If it wasn't for that elephant in the room, Maggie and I would have a perfect relationship. In all other respects we get along great. She's lost that all-too-serious bedside manner when she's around me, except when she's acting professionally in her job at Woodlands. We enjoy each other's company, and we make each other laugh. The sex is good, too, and that can be *oh* so important in keeping a relationship going.

She's going with me to Carol's wedding. Having a gorgeous woman like her at my side will keep me from being a basket case.

I'd never been inside Ross's house, but it could have been the Playboy Mansion—it was so huge. He had an expansive lawn in the back, but the cold weather necessitated the wedding being held indoors in a grand foyer. The reception took over the dining room, the living room, and a music room that held a grand piano. There were approximately sixty people in attendance. I knew maybe a third of them because once upon a time they were friends that Carol and I had. I didn't stay in touch with them much, although I'd run into the guys every now and then. Carol obviously remained closer. Most of the people were Ross's friends and family. Carol's older brother Gary—he's my age—was here from California. I hadn't seen him in years. He was friendly, but I don't think he ever liked me anyway.

It was very nice having Maggie there. I would have felt more out of place and like "the first guy the bride dumped" without her. She looked great, too. I told her she could be a fashion model instead of a doctor and she just laughed and punched my arm. I think the people who knew me were impressed. Ross certainly was. I thought he was going to call off the wedding and propose to Maggie instead. Well, not really. He did seem taken with her, though, and he was very cordial to me. What can I say? He's a successful and handsome guy, and I can't help but feel a little envious—"jealous" is the wrong word—but I'm happy for Carol, really I am, and I hope it works out better for her than our marriage did.

Gina looked beautiful. If you ask me, she was the belle of the ball. She was also very warm and friendly, talking to everyone and being charming as hell. You'd never think this was a girl who'd been assaulted in a New York park three months earlier. The anger I'd seen when I was there was gone. Carol noticed it, too, and said something about it to me.

"Gina's doing well, don't you think?" she asked.

"Seems to be. How is she at the house?"

"Fine. She's being lazy, which is understandable since she's on Christmas break. But she seems happy."

That was good to know.

"I think that martial arts class she's taking is good therapy for her," Carol said. "It helps her work out a lot of issues."

Yeah, just like my mother did.

Maggie and I sat with Gina when we noshed on wedding cake and had champagne. Gina's not old enough to drink alcohol, but I didn't mind if she had a little bubbly on this occasion.

"Oh, guess what," she said.

"What."

"You know that guy Gilbert Trejano? The one who had me arrested?"

"Uh, yeah?"

"*He* was arrested! For *rape* and *murder*!"

"What?"

"Yeah, it happened just before I came home. Boy, do I feel vindicated. I knew I was right all along."

That news hit me in the chest. I didn't know what to say at first. Maggie asked, "You mean he was the one who attacked you?"

"*I* believe he was, but the police aren't saying. He was caught for another crime."

"How did they catch him?" I asked.

Gina rolled her eyes. "Well, *they* didn't catch him exactly. Someone assaulted *him* in his apartment and made him give up evidence that was hidden there. It was like a confession. The police got an anonymous tip and found him there, all tied up, with the proof that he'd killed a girl on the Upper West Side."

My heart started pounding. Her story was *too* familiar.

"Who did this to him?" I asked.

Gina shrugged. "I don't know. I'm gonna have a tiny bit more champagne, okay, Dad?"

"Just a little."

She got up and went to the bar. Was she avoiding my question? *Was she more like her grandmother than I wanted her to be?*

I realized I was jumping to conclusions and had no reason to suspect that Gina—aw, hell I can't even say it. It couldn't be what happened. Was that why she was in such a better mood than she'd been in New York? Was this the reason the anger had dissipated?

"Martin, what's wrong?" Maggie asked.

I did my best to push away the anxiety attack by changing the subject. "Oh, nothing. I just suddenly feel like taking you home and ravaging you."

She laughed. "Weddings do that to you, too?"

I raised my eyebrows. "Oh, is that what's going on here? Are you telling me weddings make you horny?"

"Martin!" she whispered. "Stop it," she said, but I knew she enjoyed the flirtation. Nevertheless, I was dying inside and I was determined not to let Maggie see it. I was afraid I'd break out in a sweat, like I've done before.

"No, I'm not stopping it," I said. "Let's get out of here and go pretend we're rabbits."

So we made our excuses, said our goodbyes, wished the bride and groom well, and went to Maggie's place. But on the way there, the back of my mind was full of images of Gina running across New York City roofs in my mother's costume.

43
Judy's Diary
1960

DECEMBER 14, 1960

Gosh, it's been a month since I last wrote in the diary.

The big news is that today Billy and his mom moved into their new apartment in Chinatown, this time out of Flying Dragons and Hip Sing Tong turf. Actually, it's technically not in Chinatown, just a little north and east of Little Italy on Elizabeth Street near Grand. But I'll get to that in a moment; let me catch you up, dear diary.

Thanksgiving was a fun day, well, until something happened. Freddie and I hosted a big dinner at the gym and invited all the regulars. Lucy and Peter also came, and I invited some of my friends from Kennedy HQ, who stayed in the city for the holiday. Louise showed up, but Betty went to see her folks. Not surprisingly, a lot of the guys flirted with Louise, and she ate it up. Then it happened. Jimmy arrived and shocked us all by bringing his *wife*! No one knew he'd gotten married. She's a pretty Negro girl, but very shy. Her name is Violet.

I was shocked.

When I was at the buffet table helping myself to seconds, Jimmy happened to be piling turkey and green beans on his plate, too. I asked him, "So when did y'all get married?" He sheepishly replied, "Two years ago."

I nearly choked. "*Two years?* You mean you've been *married* all this time?"

He nodded. "I'm sorry, Judy."

Gawd, I would never have done what I did with him in the locker room that day if I'd known he was married. "Why didn't you *tell* me?" I said through gritted teeth.

"I don't know...I just...I didn't get the chance...I..." The poor guy stumbled all over his answer.

"What, you just wanted to do it with a white girl, is that it?"

"No! That's not it. I wouldn't have done—I didn't—oh, Judy, I was so confused. That was during a time when Violet and I, we was havin' problems. I was sleepin' on the couch. I was all messed up. That's why havin' the extra job at the gym was so good for me."

That didn't make me feel any better. No wonder he wouldn't go near me at Lucy's wedding. I felt like a fallen woman, a bad girl, an S-L-U-T, and I didn't like it one bit. I wouldn't talk to him the rest of the dinner and for several days after that. Needless to say, I had my fill of wine for dinner. I don't remember going to bed that night, but that's where I woke up the next morning! Sheesh.

On the Saturday after Thanksgiving, I dressed as the Stiletto and went out. It wasn't an eventful evening, although I chased away some punk teenagers from Washington Square Park. They were drunk and disorderly and making all kinds of racket. I should've let the cops handle them, but I felt like doing *something*. Aside from that, I didn't find any crimes in progress. I stayed out of Chinatown.

The rest of the time I've just been working at the gym. Last Sunday night Freddie and I watched *The Wizard of Oz* on TV. I loved it so much last year that I had to see it again. Freddie had seen it in the movie theaters a long time ago, but he still enjoyed it. "I bet they start showing it on TV every Christmas," he said. Maybe they will, and I'll be sitting in front of the set each time they do!

Now, back to Billy.

He got out of the hospital just after Thanksgiving. As the Stiletto, I went to see him and his mother at the old apartment. I gave them enough of Mitch Perez's money to start again—and kept some of it for myself, too! The Lees were able to move to a more up-scale apartment, although Billy's Mom refused to stray too far from Chinatown. Moving day was yesterday, and tonight I went over to see them.

Mrs. Lee had always treated me like the devil incarnate, but now I was her new best friend. Even though she didn't speak English, she smiled broadly and chattered on and on in Chinese. She wouldn't stop serving me tea. She insisted that I eat a late dinner with them— it was 11:00 at night—but I politely declined.

Billy looked great. There were some scars and bruising, and he still had a cast on his arm. He also has to wear a tight bandage around his chest, underneath his shirt. But hopefully by New Year's it'll be gone.

When we were alone, he asked me why I did what I did. "You needed some help," I answered. "And you're a friend. I help my friends."

"My mother and I are very grateful. You have—you have changed our lives."

"I hope it's for the better, Billy. I was happy to do it."

"I have some other good news."

"What's that?"

"Lily and I will be married as soon as we're out of high school."

That took me by surprise but I managed to say, "That's wonderful!" Frankly, I thought they were too young to get married, but what do I know? That's when most people get married. At any rate, they still had a few years.

"And we're going to open a new restaurant. Lily's brother is a chef. There's enough money left over from what you gave us that we can rent a space and start again. My mother will manage it at first until I graduate. Then I'll take over. It'll be a family business again."

For me it didn't seem like much of a life, growing up in a small corner of Manhattan, marrying, and staying in the same spot until it's all over. Would he ever travel? Would he try to go to college?

"Is that what you want, Billy?" I asked.

He didn't answer at first, but teasingly he put his fingers to his chin and looked skyward, as if contemplating the question. "Hmmm," he said. Then, abruptly, he nodded at me and said, "Yes." He meant it, too.

"Then that's great news, Billy. I'm so happy for you."

I didn't want to stay long. When my teacup was empty, I made my excuses to leave. Mrs. Lee fussed over me, but I simply stepped out the window onto the fire escape to avoid her following me farther. Billy said, "You could use the stairs, you know."

I laughed and replied, "Thanks, but I'm used to this. Goodbye, Billy, and good luck."

He stood on the fire escape platform and watched me descend to the street and then head east. I don't think I'll see him again. I've interfered in his life too much already. And, to tell the truth, I'm still not very comfortable in Chinatown. It truly is a different world. I have to admit it—the criminal element is too big for the Black Stiletto. The mafia and the Harlem gangsters were walks in the park compared to the Tongs. The Chinese gangs are like bees—they're a swarm that smothers you and stings you to death. There's also that language and cultural barrier that makes it particularly difficult for me to comprehend. I don't think I'd ever make a dent in what happens in Chinatown. I may have kicked Pock Face's posterior, but he still got away with murder. The only way I can live with that is by not going back there.

Except to eat.

44
Martin
The Present

It's Christmas Eve.

Mom moved back to Woodlands today. I followed the ambulance that took her from the hospital to Riverwoods. She's doing fine. The docs have her on some new medications and want her to try and get a little more exercise—which for her means more walks through the nursing home. She's talking more. Some days she seems confused about everything, but other times she's more lucid than ever. The doctors said I'd notice a change for the worse in the Alzheimer's symptoms, but from what I've seen so far that's not the case. I think the docs are as clueless as anyone. There's no rhyme or reason to the disease.

When she got to Woodlands, she didn't remember that it was her "home." She must have thought she was going back to our house in Arlington Heights. However, once she was in her old room for about an hour, it was as if she'd never left. The framed photographs were familiar, and she recognized the nurses and staff as people who cared about her.

Gina had been with Mom at the hospital prior to the discharge. Seeing her granddaughter so much recently put Mom in a very positive mood; the hospital staff gave her surprisingly good marks as a cooperative and pleasant patient! My daughter didn't accompany us to Riverwoods. She had Christmas Eve plans with some old high school friends. I'll get together with her tomorrow after she spends the morning with Carol and Ross. I plan to spend the night at Maggie's, and we'll have Christmas morning together. I haven't had a Christmas morning with a woman in, well, a long time. What a concept!

I stayed with Mom through dinner. Her spirits were good, especially when I gave her a gift. Her eyes brightened like a schoolkid's and she asked, "For me?" I said, "Sure it's for you, you're my mom and it's Christmas Eve!" And then she surprised me by saying, "I guess I've been a good girl, then." We both laughed, and I think that's the first time in months, maybe years, that we've shared a joke. It also meant she comprehended the gift-giving ritual.

The present was a black pearl necklace. Mom said, "This is beautiful!" as she held it up to examine it. I explained what it was and she let me fasten it around her neck. She stood and looked in the mirror. I do believe she liked it very much. And then she hugged me and said, "Thank you, Martin."

Wow. She called me Martin. I don't think she'd called me Martin since she started living at the nursing home. I guess today was just one of those good days.

The staff helped her get ready for bed around 7:30, and I sat with her until she fell asleep at 8:00. She looked so peaceful lying there, so I took her hand and held it. I don't know why, but my heart became very heavy and I felt like crying. After all I'd gone through since last spring when I learned Mom's secret, I think I've finally come to the conclusion that there's something I have to do before I can vanquish my demons and start living my life with some sense of normalcy again. I made my decision last night, but—and this is the crazy part—I have to run it by my mother first.

"Mom," I said softly. She didn't open her eyes, so I continued. "You know I love you, right? I do, I really do. I think you're an incredible woman, and what you did—back then—was extraordinary. But I have to say, Mom, this Black Stiletto stuff is killing me. It's eating away at my soul. It's too big a secret for me to keep to myself. I have to share the load. It's why I've been sick lately."

I paused, trying to keep myself from breaking up.

"Mom, I've been reading the diaries. I'm nearly finished with the third one. I've learned so much about you, but there are so many unanswered questions. I suppose all will be revealed as I continue to read, but I gotta tell you, I'm afraid to keep going. Some of the truths I desperately need to discover are frightening to me. Like, who is my father? Is that something I'm going to learn by the time I'm done?"

I couldn't help getting a little choked up. After some deep breaths I managed not to start sobbing like a baby.

"Anyway, I hope you understand that I promise I'll do my best to keep your secret safe, but I just can't do it alone anymore."

Then I realized Mom was awake and could hear me. A single tear rolled down her cheek.

"Mom?"

She opened her eyes and looked me. There was a deep sadness in them, and that made me start to cry, too.

"Did you hear what I was saying?"

Judy Talbot didn't answer, but she did manage to smile at me. Then she squeezed my hand.

"You look pale. What's wrong?"

I walked in to Maggie's place and put my arms around her. Sighing, I said, "It's just Mom. You know. It's hard."

"I know, Martin. Did she get settled back in okay?"

"Yeah. It took an hour or so, but then she was fine. She loved her gift. And, get this, she called me 'Martin.'"

"Wow! That's wonderful."

"Yeah. Made me feel good. And sad, too. You know." Maggie led me into the living room and I smelled the turkey roasting. "I'm not too late, am I?"

"Nope. We tend to eat like Europeans anyway, so I timed it perfectly. I hope you're hungry."

I wasn't. I had no appetite. "You bet," I answered.

"Great, you can help me in the kitchen," she said as she headed that direction, but I don't think I heard her really. I stood in the living room, staring at the lights on the Christmas tree and suddenly feeling distressed and helpless.

"Martin?"

When I didn't answer, she came back in to face me. I must have had tears in my eyes. Maggie held me at arm's length and shook her head. "Oh, Martin. It's happening again, isn't it?"

"I don't know."

"Martin, I didn't want to bring this up now, but it looks like I have to."

"What?"

She let go of me and moved away. "You're doing it again. Just what I've been talking about. You're hiding something again. You've . . . you've been hiding something all along. I know it, Martin. There's something in the past that you don't want me to know. It's been eating at me for weeks and today, especially, I've been feeling pretty anxious about it. Oh, damn it, I don't want to ruin our Christmas Eve." She turned her back to me and started to cry. My, there were a lot of tears being shed today.

I went to her and wrapped my arms around her waist, but she took my hands and held them close to her chest. The feel of her breasts underneath her bright red-and-green sweater went a long way toward arousing me, but I was too nervous and antsy to go there.

"Maggie, I'm glad you brought that up," I said. "I know it's been on your mind, and it's been on mine, too. There *is* something I've been hiding from you."

I felt her tense.

"Why don't we sit down?" I pulled her to the couch and we sat next to each other, holding hands. It was like one of those soap opera scenes in which a guilty husband says to his wife, "Darling, I have a confession to make—"

For a moment I didn't speak a word, though. I wasn't sure how to tell her.

"Well?" she asked.

"Maggie, what I'm about to tell you must never leave this room. I need you to promise me."

"Of course, Martin. Sweetheart, you can trust me."

"I *really* mean you can't tell anyone. This is, well, it's big. I'm about to drop a bombshell on you, and I want you to know I love you and I'm telling you this *because* I love you. I can't keep it to myself any longer."

She squeezed my hands. "Then tell me. I'm listening."

"All right, here goes." And then it struck me as funny. I started to laugh a little.

"What's so funny?"

"You. *You're* the one who's going to laugh and I'm just anticipating it."

"Come on, Martin, stop kidding around. I'm on pins and needles here."

"Okay. Listen. You've heard of the Black Stiletto, right?"

Her brow wrinkled and she blinked. "Huh?"

"The Black Stiletto? The costumed vigilante from the fifties and sixties? There was a movie about her, there've been comic books, you see images of her all the time, she's kind of a legend—"

"Yes, I know who she is, Martin. What does she have to do with—?" And then she froze. Maggie looked at me with the most incredulous expression I've ever seen. "You don't—wait—"

"I think you've got it," I said.

"No, I don't. Tell me. I have to hear it."

I sighed and finally said it aloud. "My Mom was the Black Stiletto."

I expected her to hit me and accuse me of making up a crazy story. Instead, she put a hand to her open mouth and stared at me wide-eyed.

I nodded. "It's the truth."

"Martin, my God, of course. It all makes sense now. Her scars. The gunshot wounds. Oh my God, Martin. Oh my *God!*"

"No one else knows. Well, there's an old FBI guy in New York who knows, but he's not telling. There could be others who might know, but I'm not aware of them. My mom has certainly kept it a closely guarded secret for fifty years. I mean to keep it that way while she's alive."

"How long have you known?"

"Just a few months." I explained how I acquired the diaries, her costume, and other stuff. "When the bank opens day after tomorrow, I'll take you there and show you what's in the safety deposit box. Hell, I'll let you read the diaries. They're fascinating."

A buzzer went off in the kitchen. "That's the turkey," she said.

"So you believe me?"

Maggie tilted her head, made a face, and then nodded. "Yeah. I do." She didn't move for a moment.

"Shouldn't we get the turkey?"

"Jesus, who can *eat* after hearing something like that?"

"I can. I'm starving." And I was now. The relief I felt was palpable. Telling Maggie about my mom made it the best Christmas in a long, long time.

45
Judy's Diary
1960

December 31, 1960

It's that time of year again, dear diary. Once again, Freddie and I are throwing the annual New Year's Eve party downstairs. It's become a routine to always make a run to my room for a few minutes to jot down some final thoughts on the past year before I get too drunk, ha ha. I can't stay long, so I'm going to make this quick. The usual crowd is here—Lucy and Peter, Clark, Louis, Corky, Paul, Wayne—plus Louise and Betty from HQ, along with their dates, and good old Chip who's here with his wisecracks. Jimmy came with Violet. I'm not as mad at him as I was. Even though he's a grown man, he's like a child when it comes to handling life. It's hard to stay mad at Jimmy because basically he's a really nice guy. When Violet was out of earshot, I asked him why he never brought her to other New Year's parties or ever mentioned her. He said she was too shy, especially around white people, but he's been trying to fix that. Like me, she's become interested in civil rights and is following Dr. King. That poor Dr. King sure has his share of troubles. In the midst of the presidential campaign a couple of months ago, he was arrested in Georgia and put in *jail* for a stupid traffic violation. Kennedy and his brother helped get him released. Anyway, Jimmy apologized to me once again, and I told him to forget it, even though it was really my fault. I'm the one who initiated it, and it didn't matter if he was married or not. "We'll just pretend it never happened," I said. And that's what I'm going to do. I hope he can manage that as well.

Lucy had some news—she and Peter are going to Los Angeles for a week in January or February. Peter has some business out there and she's tagging along for fun. She asked me if I wanted to join her! She said we could go to Disneyland together since Peter will be busy. Wow, I'd love to see Disneyland. I told her I needed to check with Freddie to get the time off, but I'm pretty sure it won't be a problem. California! Oh boy, that sounds like so much fun. Can you imagine the Black Stiletto socializing with Mickey Mouse and Donald Duck? Maybe I'd get discovered at Hollywood and Vine!

There's no question this year was an eventful one for me. I didn't have much in the way of romance, but maybe that stuff's overrated. My expeditions into the world of Chinatown were eye opening and scary. I didn't like the underbelly I found there, but I'm happy I was able to develop some new fighting skills and help a nice family. Billy is such a good kid and I'm glad I was part of his life for a little while. Working on the presidential campaign was wonderful. I loved being a Kennedy Girl. I learned a lot and made new friends, and the Black Stiletto saved the senator's life—and he doesn't even know it!

I think we're going to see a lot of changes in this country. John F. Kennedy will be a great president, probably serving two terms in office. I'm looking forward to next year with curiosity and excitement. I don't know what 1961 will bring, but you can bet there will be more trouble with the Communists, more conflict on civil rights, more crimes to stop, and more Elvis records!

Happy New Year!

ABOUT THE AUTHOR

Raymond Benson is the author of twenty-seven books and previously penned *The Black Stiletto* (2011) and *The Black Stiletto: Black & White* (2012).

Between 1996 and 2002, he was commissioned by the James Bond literary copyright holders to take over writing the 007 novels. In total he penned and published worldwide six original 007 novels, three film novelizations, and three short stories. An anthology of his 007 work, *The Union Trilogy*, was published in the fall of 2008, and a second anthology, *Choice of Weapons*, appeared summer 2010. His book *The James Bond Bedside Companion*, an encyclopedic work on the 007 phenomenon, was first published in 1984 and was nominated for an Edgar Allan Poe Award by Mystery Writers of America for Best Biographical/Critical Work.

Using the pseudonym "David Michaels," Raymond is also the author of the *New York Times* best-selling books *Tom Clancy's Splinter Cell* and its sequel *Tom Clancy's Splinter Cell: Operation Barracuda*. Raymond's original suspense novels include *Evil Hours, Face Blind, Sweetie's Diamonds* (which won the Readers' Choice Award for Best Thriller of 2006 at the Love is Murder Conference for Authors, Readers and Publishers), *Torment*, and *Artifact of Evil. A Hard Day's Death*, the first in a series of "rock 'n' roll thrillers," was published in 2008, and its sequel, the Shamus Award-nominated *Dark Side of the Morgue*, published in 2009. Other recent works include novelizations of the popular videogames, *Metal Gear Solid,* its sequel, *Metal Gear Solid 2: Sons Of Liberty, Homefront: The Voice Of Freedom*, co-written with John Milius, and *Hitman: Damnation.*

Raymond has taught courses in film genres and history at New York's New School for Social Research, Harper College in Palatine,

Illinois, College of DuPage in Glen Ellyn, Illinois, and currently presents Film Studies lectures with *Daily Herald* movie critic Dann Gire. Raymond has been honored in Naoshima, Japan, with the erection of a permanent museum dedicated to one of his novels, and he is also an ambassador for Japan's Kagawa Prefecture. Raymond is an active member of International Thriller Writers, Inc., Mystery Writers of America, the International Association of Media Tie-In Writers, a full member of ASCAP, and served on the Board of Directors of The Ian Fleming Foundation for sixteen years. He is based in the Chicago area.

www.raymondbenson.com

Look for the next installment in *The Black Stiletto* Series.